THE ETRUNIA SAGA

Book One:
Through the Portal

Ing-Marie Stengle

THE ETRUNIA SAGA

Book One:

Through the Portal

THE ETRUNIA SAGA Book One: Through the Portal © 2022, Etrunia Publishing House

ISBN: 979-8-218-10898-4

Published in the United States

Cover art: Elena Dudina

Interior formatting: Don Consolver:

Fiction/Adventure/Young adult fantasy

Available at Amazon.com and other retail outlets

Dedication:

To those with brave hearts—past, present and future.

Special thanks:

To my wonderful husband Steve and my children Samantha, Philip, and Shari, who provided the inspirations for some of these characters. Thanks to LA Justice for her editing and encouragement.

THE ETRUNIA SAGA

Book One:

Through the Portal

Ing-Marie Stenglein

CHAPTERS

CAST OF CHARACTERS

In America

Michael and Elizabeth Sinclair
Makka Sinclair, their daughter
Eddie and Anne, her brother and sister
Brian and Rose Abadon, the twins
Royal and Augusta Abadon, parents of the twins
Jesper, the garden gnome

At the Morass

Thio the Fair, the powerful and peaceful overseer of The Morass
Captain Lourdes, captain of the soldiers

At the Armory

Magnus, the forger
Khana, Whit, Tor, Tajari & Modie, weapons instructors

In the Tower of Nideon

Nideon, keeper of the precious Cvector
Melker, Agmar and Thorvi, wounded soldiers

In The White City at Lovenfell

Gareth Woodenwood, the Gate Master

At Blackwater Castle in Southistle

Lady Eyrie, the evil ruler of Etrunia
The Grand Wizard Archite, her trusted teacher of magic

Councilor Simeon, her trusted advisor
Dottir Dumbledale, a kitchen servant
Bodie, her younger brother
Orn Wittenberg, a soldier in training for Lady Eyrie

At The Black Fortress

Eric and Anders, two brothers
Lord Hviti, the most hated and feared person in Etrunia

At the Refuge of Rations

The Wraiths, unseen beings of the undead

At Fort Ravenspur

Captain Alabaster, leader of the Resistance
General Mach Darogan, commander of the Resistance troops

~ PART ONE ~
GRANITE FALLS

~ 1 ~

THE BEGINNING

The SUV was packed as the Sinclair family backed out of the long, paved driveway of their South Florida home headed toward their new life in Minnesota. The moving men had packed up their grand home in The Reserve, a gated community in Fort Lauderdale, two days earlier, sweeping through it like a swarm of locust and scooping up everything that wasn't bolted down. Their precious possessions were now stuffed into two large moving vans that were miles ahead of them.

Makka's mom and dad sat grimly in the front seats, eyes glued to the highway as they headed to an unknown destination and an entirely new life. No explanation had been given and none was forthcoming. Makka Sinclair sulked in the back seat, clutching her lifeline, her smart phone with the hot pink sparkle case too shocked at the sudden uprooting to even cry. In the cargo area, their Great Dane, Sasha, whimpered as the SUV raced north. What was the rush anyway?

On this brutally hot late August morning, all Makka knew was their destination was somewhere close to Minneapolis, fifteen hundred miles away from everything she knew and loved. Makka was beyond devastated. She'd turned fourteen only a few days ago. How could this be happening to her? She fingered the diamond chip studs she'd received as a present from her older brother, Eddie. He was the handsomest and kindest brother a girl could have—and handsome, too, with long, sandy blond hair worn shaggy like Harry Styles, sometimes swept up into a man-bun—which drove their dad crazy. Eddie, christened Edgar Bjorn Sinclair, was now a freshman far away at Columbia University in New York City. Makka knew he'd be driving the girls crazy with his tall, lanky body, soft gray eyes and heart-stopping smile. If only he was here to put an end to the madness, talk some sense into her parents or provide some measure of comfort.

But he wasn't. Neither was her older sister, Ann, who was married with two youngsters and living in San Francisco. Sometimes Makka thought she was an afterthought or an accident, which made her feel even more alone.

Now, everything in the world as she knew it had turned upside down. And on top of everything she'd lose her BFFs, Ella and Tammi. A tear trickled down her cheek, followed by another. Her dad had never really explained anything in the rush to get out of town. She needed answers. SHE NEEDED THEM NOW!

"Dad, why did we have to leave so suddenly?" she blurted out. "I mean, school starts in two days. It's not fair!" Her parents glanced at each other. Her mother, Elizabeth—Beth to her friends—peered over her dark tinted sunglasses.

"It's complicated."

"I'll tell you what's complicated," said Makka through clenched teeth, "starting school where you don't know a soul and trying to fit in. That's complicated."

4

"It's hard for me, too. I've left my job as an assistant vice principal and all my friends as well."

"Then why are we moving?"

Her dad, Michael, chimed in, his deep voice tired and irritated. "It's for my work. Let's leave it at that."

"I don't believe you," Makka retorted. "You work on a computer all day 24/7. You could do that anywhere, even on the moon."

Her mother's frown was a warning to be quiet, but Makka couldn't stop. Not now. Not when every precious minute took her further away from life as she'd known it from day one!

"Don't talk to your father like that."

"And why would you just blindly follow along?"

"That's enough young lady."

"How could you give up your teaching job Mom? Aren't you going to miss it? What will you do now?"

"Life will sort itself out, honey. And I think you'll love our new home. It won't be as hot or muggy and no more hurricanes."

"It's a done deal," said her dad. "We're moving and that's final."

"But why Minnesota? Do you know how cold it gets there? A person can freeze to death in just minutes."

"Let's cross that bridge when we come to it," said Elisabeth.

As everyone settled down to contemplate their respective futures Sasha whined. "I think Sasha probably has to pee," said Makka, and I'm starving.

Hearing her name, Sasha lifted her huge black and white head over the seat and licked Makka's cheek with a slobbery pink tongue. "Ugh, hey." Makka pulled out her cell phone and took a quick selfie, texting it to her friends with a cryptic note. *MISS U ALREADY. THIS SUCKS.* She added a few sad emoji, three bombs, two kisses, four piles of poop and hit SEND. Makka scratched the dog's head and whispered, "We'll get out of this somehow."

Her dad peered at her in the rearview mirror. "Listen, sweetie, I know you deserve a better explanation, but I really can't tell you much. We're moving to a small town outside Minneapolis called Granite Falls."

Makka had no way of knowing that her parents had a terrible secret they could not divulge to her—or to anybody. And once events began unfolding—events that would put her in mortal danger—they would have no way to protect or keep her safe.

As evening approached, Makka asked if they could stop for the night. "We found a hotel that takes dogs a little further on," said her mom. "Just try to be patient."

Patience wasn't one of Makka's best qualities. She was always antsy, always wanting to do something or go somewhere—just not Minnesota. She opened the phone and read the texts from her friends and replied: I'VE BEEN ABDUCTED BY A BUNCH OF CRAZY MANIACS...SAVE ME!

Little did she know how close it was to the truth.

~ 2 ~

MAKKA

Makka Sinclair was tall for her age, with long, muscular legs and a neck that stretched forever. She stooped to make herself appear shorter so her friends, Ella and Tammi, wouldn't have to look up when they talked to her. All of the Sinclairs were tall so it didn't really come as any great surprise. "You're statuesque," her mother said, as if that made it any better. Everyone said she was stunning with her long, slender nose and full lips. Her straight blond hair was usually caught up in a high pony tail and Makka rarely wore makeup, just a little eye liner, lipstick and a hint of tickle-me-pink blush over her flawless peaches-and-cream complexion. Her sapphire blue eyes and long lashes were highlighted by gracefully arched eyebrows and her ears had been recently pierced after a hard-won battle with her mom.

Makka had only one choice: Accept the inevitable or die trying. The Twin Cities of Minneapolis and St. Paul are located on the north shores of the Mississippi River with a population of about three million. But they were not going cosmopolitan. No, they were headed to the sticks, some small town far outside the city limits with the gawd-awful sounding name of Granite Falls.

As they got closer and were off the highway they passed a church that looked like a cross between a medieval castle and a gothic hall. She snapped a photo and texted it back to her Florida friends. She took another as they drove over the great Mississippi—sealing her fate forever.

Near the end of the long drive her mom pointed out the window toward a lush green lawn and sprawling two-story redbrick building. "That's your new school." Makka snapped a photo of the hideous redbrick building and sent it to her friends adding more piles of poop and three thumbs-down emojis as Sasha sat up and began growling.

"What's wrong girl?" asked Makka as her dad took a sharp right and pulled into a long, circular driveway behind the long-haul moving vans. The movers were unloading their belongings, Makka hated those strange men touching her things. She needed a case of Lysol wipes to scrub off their germs.

The humongous fieldstone house was even larger than their home in Fort Lauderdale, set back from the street smack in the middle of a huge stately lawn. To one side was a copse of deciduous trees and beyond that dense forest of conifers. Makka's mood brightened considerably as she imagined having an entire wing of the house to throw parties. But her enthusiasm dissolved as Sasha bolted from the SUV, stopped, peed on the lawn, and sat down whining as though her heart were breaking. Makka knew exactly how she felt.

Sure the house seems nice, but I don't know a soul and nobody knows me, she thought as a tear trickled down her cheek. How will I survive in this strange and awful place? I must, MUST, convince Dad to move back ASAP.

But Michael Sinclair was not the person she believed him to be and if Makka had known what lay ahead, she might have stolen the family car and driven back to her old house in Florida—if only she knew how to drive.

Even if she had, everything had been preordained.

Nothing was as it seemed.

And nothing would ever be the same again.

~ 3 ~

BRIAN & ROSE

As the moving men hauled the furniture off the truck, Elizabeth, who was accustomed to giving orders in the school where she'd worked, directed the burly men with authority. Makka watched her mom for a few minutes as the dynamo with her light blond hair and hazel eyes took charge. She'd be fifty on her next birthday and although they didn't always agree, Makka thought she was a pretty amazing woman—for her age.

She watched as her cherry red BSA Mach City Racers bicycle was unloaded—a birthday present from her dad. It had all the bells and whistles, including twenty-one gears, which was great for the rolling hills of Minnesota and totally the opposite of Florida, which was flat as a pancake! Now she wondered if he'd bought it because he knew it would be her primary means of transportation here!

Over the banging and scraping of the couches being unloaded, Elizabeth called out: "Why don't you explore the neighborhood? There's a family with two kids your age just up the road."

Makka nodded blankly. *How did she know that?* Something was definitely fishy. Even so, she was anxious to get away from the chaos. "Stay!" she commanded Sasha, who sat up bright-eyed. "I'll be back soon." The wagging tail swished on the overgrown grass as Makka hopped on her bike and pedaled up the street to meet the mysterious neighbors. She had no clue about how weird they were as she passed half a dozen picture-perfect homes. She looked for neighbors tending their gardens or sitting outside on lawn chairs, but didn't see a soul.

The wind picked up and the temperature dropped as the clouds scudded across the sun. Dressed in cutoff jean shorts and a lime green sleeveless tank top, she was suddenly freezing. it had been ninety-five degrees in Florida and today, in Granite Falls, it was down in the low seventies.

"Hey, over here." Makka looked up the street to see two teenagers waving at her. "Are you the new kid on the block?" They laughed at their silly joke as Makka approached. She stopped the bike without getting too close.

The girl was tallish and slim maybe five-nine, long legs, brown long hair, tawny eyes and rosy cheeks, with a wide and friendly smile. The boy stood a few inches taller, trim with an athletic build. He had dark blond hair that hung over his eyes while hers was held back by a bright red headband. She wore black leggings and a baggy long-sleeve crimson top; he wore jeans and a gray hoodie with some kind of insignia.

"I'm Rose Abadon," she said. "We live right up the street."

"I'm her brother Brian."

Rose smiled broadly, revealing straight white teeth. "We're twins."

"Twins?"

"Yep, but I'm older," Brian boasted.

"Only by two minutes. Why do you have to say that every time?"

Brian winked at Makka. "Because it's true."

Makka introduced herself and rubbed her bare arms.

"You must be freezing," Rose said. "I hear you're from Florida."

Makka's jaw dropped. Secrets would be hard to keep hidden. She nodded. "We just got here."

"Come with us, I'll loan you a sweater," Rose offered kindly.

"Yeah, come meet the crazy family who lives in the only castle on the block."

Before she could reply, she saw Brian's eyes open wide. "God almighty, is that a dog?"

Without turning around, she knew what he meant. "Yes, that's Sasha. She must have followed me. I forgot to tie her leash to something."

"Looks like a pony. I bet she eats a ton," Rose quipped.

Brian teased, "Hope you don't have to scoop the poop."

They all laughed and the ice was broken. They seemed nice enough and Makka began to relax. Although she ordered Sasha to go home, the dog was confused at her surroundings and loped happily alongside, sniffing the new Minnesota smells and making everyone smile as she rolled in the grass or marked random lawns, wagging her tail proudly.

Every now and then Sasha stopped short, sat on her haunches and let out a blood-curdling howl, as though she could smell danger up ahead. Each time, Makka had to get off the bike and calm her down. Soon enough, Makka would come to realize that while Apple Tree Lane sounded like a friendly place to live, nothing was as it appeared in Granite Falls.

~ 4 ~

GNOMES

By the time they arrived at Rose and Brian's house, Makka was absolutely freezing—and terrified. She had never seen anything so imposing as this thing they called "home." It looked like a castle—sinister and foreboding. Brian gallantly took off his hoodie and draped it over Makka's trembling shoulders. "Do you have a bunch of brothers or sisters?" asked Makka, wondering why anybody needed so much space.

"Just us and our mom and dad," said Rose cheerily as she stowed her bike between the iron bars of the ornate gate that surrounded the property. The entryway was flanked by two decorative towers with an elaborate letter "A" in gold-plated steel and topped by a crest. Makka found the whole effect weird.

Brian punched in a security code and the gates swung open. Sasha bounded in as Makka and the twins wedged their bike wheels between the bars and strolled onto the property. The gate closed with an ominous click and as Makka briefly wondered if this was a good idea. Probably not. But her mother wanted her to meet new people so she was only being the dutiful daughter— wasn't she?

"We'll both be going to the same school next year," said Rose as they pushed open the massive front doors. "I'll introduce you to all the cool girls, even though I'll be a year ahead of you."

"I'll fix you up with some of my friends," Brian offered.

"My mom doesn't think I'm ready to date yet," Makka admitted. "She thinks I'm a young fourteen, whatever that is."

"Moms are just overprotective," said Rose, rolling her eyes.

"But not ours," added Brian. "We can do anything we want to."

"Anything?"

"Anything! In fact, pretty soon we'll be helping with an assignment."

"For school?"

"For Etrunia," said Brian.

"Etrunia? What's that?"

"All will be revealed in time," said Rose cryptically. "Come on, I'll give you the grand tour."

Makka looked up. A tower loomed over weathered wood doors and she thought she glimpsed someone peering down from the tower window as they opened to reveal an inner courtyard ablaze with a riot of colorful late-blooming summer flowers and a collection of unusual gnomes. She reached for her cell phone in her back pocket, but changed her mind before pulling it out. Was it rude to take photos?

"These are so cute," she said, running her hand over a gnome's pointed hat.

"I call the one with the lantern Doc," said Rose.

"And that's Bigfoot," added Brian, pointing to a tall one with a bushy gray beard.

Sasha was at the far end, busy sniffing one with a red cap, green belted jacket and blue pants swinging a golf club. She called out, "Stop that Sasha. Here girl." Sasha refused to budge and lay down whining.

Rose and Brian exchanged glances as Makka took three long strides over to the dog, glancing quickly at the gnome, and stopped in her tracks. She was sure it blinked at her. *No way!* Garden gnomes don't blink! Makka strode over and grabbed the dog's leather collar.

"Stay."

She pulled out her phone, took a photo, and sent a quick text to her mom: *With the neighborhood kids, Sasha, too. CU soon.*

Little did she know this would be the last text she would ever send from her phone with the hot pink plastic case.

~ 5 ~

HOME STRANGE HOME

Inside the mansion, Makka was overwhelmed by the view before her eyes—as if she'd stepped back a few centuries. She clung to Sasha's collar with both hands as the dog pulled forward toward the impossibly huge fireplace. Makka felt safe with this beast at her side, even as her arms ached from holding her back.

"What do you think?" asked Rose cheerfully. "It's a bit much, I admit."

"Over the top for sure," added Brian. "This place freaks people out, that's why we never have company."

For once Makka was at a loss for words. She felt as though she'd just walked into a castle in a faraway land. The gray stone walls were adorned with colorful banners interspersed with sharp metal swords, crossbows and lethal-looking weapons. Brocade covered couches were strewn with pillows adorned with heraldry designs. From the ceiling, a circular chandelier glowed not with bulbs but with candles, flickering in the breeze created by the open door. On the wall leading up to the second level was an elaborate candle sconce and on the opposite corner was a suit of armor. The fireplace, which was not lit, was spacious enough to roast a

17

whole cow. A huge cast iron cauldron was suspended from a hook and beneath it were the telltale ashes of a recent fire. What could they have been roasting? She didn't want to know as her sapphire-hued eyes stopped roaming and her jaw dropped. There was a horse and rider! Were they real? She dared not ask, but Rose seemed to read her mind.

"Don't worry, we don't kill people here and put them on display." The explanation did little to quell the growing anxiety in Makka's gut. She felt her knees go weak and plopped down on a worn leather hassock.

"Welcome to the humble home of Royal and Augusta Abadon," said Rose, calling out, "Mom, Dad, we have company."

A minute passed and then two as Makka continued to gaze around the room, her jaw agape as she wondered, *who lives like this?*

A rustling sound caught her attention. She looked up and saw two extraordinarily tall people, both appearing so noble and regal she felt as though she should kneel or curtsy. They were imposing, both well over six feet tall. She assumed these were the parents—the lord and lady of the manor.

Augusta Abadon was exquisite—from her jeweled sandals to her emerald green eyes and platinum hair pulled tight in a bun. She was draped in a crimson flowing gown tied with a gold braided belt. Her fingers were covered with expensive rings and the nails were polished like red talons. Lady Abadon was rail thin with high cheekbones and arched brows.

"Welcome darling," she said in a breathy voice, the way an old movie actress would. For a moment Makka wondered if this was a practical joke they were playing on her—an initiation to Granite Falls.

Then a deep voice boomed over her head. "Pleased to meet you."

Royal Abadon held out a meaty hand. Sasha barked once, then lay down and whined pathetically. Makka slid her hand into his and watched it disappear. He was a giant, taller than his wife by half a foot, a solid man with florid cheeks and thinning dark hair slicked back. His stomach bulged out from under his navy blue velvet robe emblazoned with a red and gold crest, the same one that seemed to be everywhere—on the cushions and banners, the front gate and even on Brian's hoodie!

Mr. Adabon wore dark leggings, which Makka thought bizarre. Never in her life had she seen a man in leggings, except at the ballet and Mr. Abadon was no ballet dancer, not by a long shot.

"Welcome to the neighborhood," he said, his belly shaking and his black eyes blazing into her soul. "I'm looking forward to meeting your parents."

Makka's throat was so dry it was impossible to swallow. There was no way her that her father, an intensely private and quiet computer programmer, and her mother, a studious and serious school administrator, would ever be friends with this bizarre couple from ages past. No way in hell—even if it froze over— which it certainly would in the bitter cold Minnesota winter.

"Come, let's go to my room," said Rose, pulling her hand. This house was as magical as anything she'd ever read about and she couldn't wait to see more. Was this really happening to her?

"I think Sasha should wait in the courtyard," Makka said. "Can you get her a bowl of water?"

While Rose ran the tap, Makka led the dog out through the doors and into the lush garden.

For a second she wondered if she should be frightened, but she pushed the feeling deep inside, laughing at her silly fears. Rose and Brian seemed so normal. Maybe Granite Falls was a little strange, but she had to rein in her imagination. Perhaps it was the newness of it all, the strange house she was in and the odd couple who owned it.

If there was something mystical happening, how could Rose and Brian appear so average, so friendly?

Did they have a secret plan to chop her into pieces and boil her in the cast iron pot downstairs—make her into a stew and invite her parents over? God forbid! Perhaps they had a secret passageway that led to some underground prison.

And then Rose opened the door to her room and Makka felt as though she was in heaven.

~ 6 ~

HEAVEN & EARTH

Makka walked into Rose's room and gasped with delight. The floor was made of stone, the ceiling was vaulted with beams, and the walls adorned with ornate sconces. Dominating the center of the room was a four-poster queen-sized bed with an elaborately carved wooden maple frame. Blue and tan gauzy curtains floated delicately, like butterfly wings, in the breeze that came in through an open window. Heavy drapes had been tied back with golden ropes that ended in large tassels. The spread and matching pillow shams reflected the colors of the curtains giving the room a delightfully light and airy appearance, despite the heavy wooden furniture. Makka vowed to give up all Christmas presents and ask for a bed just like this for her new room.

She walked around the room brushing her hand lightly over everything, getting a sense of Rose and feeling more than a tad envious. It wasn't her style but it was gorgeous.

Rose called, "Come over here; let me show you the closet."

Makka watched with big eyes as Rose flipped a switch revealing a gigantic closet packed with gowns and fancy dresses. One wall had shelves filled with low-heeled pumps in every color of the rainbow, some with feathers, others with bows and sparkles. Another shelf held an assortment of tiaras; a humongous carved wooden jewelry case sat atop a dresser amid an array of perfume bottles and small crystal balls.

"OMG," Makka exclaimed. "This is totally awesome."

"It's nothing," Rose replied. "You should see my mother's room."

"I don't know if I can handle any more surprises today."

"Just one more," said Rose, lowering her voice. "Come with me."

Makka felt her tummy churn again. She should really head home. It had been hours since she'd left her parents and their new house.

Rose lowered her head as she moved toward the back, the ceiling slanting downward. She pushed aside a rack of dresses to reveal a small door with a handle and a key poking out of the keyhole.

Makka crouched down beside her. "Where does it go?"

Before Rose could answer, they heard Sasha barking outside. She sounded agitated and Makka dashed out of the closet to the window overlooking the garden where she caught sight of Sasha galloping across the lawn chasing one of the gnomes. One of the gnomes? That was clearly impossible and yet there it was.

"I've gotta go," Makka exclaimed, turning around and smacking right into Rose. "Excuse me. I have to catch her. She doesn't know her way around this neighborhood."

"She'll be fine," said Rose calmly, as though pony-sized dogs chased after running gnomes every day. Maybe that was life here in Minnesota. Makka had a lot to learn.

If only she knew.

~ 7 ~

WEIRDER & WEIRDER

At home, Makka stopped in the doorway and tried to catch her breath. The bike had been ditched on the lawn and if her father saw it, she'd be in trouble. She hoped he was too busy to peek outside.

Elizabeth peered up at her daughter over her glasses. "Did you have fun?"

Makka was at a loss for words. Were human gnomes, hidden passageways and two of the oddest people she'd ever met classified as fun? "I guess."

Her father looked up sternly. "Did you or didn't you?"

Makka thought Michael Sinclair was one of the handsomest men on the planet with his trim, muscular build and perfect face—straight nose, thin lips, ice blue eyes and light brown hair, worn in a buzz cut, military style. But he was a no-nonsense kind of dad. You did or you didn't. Yes or no. This or that. There was no shading or gray area and yet, even at fourteen she knew there were times when round pegs didn't fit in round holes. This was one of those times.

Michael had served in the military, perhaps everything was cut-and-dry in the service, but in real life there were loads of wishy-washy times. Like now. Makka had grown accustomed to his secret military life. He remained steadfast and tight-lipped about it, refusing to talk about it.

Now, as she stood there waiting for the other shoe to fall, she watched his eyes travel to the insignia on Brian's hoodie.

"What's that?" His voice was flat and hard. Makka stared at him blankly. Who was this man? Could this day get any weirder and what kind of stupid question was that?

"It's Brian's hoodie."

"Brian Abadon." It was a statement, not a question. *How did he know?* "And I suppose you met Rose, too."

Makka nodded blankly. *What was going on?*

"That's quite an elaborate design," said Elizabeth, pointing to the gold crest with the bright red sash and four stars.

"I guess so," Makka agreed warily. "They had crests all over the place."

Her mother's voice was unusually shrill. "You went into their house?"

"Castle is more like it. I've never seen anything so bizarre."

Michael rubbed the stubble on his chin thoughtfully. "So you met the parents?" Was it her imagination or had his whole demeanor changed?

"Yes, Royal and Augusta Abadon. They seemed nice, but definitely odd."

"Odd...in what way?" asked Elizabeth cautiously.

"First, they're not your traditional Midwesterners, that's for sure. Their house looked like a castle and they appeared to be dressed up as a queen and king."

She watched her parents exchange guarded glances.

Slowly, her mother approached Makka and placed her hands gently on her shoulders. "You'd better check out your room and make a list of what you need to make it feel homey," she said. "We'll finish up down here and then we'll go out for dinner. Okay?"

Anything that seemed halfway normal, like eating out at Cracker Barrel or digging into a crusty pizza dripping with cheese, was fine with Makka. Bring on NORMAL!

As she headed upstairs to check out her room and see if a massive four-poster complete with netting would fit, she reached into her back pocket to retrieve her phone and text Ella and Tammi about her unusual first day in Minnesota. But her pocket was empty. Where did she lose it? Her mind flashed back to her emergency exit from the house, running after Sasha, the gate opening automatically as she approached it, grabbing her bike from the fence posts and racing through the new neighborhood. It could be anywhere, but hopefully, it was still in Rose's room.

She laughed aloud wondering if the gnomes had it. Were they watching her silly videos? *Wait! Gnomes don't use cell phones, do they?* She didn't even have Rose's number to call and ask her to search around with Brian. That left only one alternative: Early the next morning she would ride back to the Abadon's to find her lifeline. It was bright pink so she should be able to spot it easily.

She might as well just curl up and die right now if that phone wasn't located ASAP. Her heart ached to talk to a familiar voice, even her brother in college, but she couldn't.

Makka felt isolated, alone in a strange land.

Weird noises, the unfamiliar creaking and groaning of the house, the scratching of raccoons and foxes outside and Sasha snoring at the foot of her bed kept her up all night. And what if her phone was never found?

She couldn't go there!

Early, before the sun was fully up, she slipped out of bed intending to find her phone, return the hoodie and then sever all ties with the Abadons and their supreme weirdness—even though Brian was hot stuff.

Events, however, were already unfolding and before the end of the day, the bottom of her world would fall away, leaving her suspended in time and space.

~ 8 ~

THE MAGIC BEGINS

At precisely nine o'clock, Makka arrived at the gate to the Abadon estate and parked her bike between the rails. She rang a bell located on the post near the hinge and the wide iron doors parted like magic.

She used the lion head knockers and the doors were opened by a small, older woman dressed in black. Without a word, she turned and beckoned Makka to follow. In the gnome garden, Makka was surprised to find that none of the gnomes were in the same places as the previous day. She wanted to ask the woman whether they moved the statues or if they statues moved themselves. That silly thought made her laugh out loud.

The housekeeper, at least that's who Makka assumed the woman was, turned and frowned. *No laughing allowed here.*

She made a mental note to ask Brian, the sensible one. Suddenly, she felt embarrassed to be back here so early. What if they were late sleepers? What if they were enjoying a quiet family breakfast?

The housekeeper showed Makka to the living room and pointed to a rich burgundy and green brocade couch that looked lumpy and uncomfortable. Gingerly, Makka lowered herself down and felt it crunch under her. Was that sawdust or crushed bugs? She didn't want to know. A few minutes passed. *Tick...tock.* The steady clicking of a clock's metronome somewhere deep in the home kept time with her beating heart.

Without asking if she was hungry, the diminutive woman in a stained black dress brought a small plate with a sandwich and glass of red liquid. Although she wasn't hungry, Makka accepted the food and looked for a place to set it down. There was no coffee table so she balanced the ceramic plate on her lap and sniffed the drink hoping it wasn't bat's blood or poison. She placed the glass on the floor and as she bent over, she saw the sandwich on the plate move. MOVE? *No way.*

No, sandwiches don't move. But yes, this one did. It looked like two slices of bread with a butterfly wing caught in the center. Gingerly, Makka lifted off the top piece of bread and a butterfly flew up and into her face. Shocked to the core, Makka jumped up, kicking over the glass and spilling the red liquid, watching in horror as the ceramic plate crashed to the stone floor and split in half.

The sharp cracking noise echoed through the living room like a sonic boom. Makka wanted to dash out of the house and never come back. Then she remembered the missing phone and took a deep breath. She had come for a reason. She could not leave without it.

As she sat back on the couch, tears streaming down her cheeks, holding the two pieces of the plate, one in each hand, she saw the red liquid on the floor evaporate right before her eyes. The puddle, which would have left a nasty stain, shrank from platter size to thimble size and then to nothing at all. *What the?*

The two pieces of the plate, now without the butterfly sandwich—ugh, did they really want her to eat that?—fit together perfectly. Makka held them in place, wondering how to hand it back without the housekeeper noticing that the plate was broken.

With a hissing sound, a red line appeared, beginning at the outer edge and running straight down the seam of the splinted halves. Makka could not believe what she was seeing. In only a few seconds, the spill on the floor had vanished and the plate had somehow mended itself. Without waiting for another disaster, she snuck into the kitchen and put the glass and plate down on the counter and left without a word.

On the way back to the living room, she found the staircase and headed up the steps and down the hall toward Rose's room. It was bold, she knew that. This was a huge NO on her mother's NEVER DO THIS list. But she felt she had no choice.

She wore shorts again and a lightweight sweater with suede fringed sandals, her long blond hair was pulled into a pony tail as usual and she was carrying Brian's hoodie over her arm as she tried to locate Rose's room.

As she approached the closed door, her new friend yanked it open and tugged Makka inside. "What took you so long?"

"How did you know I was here?"

"Duh!" Rose pulled Makka to the window where she could see over the courtyard to the fence where her cherry red BSA Mach

City Racer was parked. "Hard to miss that first thing in the morning."

"Have you seen my phone?"

"I found it in the gnome garden last night."

Makka hesitated. "About those gnomes…"

"Cute, aren't they?"

"Tell me they don't move around at night."

Rose didn't reply. "Do they?" she prodded, not wanting to know the answer.

Rose threw her head back and laughed out loud; she giggled until tears rolled from her eyes. "You're hysterical, Makka. I love your sense of humor."

Makka realized that her new friend hadn't answered and changed the subject. "Well…okay then. Where's the phone?"

"On the dresser." Rose pointed to the heavy wooden piece against the wall. Yes, there it was. She breathed a huge sigh of relief.

"Hey, thanks for bringing Brian's hoodie," Rose said. "It's his favorite."

They sat in silence as a minute ticked by and until Makka summoned up the courage to ask: "Is this castle, I mean, is your house haunted?"

Even as the words spilled from her lips, she felt foolish. Still, there were so many unanswered questions.

"Come, sit down," said Rose, patting the bed, which, while they were talking had miraculously made itself. Makka sat down as they faced the window. The cell phone was still on the dresser and as Rose began to talk about life in Granite Falls, Makka heard a strange noise behind her. Assuming it was Brian coming to say good morning, she didn't turn around right away—not wanting to appear too eager to greet the good looking teenager. She was already feeling flutters in her tummy every time she looked at his thick, wavy hair and green eyes with gold flecks. His nose was perfect and his skin had a glow to it. He was, in a word, perfect.

Suddenly, from the corner of her eye, she saw a flash of green and watched in horror as a small hand snatched the pink case right off the dresser. Makka was up in a flash. "Hey, hey you, put that down right now. I said PUT IT DOWN! Give it back right now!"

Instead of obeying, the same gnome that Sasha had chased the day before turned toward her, stuck out his tongue and raced into Rose's closet. With her heart pounding, Makka sprang into motion, dashing into the closet and watching with dread as the weirdo gnome opened the secret passageway door and shot like a cannonball into the gloom.

~ 9 ~

THE PORTAL

Makka screeched to a halt as he disappeared into the gloomy passageway. Every fiber in her body told her to let the phone go—it was *only* a phone—her parents would buy her a new one. Or maybe they'd accuse her of being careless and teach her a lesson by not replacing it.

With no phone she might as well curl up like a millipede and die right there in Rose's closet. What was the point of living without social media and texting and taking selfies to share? She couldn't go a day without posting a dozen at least. And now her most precious possession had vanished.

"Stop!" she yelled to the fleeing figure that was just a shadow in the distance as she raced down, and further down a spiral staircase,.

It was darker and damper as she descended, but she could still hear his leather slippers slapping the stones and the clank of the phone hitting the handrail. *Please don't shatter the glass,* she prayed. Please, pretty please with a butterfly sandwich on top.

Incredibly, soft spotlights lit up every sixth step to guide her. The click clack of her sandals echoed in the narrow confines and she was sorry that she hadn't opted to wear her Nikes.

As she neared the bottom, which reeked of mold and mildew, she saw that the stone walls had an orange glow. At the bottom there was a small tiki torch. She grabbed it by the base and, holding it gingerly so she didn't burn her clothing or hands, she continued the chase.

Without a nanosecond to spare, she tore around yet another curve only to realize the passageway was now angling upward. She caught a glimpse of brown as she huffed and puffed upward, the slant getting stepper.

Her legs were on fire, every muscle burning, aching as the leather strap of her fringed sandals dug into her delicate skin. Sweat dripped from her forehead and into her eyes.

The royal blue sweater, which she had worn to impress Brian, was suffocating her. As she ran even further up, now climbing a narrow stone stairway gasping for air, she noticed a crack of light up ahead.

She had to catch the thief or he would disappear with her phone for eternity. He had to stop for a moment and unlock an iron gate and she gained a few yards on him. Spotting another recess in the wall, she put the torch down quickly and got ready for the final sprint.

Ahead, through the opening, she saw what looked like a thick pine forest. She hadn't noticed one growing behind the Abadon house and she puzzled over that for only a split second before springing forward and reaching out for his jacket as he zipped through the gate and disappeared into the dense trees.

Before Makka could even slow down, she heard the gate slam shut behind her. Quickly, she turned back and tugged on the heavy metal as her knees buckled. "Rose, Brian, help. HELP ME!"

Unwittingly, she had passed through the portal into Etrunia. Yet strangely, she was exactly where she was supposed to be, even if it was only four days before starting her freshman year at Granite Falls High School.

But this had all been ordained long before she was born.

~ 10 ~

JESPER

Makka felt like a fool. Why had she followed a weird gnome through a secret passageway and into the land of…the land of…where was she anyway?

Thirsty, tired and in need of a friend, or even a stranger, to tell her how to get back to Granite Falls, she pushed herself up, but after taking only a few steps, she realized that it was better to stay hidden so the ugly gnome and his dreadful friends wouldn't see her. They might want to do awful things to her, horrible things she dared not imagine.

Her only hope was that Rose and Brian would come barging through the portal and lead her back to safety. "Please, pretty please with a pink cell phone on top," she muttered aloud. But that was not going to happen.

With trembling knees, she stood atop a small hill of broken rock fragments wondering where to go and what to do. No road was visible from her vantage point. Turning around, she could not see the portal and, therefore, there was no going back. Easing herself down the embankment, trying not to slip and fall on the loose shards, she spotted a hut not too far away—just through a small copse of trees and over a small brook. Perhaps they had a phone or some way she could contact the authorities to help get her back to Apple Tree Lane.

Little did she know she was in Etrunia and there was no going back—not until her mission was accomplished.

But the air was fresh, smelling of pine, and the day was perfect —not too hot nor too cold—as a gentle breeze blew her pony tail, her worries began to subside. Help couldn't be far away and once her dad realized she was missing, they would move heaven and earth to find her. Comforted by the thought of rescue, she began to hum when suddenly a figure darted out from behind a tree and shouted, "Well, well, you're finally here!"

Makka shrieked with fright, as roosting birds flew into the air with loud squawks. A nearby squirrel gnawing on a nut scampered up a tree. Before her stood the gnome.

"Who are you? Where am I? And where is my phone? I demand answers." She tossed her pony tail and stamped her foot. *"Owww."*

Gazing down, she realized her feet were bleeding, ruining her expensive sandals. "Now you owe me a new pair of shoes."

The gnome grinned at her silliness. "You may call me Jesper and if you ever want your phone back you must listen to me very carefully."

"Why should I listen to you?"

"Do you know where you are?"

"No, Jester, I don't have a clue. Please, enlighten me."

Her sarcasm was not lost on the little man, his red cap tilting to the side. "First of all, it's not Jester. It's Jesper with an "s" and the attitude won't help you get through this ordeal."

"What ordeal?" Makka's heart began pounding. What was going on?"

Jesper plopped down on the pine needles and patted the ground next to him. "Sit down, it's a long story. I'll explain it all and then you can decide."

"Decide what?"

"Decide nothing. This is all preordained."

"What does that mean?"

"It means it's going to happen no matter what, so listen carefully."

Then Jesper, the gnome who acted like a human being, the very one who'd stolen her precious cell phone, told her about the past. "And now you will change the future."

He continued, explaining that she was in a sprawling country located off the grid and not on any map in any atlas or on Google Earth. "Etrunia is shaped like a triangle with the point at the bottom," he said. "You've come through the mountains on the northeast side, not far from Northgate where the castle belonging to the Great Pharmakeus is located."

Jesper pointed as she followed his finger. "There's the cathedral tree, you see it over there?" He indicated an enormous spruce tree with multiple branches forming spires. "You can see that from a great distance and find your way back to the portal. Of course…"

"Of course, what?"

"If you're joking, it isn't funny."

"Did you know that the path we're on is called the Trail of Fears?"

"How could I possibly know that?"

"I may look funny to some people, a short man dressed like a gnome. But I'm deadly serious. We must get the Great Pharmakeus and his beautiful wife back to Etrunia. They were kind and fair and the people lived in great harmony. But his evil sister, Lady Eyrie, had her army overthrow his and he was exiled, never to return."

Jesper explained that Lady Eyrie lived at the apex of the triangle, down in the south portion called Southistle. "She has an enormous castle and hundreds of guards. She's a vile and malevolent ruler—so is Lord Hviti. I wish death upon both of them."

"That's a terrible thing to say. My mother says never speak ill of people."

"Your mother? Elizabeth I believe."

Makka was startled. "How do you know my mother's name? Tell me now. This very minute."

"Not now. Come let's hurry and I'll explain." Jesper popped up, grabbed her hand and pulled her down the Trail of Fears as Makka prayed they didn't run into any werewolves, vampires, goblins or zombies.

"I have get back home now." She pulled up short and turned around. "Rose will be worried about me."

"Rose knew this would happen."

"No way! You're lying."

"Michael has warned you about lying."

"Say what? You know my father, too? You're scaring me."

"Hah! I haven't even started."

He grabbed her hand and yanked her forward, then scurried along the path even faster as she struggled to keep up.

"Your life will depend upon your bravery, your skill with a sword, and your cunning," he gasped.

Makka had neither skill with a sword and had, in fact never held one, nor was she cunning—except in making excuses to her mom for the times she slipped out of the house after dark to go out with her friends.

This wasn't anything like that. Her nerves were raw and her body trembled with fear.

"Lord Hviti and Lady Eyrie are determined to ruin Etrunia and bring it under their evil spells." Jesper dropped his voice. "The most treacherous of them all lives in the northwest part in a hideous castle in the middle of a lake. It's known as Valgard but we all call it the Dark Fortress because of the evil that goes on there. To get there you must go through the Forest of the Damned."

"Well I can assure you that I'm not going anywhere near there," Makka said. "No way, no how."

"You'll have no choice when the time comes."

"I always have a choice."

"No. You are here to save us."

"Okay Jesper, stop with the jokes already. "There's no way on earth I'm going through the Forest of the Damned to some godforsaken castle in the middle of a lake where all kinds of evil takes place. I'm just a nice girl from Florida who's looking for her phone. Can you please just hand it over so we can stop this charade."

Ignoring her, he continued to scurry along.

"I'm going to take you to a safe place for the night, but we have a long way to go. Hurry up! Hurry! We can't have you out in the dark. It's too risky."

"Why? Where are we going?" She took a few long strides to catch up to him. "I'm hungry and tired. My feet hurt, my head is throbbing. Why can't we stop and eat?"

"All will be revealed in time."

Makka's imagination went into overdrive, but her survival instinct overrode all her heart.

There's no way I'm dying here, no way, she vowed. I have got to make it back home, somehow, someway—*even if it's the last thing I do*!

~ PART TWO ~
ETRUNIA

~ 11 ~

CHLOE

Up ahead, at the crest of a hill, was a small cabin with a thatched roof. A young woman came out wiping her hands on a stained apron that was once white, but was now yellow with age. "Makka?"

Jesper pushed the reluctant girl forward. "She has finally come to save us. It's taken long enough." Makka was surprised at his exasperation—after all, he was the reason this was all happening.

She retorted angrily: "I just want my phone back and then I'm outta here."

Jesper fell over laughing, as though she had told the funniest joke ever. "Leaving? No way. Not after waiting so long for you to get here."

The woman, who Makka judged to be in her mid-twenties, came over and took Makka's hand. "I'm Chloe. I have warm food waiting for you and a change of clothes."

Jesper pulled himself together and with a sweep of his hat he turned on his heel, skipping along the Trail of Fears heading north and leaving Makka bewildered. What was she doing here and why were they waiting for her? She could not imagine why. She still didn't have her cell phone and now she was sick to death that her parents would call the police and send out an Amber alert. Could this get any worse?

Yes. If she knew all the terrible things that lay in her future, she would have clawed her way back to the portal and somehow squeezed through.

"Hey, wait!" she cried after Jesper. "My phone; I want it back. You promised!"

"Let it go," said Chloe softly. "It's no longer important and will not help you on your quest."

She stared at Chloe who smiled benignly as Makka took a deep breath. "I have no quest," she said, yet even as the words tumbled out, she realized she had been brought here for a higher purpose.

Chloe was a thin, angular woman with a sharp chin and ears that were pointy at the top. Her neck was as long as a swan and her hair was curled in dark kinks cut close to her long face. Her cheekbones were high and her lips full; the color of her skin reminded Makka of coffee with a touch of cream. When she smiled, Chloe's teeth gleamed like the full moon in a dark sky. But her eyes were the most fascinating – copper-colored. Stunning! Makka stood transfixed.

"I need to call home," she said, her lower lip quivering, a tear rolling down her cheek.

"She knows. And she also knows that right now you're safe here with me."

"How do you know?"

Chloe said, "You're here now, here to fulfill your destiny, you...no one else. Right now at this moment, you're safe."

If only she could call Rose and Brian to rescue her. *But no.* There was nothing to do but pray that Chloe was right, that she was really safe and not doomed.

"Hurry, come in, let's get you cleaned up and out of those clothes."

"What's wrong with what I'm wearing?" Makka protested defensively. She had picked the sweater purposely because it showed off her eyes. She'd hoped Brian would notice, but everything had gone to hell faster than she could say *cell phone.* Chloe ushered her inside.

The fireplace was not as wide or high as the Abadon's, but it had a similar iron cauldron hanging over a low-burning fire. It was toasty warm and smelled delicious. By her calculations, it should be around noon and yet the sun was setting and a small table was set for dinner. Weird how time flies when you're lost in some strange triangular country in middle Earth, or wherever the heck she was.

Just as suddenly, she realized that school was due to start soon and she still had to shop for clothes. Her mom had promised a new wardrobe as a consolation for leaving her friends. She vowed to make her parents buy her a four-poster bed for her room, just like Rose's. Where was Rose anyway?

Makka's head spun with the possibility that she had been duped. But the aroma from the food was enticing and she prayed it wasn't fox tails or possum stew or something made of dirt and berries. As she waited for Chloe to stir the cauldron, her eyes swept over the floor which was made of wide planks with a small cowhide rug near the narrow cot along one wall. The bed was decorated with a colorful quilt, patchwork squares like her grandma used to make from their old clothing.

On top of the spread were a burnt orange jumper and a long-sleeved blouse to wear underneath made of cream-colored, rough-spun cotton. There was also a leather belt and fringed leather bag with decorative beads meant to the carry credit cards, lipstick and the cell phone she no longer had

The hideous orange jumper looked eerily like the burgundy one that Chloe wore, but without the soiled apron. Makka had the sinking feeling that she was giving away her only spare piece of clothing since she saw no closet, but only one hook in the corner.

A pair of handmade leather shoes with a metal buckle was tucked neatly under the cot. She assumed that those completed the ugly and impossibly unfashionable outfit. Her feet were so sore she could only pray the dreadful shoes fit. If not, she'd have to go barefoot.

"I hope you don't expect me to wear that," she said testily, pointing at the clothing.

"You can't go around Etrunia wearing that." She pointed at Makka's shorts.

"Why not?"

"It's not accepted here."

"What will happen if I do?"

"I cannot even imagine. Please heed my advice."

"Will they kill me?" Makka asked sarcastically.

"There's no telling what the evil Lady Eyrie would do. Her jealousy knows no bounds and her wrath should be avoided at all costs," said Chloe. "Anyway, the long skirt will afford better protection when you run through the Forest of the Damned."

"Is that meant to scare me?"

If Chloe was trying to frighten Makka she was doing a good job.

Makka rolled her eyes up to the thatched ceiling, hoping it wouldn't rain and soak her to the skin. This was wrong on so many levels. "Listen, I have to go home immediately, if not sooner."

Chloe's eyes danced merrily.

"You have a lot to do here in a short time and we've been waiting ages for you. We've lost track of how long it's been."

"Why would you be waiting?"

Ignoring the question, Chloe continued. "Since you don't know the layout of the land or the way things work around here, and since you are basically all alone and on your own, what I'm telling you is for your benefit. Pay attention. You're not in Granite Falls anymore."

"You sound like my mother, always telling me what to do."

"What does it matter if you wear this dress you call ugly? It will keep you warm and prevent you from sticking out like a sore stump."

"Sore thumb."

Makka tossed her ponytail defiantly and squared her shoulders even as her confidence dissolved into a puddle of fear and doubt.

Little did she know that by the morning she would be on the Path of Peril and sooner than she could ever imagine she would be face to face with the strangest person she had ever met, even odder than Jesper who, it turned out, was okay—for a gnome, that is.

If only she had her phone to take a photo of Chloe and the hut and even one of Jesper. Then she'd be able to prove this was really happening...or was it?

~ 12 ~

THE PLOT THICKENS

Chloe was up before dawn, tending the fire and heating porridge for breakfast. The sound of her moving around awoke Makka, although she could've sworn she never actually fell asleep. She didn't see another bed and wondered if the hostess had slept on the floor or in one of those back-breaking wooden chairs. For a moment she felt ashamed, but then she realized NONE of this was her fault. Besides, she would be going home today, so it didn't really matter.

Chloe helped her lace the front of the orange jumper and adjust the belt and fringed purse. The leather shoes were snug, but Makka had no choice. Her favorite sandals were ruined from yesterday's sprint down the secret tunnel after Jesper. Now she was paying the price for her impulsive foolishness. She raked her fingers through her blond hair and pulled it back in a messy pony tail.

The small, wooden table was set with napkins and hand-crafted clay mugs filled with hot tea. Chloe ladled a glob of oats into each bowl and offered a honey pot to Makka who stared at the mess as though it was poop. She hated the way it stuck to the roof of her mouth; it made her gag. She pictured that little weasel Jesper in a big vat of oatmeal, struggling to get out.

"Something funny?" asked Chloe, cheerfully. How could she be so jolly at this ungodly hour?

"Where's your TV? I don't see one here."

Chloe cocked her head to one side. "I'm sorry, I don't understand."

Makka flushed. There was no electricity. It was like being in the Middle Ages. Her class had studied about the "olden days" in middle school. It was a dangerous time, filled with intrigue and wars with knights in armor, fair maidens being captured, castles being stormed and the dreaded plague. Makka broke into a sweat. She had to get home—correction, she had to retrieve her phone and then get home. There wasn't a minute to waste.

"Do you have any bread?"

Chloe smiled. "I know. Porridge is nasty stuff."

Was she that obvious?

"Not my favorite," Makka acknowledged spooning honey into her tea as Chloe went to a nook over the fireplace. She pulled out a stained cloth and unwrapped a crust. Makka was ready to gag. No way was she eating that moldy thing.

"I guess there's no refrigerator."

"A what?"

Makka made a mental note to stop asking questions and behaving like an ungrateful brat. Ruefully, she accepted the rock-hard chunk.

"Better dunk it or you'll break a tooth."

"Ever hear of a chocolate doughnut?" asked Makka.

Chloe shook her head.

"Pancakes, waffles, French toast, bagels?"

Chloe appeared crestfallen. "I'm a terrible host, I don't get much company."

"This is fine, yummy in fact." She took a bite of the soggy mess and found, to her complete surprise, it had a sweet, nutlike flavor.

Chloe smiled. "Let me tell you about Etrunia."

Makka needed to know what was going on here—in this stranger-than-strange land—not that she was staying.

"Long ago, the Great Pharmakeus was our ruler. He was a gentle giant and his wife, Augusta, took our breath away with her flawless beauty and exquisite gowns. They lived north of the secret portal, beyond the mountains in Northgate. Their castle was astounding, modern for the times and impeccably clean. I was invited there twice and I can still picture the banners and tapestries, the large halls, staircases and bedrooms with brocade spreads. They even had a closet with a potty. Can you imagine?"

Yes, Makka could imagine. How did people live without bathrooms?

"But then Lady Eyrie put a bad curse on them."

"Curse?"

"Yes," Chloe nodded emphatically. "She joined forces with the diabolical Lord Hviti and his army of ghouls. Together they drove out the Great Pharmakeus and Augusta, along with the second in command the Viceroy and his wife the Vicereine, a lovely woman named Elizabeth. We adored her."

The room fell silent as Makka was lost in thought. Her mother's name was Elizabeth. Was that too weird a coincidence? Yes. Probably. And hadn't Jesper mentioned her name as well?

What the heck was going on here?

Makka prodded Chloe to continue. "Then what happened?"

Before Chloe could explain, she whipped her head around and put her finger to her lips. "Shhhh. I hear something. Come!" She grabbed Makka's hand and pulled her out of the chair. "We must leave right this minute. They have us surrounded!"

"Who?" Makka trembled with dread. "Who's here?"

"Lady Eyrie's soldiers. They keep a close eye on this cottage, they know where and when I leave."

Without another word, Chloe yanked up the small rug and tugged at a heavy metal ring in the floor. Suddenly, the trapdoor opened and she pushed Makka down into the darkness as she herself followed pulling the door shut as she descended. The pitch black was suffocating. Makka stood rooted to the spot as Chloe lit a small torch illuminating a stairway leading straight to hell.

"Go, hurry. We must get to Thio's castle before they catch us."

~ 13 ~

THE TRUTH SPILLS FORTH

"Come, quick!" Chloe raced down the steps at breakneck speed as Makka prayed she didn't trip and pitch forward into eternity.

"Are we going to the portal?" she asked, gripping the hem of her jumper.

"No, only Jesper can get through the portal."

"Where is he?" she gasped.

"The Tower of Nideon."

Tower of what? Makka couldn't wrap her head around this bewildering nonsense. *Who* were these people and what did they expect *her* to do?

Chloe felt awful. This race for their lives wasn't the way she had planned to introduce Makka to Etrunia. Not by a long shot, but now there was no choice. Makka seemed like a sweet girl, trustworthy, willful and kind-hearted, despite her snooty attitude. They ran for what seemed like forever in the darkness through twisty corridors, around tree roots and through sticky and slimy spider webs. Makka felt as if she had hundreds of spiders

Ing-Marie Stenglein

crawling all over her. The air was oppressive, hot and humid, smelling musty—like mushrooms and mold. Makka sneezed.

"Here," Chloe suddenly veered to the right and Makka, not being able to see where they were headed, tripped and slammed into the dirt wall.

"Ouch, damn, that hurt." She rubbed her forehead where a bruise had begun to blossom. Chloe turned around; her face glowed in the firelight.

"Are you okay?"

"Yes, I guess."

"Good, we're going up to daylight so shield your eyes and for god's sake, don't speak. The soldiers could be anywhere."

"Soldiers?"

"Lady Eyrie's army! I told you before. Shhhh."

Army? Soldiers. Makka's knees buckled, but she caught herself and crept forward, upward on a ramp. Chloe lifted a small hatch revealing a tiny patch of blue high above. Makka shielded her eyes from the sudden light and climbed out. Chloe replaced the moss cover and they crept into a copse of beech trees.

"Come, hurry! Stay close."

Makka did as she was instructed. From the corner of her eye, she saw a fluttering. A leaf? A chipmunk, squirrel or bird? She wasn't sure. There, there was another one! Something moved up ahead. She heard branches crack and realized she wasn't watching where she was walking. Chloe turned around and gave her a silent warning. Birds trilled and flew from the treetops into the bright, crystal blue air.

The day was clear and crisp and the extra fabric of her jumper swished around her bare legs—something she wasn't accustomed to. But the forest was rich with small clusters of tamarack trees and Makka marveled at the intense colors of red, orange, gold and green. Despite her predicament, it was simply gorgeous.

Chloe pointed to a path to their right. "That's the Pristine Path, it welcomes newcomers to Etrunia. Just north of the mountains behind us, it turns into the Royal Road."

Both women stopped and turned around to stare at the snow-capped mountains behind them. "The portal is in there, right?" asked Makka.

Chloe nodded. "And there's a tunnel that goes through the rock leading to the Royal Road. It was intended to keep invaders out. But, of course, Lady Eyrie was familiar with all the ways to get in and out of the castle, being the sister of our illustrious ruler."

They continued forward as Chloe continued the story.

"Since this peaceful country was always under attack from invaders who wanted to poach our fertile land for farming, as well as the rich ores to make weapons and the magical crystals that abound here, Lady Eyrie was put in charge of guarding the sprawling city of Southistle at the southern border. Pharmakeus guarded the north. To the east is the Desert of Lost Souls."

"That sounds scary."

"No worries. We're not going that way. But when the wind is blowing from that direction, you can feel the intense heat." She conveniently withheld the fact that Makka would, indeed, be going to that horribly truly frightening place before long.

Now fully engrossed, feeling a tad more confident in herself, she asked: "Then what?"

"Pharmakeus and his sister, Lady Eyrie, had different plans for Etrunia. Pharmakeus was immersed in ruling the country, defending the northern border, working out peace treaties with warring factions, trade agreements, and ensuring our progress forward toward a more enlightened age instead of wallowing in poverty and ignorance. But soon he noticed that the messengers that he sent to Lady Eyrie never returned. They simply vanished."

Makka stopped in her tracks. *No way!* Just a second ago she felt fine and now her entire body was tingling with electricity, a jolt of familiarity washed over her. Perhaps she was recalling a portion of some strange tale she'd read. But no, this was something else entirely and not in a good way.

Chloe's words filtered through her brain. "Finally he decided to pay his sister a visit. It was a long and dangerous journey. If only he had stayed home…"

Her voice trailed off.

"What happened?" asked Makka breathlessly. "Did someone get murdered?"

Chloe shook her head sadly. "Even worse than that."

"What could be worse than murder?"

Ignoring the question, Chloe said tersely, "Come, hurry. We must get to the Whip Line."

Makka froze in her tracks. Whip Line? Did people stand in line to get whipped?

No, that couldn't be. Could it? She broke into a cold sweat. She sank to her knees as a burnt umber face peered at her from the other side. She shrieked and fell backward. Her heart was beating like a hummingbird—at a thousand beats per second.

Suddenly, the woods seemed to come alive with fluttering and hoots, whistles and grunts.

Makka covered her ears and prayed that she'd wake up from this nightmare as she heard Chloe say, "Come, hurry. Your life depends on it."

~ 14 ~

THE WHIP LINE

They raced through the woods to the Whip Line like lunatics trying to escape an asylum. Things had gone from bad to worse for Makka, who said a silent prayer to her brother Eddie, wishing he was here to protect her from this craziness. Suddenly, Chloe pulled to a stop in front of a huge tree.

"Here. We're going up now."

Makka shielded her eyes as her head tilted back to see the height of this ancient tree. It seemed to stretch into the sky. In fact, she couldn't see any blue at all—only a platform way up there. No way!

"How…" Her words trailed off as she wondered if she was supposed to climb up that monstrosity.

"Come, here!" Chloe sounded desperate and fraught with urgency. As Makka worked her way around the trunk, she was dumbfounded to see a door cut perfectly in the trunk. Before her brain could compute what was happening, Chloe grabbed her hand and pulled her inside. The door slammed shut and suddenly they were moving upward in the gloom.

She heard Chloe grunting as she pulled on a rope attached to a pulley somewhere high above. The creaking and groaning was magnified in the confined space. Makka was sweating, her heart hammering. Claustrophobia ran in her family. They all had it—fear of tight spaces.

She did her best to appear brave and cool, but inside it felt as though the air was pressurized as she fought for every breath. The heat and aroma of rotted wood threatened to overpower her as she let her fingertips run over the rough sheath of wood that comprised the heart and soul of this ages-old stately pine tree.

At last, the noise stopped and the platform came to a shuddering halt. Chloe was panting from the extraordinary effort it had taken to lift two people fifty feet in the air. She pushed another trap door open and a whoosh of cool, fresh air blew in.

Makka took a deep breath as though she had just surfaced from the bottom of the sea. In a way, she had. Again, Chloe took her hand and they stepped onto a narrow ledge. Makka nearly fell off as she stepped back, surprised to see someone else already there.

This adventure was a complete shock to her system and now the worst case scenario was playing out. They had lured her into the sky as she pictured herself being tossed off the platform and splatting like a watermelon on the ground below. Even the soft bed of pine needles so far down there wouldn't cushion her fall enough to keep her alive.

There were no ambulances here. No 911 emergency line. No telephone lines at all. Only the Whip Line, which she now saw for the first time.

Chloe grasped her cold hand and squeezed it. "Settle down, Makka. We are safe here. This is Sergeant Barrett; he's here to help us get to Thio's castle."

With great effort, Makka pulled her eyes off the ground below and turned them in the direction of their escort. He was wiry and dark-skinned, about her height and dressed in camouflage that looked as though his uniform had been washed a thousand times and then put through a shredder.

Basically, they were rags and then, suddenly, she realized that was the fluttering she had seen in the forest was the fabric from the shredded uniforms.

As she studied Sergeant Barrett's face, she recognized it as the one that had peered at her by the tree a little while ago. He wasn't much older than her brother Eddie, maybe nineteen.

Any resistance was futile at this point. What could she do way up in the air, out on a ledge of a tree in the middle of nowhere in a country called Etrunia with two people that may or may not be out to kill her.

Chloe shouted, "Watch me, I'm going first. I'll meet you on the other side."

Makka watched as the sergeant helped Chloe navigate her way onto a seat that looked like the swings at the park she played in as a child. It was attached to what she now recognized as a zip line contraption going down through the treetops and ending at what was left of an old battlement station.

She turned her head to see what it looked like but saw only a bunch of stones. Her heart sank. She hoped the rope would hold and the pulleys wouldn't jam. Suddenly, Chloe was headed down at a rapid rate, her skirt fluttering in the breeze as she held onto a handle attached to the swing for dear life. Makka gasped aloud and she saw Sergeant Barrett grin. This was great fun for the young soldier, but she was terrified beyond words.

Her knees buckled and she teetered toward the edge of the narrow platform. With one hand on the pulley rope, the soldier reached out and grabbed Makka's pony tail just as she stepped toward the rim, pulling her to safety. She sank down, the jumper splaying out around her as she wiped her tears with the back of her hand.

Then she heard the dreaded words: "You're next."

With her heart thundering, she sat down on the rubbery sling seat, closed her eyes, and hurled into the void.

~ 15 ~

THE MORASS

Makka was barely settled in the swing seat when she shot forward with a tremendous whoosh, moving fast and bouncing wildly with every pull of the rope by Sergeant Barrett. Her ears popped and before she had a chance to catch her breath, she was sailing over the treetops, completely unseen from below. As she jounced around, she caught a glimpse of something on fire and realized it was Chloe's sweet little home.

She grappled with the enormity of her situation. *Was it my fault,* she wondered. Would they have burned the house if I hadn't come here? Overwhelmed with guilt and worry, she didn't see a tree branch that slashed her cheek, causing an ugly red welt; her eyes watered.

Zipping along toward a destination she could never have imagined in her wildest dreams, Makka clung with every ounce of strength as the violent and erratic ride took her further from home and deeper into the mystery of Etrunia.

After what seemed an eternity, the swing slowed and began its descent toward the remaining battlement of Thio the Fair's ruined castle. Only ugly, burnt slabs of walls remained standing, not enough to keep anybody out. The towers with the arrow loops were smashed to smithereens, the moat had dried up and the drawbridge had been scavenged for its wooden planks. The only remaining building was the keep—the enclosed area that held the kitchen, bedrooms and throne room. But the roof had been burned off and the top of the structure was damaged beyond repair. Makka wondered who could possibly live here, exposed to the elements and the enemy.

The ride ended suddenly with a screech of the wheel, a jerk of the rope and an abrupt end to the forward motion. The chair swung crazily in the air as Makka twisted in the breeze, unable to free herself. Chloe reached up to help her out.

"I know the ride's a little bumpy, but we saved half a day and we avoided being spotted by the enemy so it's worth the discomfort."

Makka grimaced in pain.

"Okay then. Follow me into the Morass."

"Morass? That sounds hazardous."

"I'll protect you."

Chloe turned abruptly as Makka wondered how the slight and unarmed girl could offer any security whatsoever and suddenly she realized Chloe was disappearing right before her eyes—her trusted guide was sinking into the earth. Only two steps behind, Makka noticed too late that she, too, was being gobbled by the spongy ground. Agitated and fearful of being smothered or buried alive, her head pounded like a kettle drum.

Down they went, further into the soggy earth as the odor of rotted vegetation and musty, rank soil became pungent and overpowering, causing a bitter taste at the back of her throat and a sneezing fit. As Makka was about to turn and flee, ready to take her chances with Lady Eyrie's guards and plead for mercy, she and Chloe entered a vast underground chamber—a great hall with a dirt floor hard-packed from years of use.

The earthen walls were supported by heavy boards, possibly from the drawbridge. The low ceiling was decorated with dangling tree roots that had been looped up and secured in order to hold lanterns. The effect was a warm and homey, like a starry night. Enchanted, Makka took a few minutes to look around, spotting a hearth along one wall and a small pond in the center. There must be a chimney leading out to the remnants of the castle above them.

"When the fortress was destroyed, Thio and her soldiers had no alternative," Chloe explained. "They simply went below ground and rebuilt everything." They took a few tentative steps forward and noticed a number of long wooden plank tables with benches on both sides that could seat at least forty people or more.

"There's a huge number of rooms, a complex labyrinth that lead off this grand ballroom to the soldiers' quarters, Thio's chambers, the throne room, the humongous kitchen, and even the livestock pen. The entire castle is underground."

Both women turned suddenly as a tall, well-built soldier with dirt on his face and shredded camo rags entered. Chloe said: "This is Captain Lourdes."

He bowed slightly, struggling not to drop something heavy that was nestled in a pillow he vigilantly carried with upturned hands.

Makka prayed it wasn't something dead or some weird food she'd be expected to eat. Again, she felt her head swimming and knees go weak. Chloe held her elbow tightly to keep her upright. She let her eyes travel around the room, distracting her mind and trying to set aside her fear of the unknown and the dangers that lay ahead.

Again, she was acutely aware of the heavy homespun dress and wished that she was in something lighter that she could peel off in a minute for a rapid escape. Not that there was any way to escape.

"Follow me," he commanded.

Chloe and Makka fell in step behind him. Captain Lourdes ducked his head to get to the next room and there, in the center, was a magnificent carved wooden throne. The masterpiece was all one huge stump, whittled with fantastical beasts and birds, flowers and designs, and polished until it gleamed in the glow of the overhead lanterns. The burl wood was multicolored in shades of ash, teak, burnt orange and mahogany.

The show was about to begin; the curtain was going up on the most mystical drama Makka could have imagined. But instead of being hurtled into space, she was sliding back in time to the days of dragons and dungeons, sorcerers and wizards, bows, arrows and Flesh-Eating Cocoons.

~ 16 ~

THIO THE FAIR

Thio the Fair seemed to float into the room from the other side of the hall taking Makka's breath away. Surrounded by four stunning maidens, each gowned in a shade of green—lichen, jade, peapod and olive—Thio gestured to the visitor. "Come closer, I won't bite you."

The dazzling woman strode into the room in total command, head high, body erect. Her pale face had a slightly greenish tint. Her lips were pink and her eyes the most amazing color of chartreuse. They almost didn't look real. Makka wondered if she was wearing contact lenses, but quickly corrected her thoughts to remember that contacts were light years in the future.

Thio's long white hair was parted in the center and trailed down over her slender shoulders like a silken waterfall. The bottom was cut bluntly and looked as though the tips had been dunked in a puddle of grass-hued dye. It couldn't be natural, but Makka accepted the shaded effect and the effect was dramatic and spectacular.

"Isn't she stunning?" whispered Chloe.

Gorgeous didn't come close to describing the ruler of this subterranean empire. She carried herself with purpose, her entire persona radiating a unique perfection of grace and ageless beauty. Her skin was smooth as glass, without a single wrinkle or blemish. Her demeanor was so reserved and mature she could have been thirteen years old or three hundred. Makka couldn't even fathom her age and didn't try to guess.

Chloe pulled Makka down to her knee as Thio the Fair strode across the room her pale shimmery gown rustling around her ankles, dotted with silver beads of dew. With a whoosh, she swept the emerald studded hem aside and slid onto the carved and polished burl wood throne. As she settled under the flickering orange lanterns, the diadem in her hair—a modest tiara was comprised of pale green quartz and deep, rich bottle green emeralds.

"So this is the lovely young lady who has come to save us all," she nodded at Makka who felt her cheeks flush crimson. "So pleased to meet you Makka. We have waited for your arrival for a long, long time. How do you like the Morass?"

Makka smiled and held two thumbs up, unable to utter a single word.

Thio the Fair smiled. "So we have your blessing. Then we can begin."

The Fair Maiden clapped her tiny, pale hands twice. Startled and overwhelmed by her predicament and the imminent possibility of her demise, Makka felt the bile rising in her throat again as she watched Captain Lourdes struggle forward with his precious cargo. He placed the pillow holding something heavy, and obviously dearly cherished, on a pedestal that had somehow magically appeared before them. He yanked off the cloth cover to reveal a green-tinted quartz crystal sphere the size of a bowling ball. It must have weighed a ton since the military man was drenched in sweat from his effort.

The ruler of the Morass leaned forward and placed her hands on the glowing orb, which throbbed and pulsated, glowing sea green, aqua, lavender, rose, ginger, citrus yellow and back to green.

Then she lifted her head and looked at Makka and said: "Get comfortable my dear. Chloe will leave soon, but you have been placed in good hands. We will protect you from evil—for now."

She wondered where her new friend would go or where she'd live, now that her cottage was just a jumble of charred wood. She felt awful for Chloe, a fearless and funny woman so filled with joy.

"Pay attention now because the story I am about to tell may save your life in the near future. You are here for a purpose that will be revealed over time and in many ways. Let me start now by telling you about this crystal and Lady Eyrie and why you have been brought to Etrunia. It was no accident."

Makka was relieved that she was still on bended knee otherwise she would have toppled over. She was stressed and starving and barely able to comprehend the torrent of information that bombarded her.

~ 17 ~

LADY EYRIE

When everyone was settled, Thio the Fair sat squarely on her solid wood throne. Chloe and Makka brushed off some dirt from their knees and relaxed on small, round stools, grateful that they could listen in comfort. Kneeling on the hard-packed earth floor had been excruciating, even for a few minutes.

Thio folded her pale hands in her lap and Makka noticed they were devoid of rings or blemishes. Her nails were painted chartreuse and matched her eyes. Did they have nail polish? Impossible! Were they naturally that color?

Thio's whispery, high-pitched voice broke through her wandering thoughts.

"Let us all welcome Makka Sinclair to Etrunia. She has come to us in our hour of need, at a time of crises when we felt all was lost—that we would be vanquished by evil forces and made to surrender to the wickedness that now abounds around us all."

Thio's face drooped as her eyes filled with sorrow. She seemed so fragile and vulnerable as she continued. "At one time we were the Forest People—proud and honest, hardworking people who lived and breathed under the loving rule of the Great

Pharmakeus. He was a wise soul who governed Etrunia with warmth, compassion and an understanding that the world was evolving around us while we were stuck in the past.

"But, trouble arose between Pharmakeus and his sister, Lady Eyrie who lived in the South. The only way to learn the truth was for Pharmakeus himself to travel from the far north, past the mountains and the portal to her castle in Southistle. When he arrived, he found that his sister had morphed into someone he didn't recognize or even know. Once considered a beauty with raven black hair and ruby lips, her eyes were now dull and clouded. Her face was hollow; her cheekbones protruded. She looked like a walking corpse."

Makka pictured a zombie as Thio's sorrowful voice filtered back into her consciousness.

"Lady Eyrie, once so fun-loving and striking in appearance, was drawn and haggard; her lovely tresses were uncombed and streaked with premature gray. When her brother questioned her about the messengers who had disappeared, she was cold and distant, refusing to answer or address his concerns. When he pointedly asked if she'd murdered the missing soldiers and messengers, Lady Eyrie replied flippantly—or so it's been rumored: 'Anything's possible.'"

"My dad always uses that expression," Makka blurted out—and then blushed violently at her enormous blunder.

Thio the Fair nodded in agreement and continued. "According to reliable sources, he learned that she had taken up sorcery and kept a powerful crystal ball on a pedestal in the great chamber."

"Like yours?"

A gasp filled the chamber as Makka's words hung in midair. A look of consternation came over Thio's face and Makka was suddenly overwhelmed with fear that she was drowning. She could barely breathe. It was a heart-stopping moment, like blurting out something in a school assembly—only worse.

"Yes, Makka. Like mine. There are only five in all of Etrunia and only the most powerful wizards can master the art of reading crystals like this *orbuculum*. See the intricate rainbows in the sphere? It makes for perfect for scrying."

"What's that?"

"Seeing the past, present and future—a form of clairvoyance."

"Very neat."

"Yes, well, only if it's used for good," Thio agreed. "But Lady Eyrie had enlisted the service of Arcite, the Grand Wizard, and together they made a formidable opponent. Even Pharmakeus with his powerful army was no match for their occult treachery."

Makka's stomach churned and she regretted not packing a crust of moldy bread in the pouch that hung from her belt. Her mouth was so dry.

"I'm so sorry," she managed to squeak out. "I'm so thirsty. Do you have a bottle of water?"

Thio's green eyes searched the guest quizzically. "Bottle of water?"

Makka flushed beet red at yet another reference to the future as Thio the Fair clapped her hand and a maiden, wearing a lichen-colored pale green jumper similar to Makka's, brought two pewter cups filled with liquid. The girl's face was pale, like

71

Thio's, with a faint greenish tinge. Makka was not surprised— after all, they lived underground. It was no wonder they looked so transparent.

She smiled and gratefully took the cup, whispering to Chloe: "Is this safe to drink?"

"Perfectly."

Too thirsty to wait one more second, she followed Chloe's lead and tilted the pewter cup upward, draining the water in a series of long, satisfying gulps. It was surprisingly sweet and tasted more pure than even the most expensive bottled water.

"The spring water comes downstream from the mountains and into the Alcazor River," explained Captain Lourdes. "It's melted snow at its finest."

Thio the Fair nodded at the Captain and continued as Makka's heart raced and beads of dread dribbled down her back, tickling her spine. She shifted uneasily on the stool.

"The meeting between Pharmakeus and his sister spiraled out of control. After realizing that the rumors were true about her sorcery with the Grand Wizard Arcite, they fought bitterly. Everyone in the castle could hear their shrieks and howls. He pulled out his sword and went crazy, knocking over furniture and splitting the wood. He picked up things and threw them across the room and pushed some of her bodyguards down, threatening to kill them. It was mayhem, total madness. It was awful. Meanwhile, Lady Eyrie cowered near the pedestal, fearful that he would destroy her most precious possession—the crystal ball. To make peace and calm his rage, she admitted that she was jealous of his power and asked for forgiveness."

Makka felt as though she knew this story already—but that was impossible.

"Lady Eyrie calmed her brother down with some silly sweet talk, reminding him how they fought as kids and said that she would defer to his authority. He softened and put his sword back in the sheath just as the Grand Wizard swooped in causing the crystal ball to glow as though it was on fire. He mumbled a chant and suddenly orange flames shot from the crystal and engulfed our illustrious leader, causing him to shriek like a wild animal and crumple into a pile of ashes. He simply vanished on the spot.

"Everyone was stunned into silence, except Lady Eyrie who began to howl and clap her hands. The Wizard joined her and, suddenly, the guards who'd arrived with Pharmakeus went up in small puffs of smoke, vaporized into thin air."

"No. That's impossible!" Makka's face was white as snow.

"Even more bizarre, his wife, Augusta, who had stayed home while her husband traveled south, as well as all of their entire staff and servants in the Northgate castle, vanished as well. Now only the rats and mice live there."

Makka was stunned. "I thought these things only happened in fairy tales, not real life," she said.

But was this real life?

Chloe placed a restraining hand on Makka's arm, indicating she should stop talking.

"If you don't focus on what is happening *here and now*," said Thio. "You will find yourself unable to cope with the perils yet to come. You will be powerless to make rational decisions when you need them the most."

"I just want to go back to Minnesota," she pleaded, a tear slipping down her face.

"Not just yet," added Thio. "You must know the rest of the story."

She sipped from a jeweled goblet that was offered to her, smiled at the man servant and continued.

"Lady Eyrie and the diabolical Lord Hviti have possession of two of the five crystal balls in our kingdom. Now they've joined forces. Nobody is safe. Their supremacy has put our country under siege. Just look around. Chloe's home was burned to the ground and we have been vanquished, forced to live here, in the shadow of our once mighty fortress."

She paused and dropped her head. Tears welled in her eyes but she blinked them back, took a deep breath and continued.

"We were once a proud community; we were the Forest People that lived on the edge of the Morass, fierce supporters of the Great Pharmakeus. Lady Eyrie knew this and you can see what happened. Our homes and castle were destroyed, our prosperous farms and land taken away and our livelihood destroyed. We were forced underground and can no longer call ourselves the Forest People. Now we are the Moss Tribe.

"But, no fear, there are Resistance Forces everywhere in Etrunia—small organized armies of rebels, who are trying to take down the evil forces to allow the return of the Great Pharmakeus. THAT is why you are here, Makka. You will help Etrunia's people come together to crush the evil leaders so we can prosper as a great land once again."

"Me? No way! Maybe you're thinking of Joan of Arc. She was a warrior. I am just an ordinary girl."

"You are the least ordinary young woman—you are the daughter of The Ancients."

"Say what?"

"All will be revealed in time. For now, just know that you have been brought here to save us from complete destruction and total annihilation."

Makka felt the blood drain from her head and a wooziness wash over her, as her heart sank to the soles of her ugly shoes.

She needed help immediately, if not sooner. Rose and Brian were the only ones who could help, especially Brian who made her feel safe.

Suddenly, the crystal ball began vibrating again, pulsating with an ungodly pinging. Even below the earth, they heard a wild groaning, throbbing and howling, as though a prehistoric monster were hovering above. Startled glances filled the room, mouths dropped open.

"Is that a helicopter?" Makka asked hopefully.

Chloe grabbed her arm, shouting above the racket. "Heli…what? What are you talking about, Makka?"

"Maybe it's a Blackhawk," she shouted, jumping off the stool and racing toward the exit, which was blocked by Captain Lourdes and his men.

As Makka skidded to a stop, she wondered how Thio the Fair knew so much about her. She hadn't seen a telephone, cell phone tower, or even a carrier pigeon since she woke up. No smoke signals or forest nymphs to herald their arrival. She was deep in the woods without a compass.

Most important: what did she mean she came from the Ancients? Ancient what? This was total craziness—and the noise was making her ears vibrate.

Unaware of the disasters that lay ahead, feeling sick to her stomach, and yet excited at her impending imagined rescue, she slipped between the guards and found the ramp leading to the path of madness, murder, magical crystal balls, and mayhem.

~ 18 ~

THE GRIZZARDS

"Makka! Makka, come back!"

A chorus of agitated voices followed her as she raced toward the exit, into the heart of horrifying noise that filtered from high above the fields down into the underground chambers. Even as her mind was tripping over itself with plans and ideas for escape, this was a moment of temporary glory as a trace of fresh air snaked up her nostrils wiping away the aroma of rot and decay.

The passageway brightened, until her eyes ached from the sudden light that assaulted her. With the truly terrifying noise from above, she didn't realize that everybody was hot on her heels, hoping to keep her safe, while viewing the spectacle firsthand.

The soldiers had already positioned themselves facing the fields and forest to ward off any sudden attack from the enemy. They could not risk losing their liberator when Etrunia teetered on the brink of destruction.

As she reached the light, the air was thick with raucous cries and what appeared to be swiftly moving black clouds that swooped and changed direction every few seconds, virtually blotting out the sunlight. Either it was a tornado or some vaporous monster approaching, intent on gobbling them up for lunch. The sky turned dark and then gray, swirling in a bizarre aerial ballet.

As they looked into the distance, a tsunami of snowy white birds, each with a six-foot wingspan and black markings swooped down, their long, red curved beaks opening and closing like crab claws. The strident, high-pitched racket unnerved Makka as she was suddenly surrounded by Thio the Fair, her handmaidens, and a host of soldiers—their bodies pressing too close for comfort. If a stampede occurred, she'd be trampled underfoot. They were all surrounded by the soldiers, pressed into a clump of bodies.

Thus distracted, nobody noticed Sergeant Barrett arrive from the underground stable with two roan-colored mares; nor did anybody see Chloe hoist herself onto one of them and disappear into the dense forest, lost from sight almost immediately.

As though the commotion wasn't loud enough, it suddenly ramped up ten decibels. The noise was deafening as everyone covered their ears and two black spots appeared amongst the flock of shifting snowy birds. The crowd watched in awe, gasping with astonishment as the two spots grew larger.

Makka knew it was a *helo*, a Coast Guard helicopter or one from the FBI, or perhaps her dad had chartered one to rescue her. They were certainly two military transports coming to save her—she even heard the familiar *thrump, thrump, thrump* of the rotors as they washed through the air.

Then, suddenly, someone in the crowd yelled: "It's the Grizzards, it's the Grizzards!" A chorus of chanting immediately began. "Grizzards! Grizzards! Grizzards!"

Makka peeled her eyes away from the spectacle unfolding above her and looked around for somebody to explain what a Grizzard was. But all the tugging on sleeves and all the pleading for someone to tell her was in vain. Every olive green face was upturned, eyes transfixed on the creatures that were heading right into the heart of the courtyard to the most likely landing spot, a bare patch of soil surrounded by the destroyed, abandoned castle's smashed walls and tumbled stones.

The crowd surged forward, pushing Makka toward the gigantic, flapping birds. She now saw they were blackish brown, with a wingspan of a small plane and hawk-like beaks designed for tearing flesh apart. As they spiraled down in circles, she noticed their black, beady eyes ringed with crimson, as though they crying blood.

The tempest of flapping wings as they descended created dry dust that flew into the air and settled on clothing, hair and skin. She shielded her eyes with her fingers and pressed her lips closed to avoid inhaling anything as the winged creatures approached for a landing, their fearsome talents as long and sharp as bear claws!

As the Grizzards skidded to a stop, a mighty cheer erupted. Both birds shook out their wings and tucked them neatly under their bodies. Then, as though trained, they lowered their heads to the ground and to Makka's utter disbelief, two people slid off—one from each bird's back. Everyone in the crowd knelt, except for Makka, who was too stunned to move. Thio the Fair with her pearly skin glowing in the sunlight strode over to greet the newcomers accompanied by Captain Lourdes who never seemed to be more than a few steps away from her.

"Welcome to the Morass," she said. "I hope your ride was smooth."

"It was pretty amazing," said the young man, dusting off his sleeves and smoothing his sandy colored hair, which stuck out at rakish angles from the windy ride. Makka, shocked to her core, felt as though she'd been zapped by a taser gun.

In this heart-stopping moment, she realized that voice was familiar, but how could it be? She stood as speechless among the crowd as Thio the Fair introduced them.

"Please everyone, welcome Brian and Rose Abadon," said Thio. "They are here to help Makka restore peace and order to Etrunia."

The crowd erupted like a human volcano with cheers and hats tossed in the air. It was extremely reckless to be this noisy out in the open. Lady Eyrie's spies were everywhere, and her soldiers were never far behind. But this marvelous happening was a moment too glorious not to celebrate. Makka felt the blood rush from her head and her knees buckled. Was it really Rose and Brian—dare she hope? How had they known where to find her?

No matter what, her faith in their friendship was restored and her grudge against Rose for being careless enough to allow Jesper to snatch her cell phone and run off with it was instantly forgotten.

She looked around for Chloe. She just had to meet her two Minnesota neighbors, but sweet Chloe had vanished into thin air. She called Chloe's name until she was hoarse and then, unable to comprehend everything that had happened since she awoke—the hurried breakfast, the flight down through Chloe's basement, the whip line ride from hell, the whole underground experience and the Grizzards landing—made her knees buckle and she sank to the ground, her burnt orange jumper splayed around her like a Christmas tree skirt.

Slowly the crowd disbursed, drifting away to their underground lair and suddenly Brian and Rose were at her side, grabbing her hands and whispering in her ear: "We would never abandon you, Makka. We are in this together, for better and for worse."

Makka smiled so wide she thought her face would crack.

Rose kissed her cheek, her sun burnt face and long brown hair were a sight for Makka's sore eyes.

"We stick together until our work is done here. Everyone agree?"

"What, exactly, are we here for?" Makka still didn't understand anything that had happened or why she had been chosen, although she took great comfort in having her new friends back at her side.

"All will be revealed in time," said Brian, the oldest and wisest of the group. "Come, let's go below and stay out of harm's way."

They helped Makka to her feet and together they went through the entrance to Thio the Fair's underground castle to learn their fate.

~ 19 ~

REUNITED

After they had all gathered in the grand chamber, Thio the Fair clapped her hands three times and the room that buzzed with excitement fell silent. "Please, pay attention everyone; your very lives depend on it."

Makka drew in a deep breath and sighed; from the corner of her eye she noticed Brian glancing at her, causing her heart to hammer in her ears. There it was—her life hanging in the balance—*again*! She was caught smack dab in the middle and there was no way out, unless she was dreaming and could wake herself up.

Thio's voice broke through her mental static like tinkling bells.

"First, I want thank Brian and Rose Abadon for joining us in our battle to save Etrunia from the wicked Lady Eyrie and Lord Hviti." She nodded in their direction and smiled broadly, white teeth flashing like pearls. "They have risked their lives for us."

She walked over to the twins, embracing each of them warmly. Makka had a close-up view of her shamrock-tipped hair and wondered if her mom would allow her to dye the ends of her sun-kissed locks blue or purple or red. *Doubtful*.

"We will celebrate your arrival in a few minutes, but first I must get serious."

"Seriously," Makka whispered to Rose, "can this get any crazier?"

Rose put her fingers to her lips and shook her head.

"I really need to get home now," Makka hissed. "I hate this."

But once again Thio's voice cut through her thoughts as she realized the crystal ball was pulsating light and glowing like something from a movie.

"There are five crystal balls in Etrunia. Alone, each is extremely powerful and each provides a visual portal to the past and future, bringing supremacy to whoever has possession, that is, if the person knows how to use and control it.

"One is here, in front of you.

"One is in the hands of Lady Eyrie and Lord Hviti has one. The fourth is in Lovenfell, located in the White City. But more about that later."

"And the fifth?" asked Makka.

Thio shifted on the throne and continued.

"Before the Great Pharmakeus left his castle north of the mountains to visit his sister in Southistle, he hid his crystal ball—the fifth one. It's rumored to be hidden in the ancient city under the sands of the Desert of Lost Souls, but nobody knows for certain. Then, he had his most trusted conjurer create an instrument that would always be able to guide him to it. This strange one-of-a-kind mechanism that would guide someone to the crystal ball and the powerful throne is known as the Cvector. Whoever is in possession of the Cvector will be able to find Pharmakeus's crystal ball and also the portal through which Pharmakeus can be brought back here to Etrunia.

"Remember, whoever has all five of the crystal balls will rule the universe. He or she will be all powerful, dominant in controlling Etrunia and the lands beyond our borders. The country as we know it will be torn apart by death and destruction if they fall into the hands of Lady Eyrie or Lord Hviti."

She paused to collect herself. There was a rustling and shifting of weight as everyone held their breath waiting for her to continue.

Makka stared at the sphere, feeling her entire being sucked into Thio's power as she beckoned to Makka, Rose and Brian to come forth and touch the pulsating orb. Startled, the three American teenagers glanced at each other and rose slowly and unsteadily, grasped hands and walked at a snail's pace toward the pedestal.

"Please place your hands on it," commanded Thio the Fair. The touch of the cool stone sent a jolt of electricity through them, as though they'd been zapped by lightning. Thio's voice, like an angel on high, chanted:

"Oh, will you be staying or fleeing in fear?
We need your strength to help us here.
Under water or high in the sky,
Without your presence we will surely die."
"Through dark forests and dead of night
Stay strong, you are on the side of right
You are here to right the wrongs
Vanquished evil forces and always stay strong."
She smiled benignly. "There, that's done."

Brian, Rose and Makka removed their hands from the crystal. Captain Lourdes stepped forward and wrapped it in an olive-colored cloth and removed it as the pedestal slid down into the earth.

"And now, it's time to celebrate." Again, the ruler of the Morass clapped her tiny pale hands.

From an adjacent room, the sounds of music being played on the harp, lute, violins and accompanied by the steady beat of a drum called a "naker" which hung around the neck of a short, fat man filled the air. A fiddler joined in, stomping his wooden clogs to the earth and yet another turned the wheel of a hurdy-gurdy, a contraption of strings and keys that rose and fell, making a veritable symphony. The eerie whine of a bagpipe rose over the melody, bringing everyone to the brink of tears.

The crowd surged into the great dining hall where long wooden tables were laid out with plates and goblets. Soldiers in their shredded camouflage sat next to fair maidens as the scullery crew brought out platters of food—a genuine feast of deep-fried meat pies, baked root vegetables, roast chicken, plates of peas, baskets of breads and bowls of oatmeal dripping with cinnamon and sugar.

Large pitchers of sugar wine were set out and pewter goblets were quickly filled. Makka's throat felt like sandpaper and she took a deep gulp, savoring the honey flavor of the burgundy liquid.

"What is this? Am I going to get drunk?" she asked Brian.

He took a sip and smiled. "Sweet wine," he replied. "Delicious and completely non- alcoholic. Made from honey and beetroot.

Bottoms up." He clinked his goblet to hers, drained the wine in a single gulp and burped from the soles of his feet.

They all dug in greedily, grabbing at the provisions with their fingers, shoving handfuls into their mouths as though they hadn't eaten in a year. Makka couldn't remember the last time she'd had a proper meal—certainly the hard crust of bread at Chloe's that morning didn't count.

As she ate, she gazed around at the soldiers and Thio's handmaidens and was shocked to find that most of them looked like teenagers! She leaned over to Rose and asked why they weren't in school.

"Lady Eyrie shut down all schools when she took power. That's one important reason that we're here—to put their lives back in order. Get these kids back to their normal lives."

That hit home to Makka. SHE should be getting her own life in order—getting ready for school, fixing up her new room. But the fateful meeting with Brian and Rose had turned her life upside down and inside out. She recalled their bizarre castle-like home, the gnomes, the butterfly sandwich, Jesper and her stolen cell phone which had led to her ending up on the other side of the portal in this bizarre scenario.

And yet it seemed so perfectly normal with everyone eating and drinking and chatting and dancing. A juggler in the corner tossed colored balls and acrobats leaped across the room doing handsprings and balancing on one another. One hung upside down from the low ceiling trying to wiggle out of leather cuffs, like a medieval Houdini.

Despite any misgivings about being in this magical world, so different than anything she could even have imagined, Makka suddenly had the feeling that everything would be all right.

No matter what came along, she would handle it.

PART THREE: THE TOWER OF NIDEON

~ 20 ~

THE FIRST NIGHT

The three friends were led down a labyrinth of halls to simply furnished rooms with low ceilings and earthen walls. Each contained a small wooden table upon which rested a pitcher of water and a basin for washing up. A wood-frame bed was in the center of the room with a straw mattress covered with a colorful quilt in earthy shades. A simple straight-back chair was the only other item in the Spartan room. A towel hung on a hook near the ewer and a cotton nightshirt lay on the bed.

Makka bid goodnight to her friends, washed her face, rinsed her mouth, unlaced the heavy cotton jumper, slipped gratefully into the soft cotton gown and fell into a fitful slumber.

A nightmarish kaleidoscope of huge flying birds, terrifying woodland creatures, pulsating crystal balls and raggedy soldiers filled her head. She imagined hordes of worms and insects crawling over her clothes and through her hair in the eternal dark of the underground fortress. She tossed and turned feeling smothered until, at some point in the night, her brother, Eddie appeared, floating above her.

"I have your back," he whispered in the pitch black. "Everything is under control, although it might not seem so, Makka. I am always nearby and you are never truly alone." A warm golden glow engulfed the chamber filling her with absolute contentment; she fell into an exhausted, dreamless slumber. Without a rising sun to announce a new day, Makka had no idea what time it was when she awoke or what lay in store for them in this crazy quilt called Etrunia.

A handmaiden knocked gently to wake her for breakfast carrying a change of clothing over her arm. Makka gratefully accepted baggy khaki-colored trousers, a rough-spun cotton shirt with long-sleeves in a periwinkle blue and a thick silver-buckled belt. Makka was pleased to see there were pockets in the front and back.

Although the material was rougher than the jumper Chloe had provided, it was nice to get away from the voluminous skirt and loose bodice. She had freedom of movement and didn't feel weighted down. Home, however, was heavy on her mind.

Makka still clung to the hope that she would be back in Minnesota by dusk, her face smothered by Sasha's wet slobbery kisses, her mother crying tears of joy and her dad stoic on the outside but melting on the inside knowing his little girl was safe.

But "home" was nowhere on the horizon for any of them. Fortunately, she knew nothing of the future as she buckled the belt and laced her brown leather shoes.

She joined Brian and Rose who were similarly dressed. Rose's pants were gray and her shirt was pale pink, making her cheeks appear even rosier.

Brian's trousers were deep blue, his shirt pale yellow. They smiled wanly, none of them looking as though they were ready and able to face another long and exhausting day; all of them exhibiting the signs of a restless night's sleep—if they could even call it sleep.

In the dining room, they were surprised to see the dregs of last night's festivities had vanished, replaced instead by bowls of porridge, baskets of homemade bread and pots of jam, chunks of cheese and honeycombs dripping with sweetness. Huge urns of hot steaming liquid made her tummy rumble loudly which was strange because Makka felt she had eaten a sumptuous feast only minutes ago.

After they'd finished their meal, gongs sounded throughout the chamber and everyone began moving toward the throne room yet again. It was disorienting, being under the ground with no light, no birds chirping or wind rustling. Thio the Fair, looking exactly like she did the day prior—her milky skin shining, her green-hemmed white robe dotted with beads of silver dew, her emerald tiara sparkling in the lantern light—asked the guests to gather round the crystal ball.

"Look closely Makka," she said. The ball glowed cherry red, jade green and violet. "Do you see that little girl playing with the large dog; he's bigger than she is."

Makka bent closer. "That's Sasha!"

"You were smaller then. Now you are tall."

"I must have been five. I was in Florida—see, there's a palm tree."

Thio smiled benevolently. "We've been keeping tabs on you for a long while—since before you were born, actually."

Makka reeled back as Brian and Rose exchanged glances.

"How? Why? What in heaven's name is going on?" Makka backed away and bumped into Brian who put a comforting hand on her shoulders. The warmth from his palms did nothing to stop her violent shaking.

"We have been waiting for you. Our hope and our future depend on you. But don't despair. I will make sure you have help along with way."

"Along what way? I don't want to go anywhere but home."

"For now, consider this home." Thio laughed, sounding as though a thousand tiny silver bells were ringing. "I don't mean here, in our underground vault. I mean out there." She gestured upward, toward the sky far above their hidden fortress. "You are here to restore order and rediscover the land of The Ancients. There is where our salvation lies."

"Ancients? Salvation? No way."

"Yes, I'm afraid so. At the beginning of our time, there were scattered clans who lived in separate villages and small cities. Our ancestors lived in the Great Forest and built a boardwalk maze to make transporting goods easier. They were quite skilled with stonework and created some beautiful and ornate dwellings, including the castle that once sat above us.

Eventually, they moved away from the area and our numbers dwindled. Then, the Ancients appeared, setting up borders and named it Etrunia. They inhabited Etrunia for many, many years.

Then, as the Ancients eventually dwindled in number, foreign fierce warriors claimed the lands though nobody knows where they came from, but, during their reign, there was peace and prosperity throughout the land."

Brian, Rose and Makka stared at each other. They could have heard a pin drop.

"Our history is still being written. But first things first: You must get to the Tower of Nideon and retrieve the Cvector. That's the key to restoring peace."

"*Cvector?*" asked Brian and Rose in sync—something they did often, being born only minutes apart.

"I think I explained part of that yesterday. It's in the possession of Nideon, a sly weasel and a traitor. He was the man servant to the Great Pharmakeus and was entrusted with this magic amulet." Absolute silence fell upon the crowd.

"But Nideon was not faithful to Pharmakeus. He joined forces with Lady Eyrie, catering to her every whim—except that he clung to the Cvector, trying to outsmart her and claim the kingdom for his own. Now he is up to something, something awful, I can feel it in my blood. You must go, get the Cvector and report back to me. Do you understand?"

Rose and Brian nodded. But Makka didn't understand at all.

"Why can't you just ask him for it?"

"If only I could." Thio's face fell and she suddenly appeared to have aged a hundred years, her fingers gnarled, her hair coarse and wiry, her eyes red-rimmed and her face creased with lines. Makka gasped in fright.

"Okay, I'll try." She turned to plead with her friends. "We'll get the Cvector. We'll do whatever we can to help."

Thio slowly looked up, her face morphing back to its natural pearly hue, her fingers softening, and her hair perfectly straight.

Did that just happen? Makka couldn't be sure, but she had made a promise. Now she was obligated to fulfill it—to do the best she could to help Thio the Fair fight the forces of evil and restore humanity to a country torn apart by wicked and immoral traitors.

Clapping her hands, Thio summoned Captain Lourdes and Sergeant Barrett.

"Please take our honored guests to the Armory and get them fitted for their undertaking. They will need lessons and weapons for survival."

The Captain and Sergeant bowed deeply to their fearlessly exquisite leader. They turned to Makka, Brian and Rose.

"Please, follow us to the Armory. We will spend the day there. Tomorrow you will leave with knowledge in the art of war and self-defense."

~ 21 ~

THE ARMORY

Makka, Rose, and Brian followed the two soldiers—seasoned veterans barely out of their teens, if that—through the dimly lit passageways until they entered a huge, high-ceilinged room filled with bales of hay, a forge, and mountains of weaponry. A stout gray-haired man with thick legs, bright blue eyes, brown beard, and a moustache stood near the smoldering forge.

He wore a leather apron around his expansive girth and pounded ferociously on a length of red-hot steel, hammer clanging noisily against the iron anvil. Nothing had prepared them for the extreme heat and intense racket after the calm of the previous day. This was crazily hectic and much too chaotic. They stared at each other, mouths agape, as if to say, *we didn't sign up for this.* Sergeant Barrett didn't seem to notice as he slapped the smithy on the back.

"This is our blacksmith Magnus, working hard as always." Magnus glanced up, holding the hammer aloft. "Hey mate, show these toadstools how it's done."

"Sure thing," Magnus replied, hiding his annoyance at being interrupted. "This is the forge," he pointed to a pile of glowing embers in a large metal trough. "When I pull this string, it pumps the bellows on the other side of the wall, and air fans the flames so they glow red hot."

He demonstrated how it was done as Makka, Brian, and Rose jumped back to avoid being burned. He held up the long sword he was crafting.

"The grip is made of coiled rope, it's simple and yet effective to keep the hand from slipping. And this," he pointed to a bulge at the top, "is called the pommel. Without it, the sword would fly out of your hands. The hilt here," he pointed to the rectangle at the top of the blade, "is as far as you can run it through a body. But the tip is the most important."

He held it aloft and they could see that it was razor sharp. "I've already drawn it out as far as it can go without compromising the strength."

He turned to Sergeant Barrett. "I think they'd be better with Quillon daggers, easier to use for the uninitiated."

Barrett nodded in agreement. "Follow me."

They were led around the circular room, noticing for the first time that the walls were covered with instruments of death: longbows, crossbows, quivers of arrows, and slings. There were long swords, lances, battle axes, short swords, bludgeons, halberds, daggers and knives in every shape and size. Some appeared to have dried, crusted blood the color of rust flaking along the blade.

Suits of armor stood like deadly mannequins with fearsome masks. All this was well and fine, but where were the grenades, AK-15 rifles, pistols, rocket launchers, tanks, missiles and the weaponry of modern-day destruction? Did they really have to use this antiquated equipment?

"That's a *glaive*," said Captain Lourdes, pointing to a lethal-looking instrument consisting of a long wooden pole with a blade affixed to the end. "You can use it to knock someone off their horse and then stab them to death."

The blood drained from Makka's face. "Why would I do something so spiteful?"

"To save your own life, or that of your friends."

"What exactly are we getting into?" asked Rose.

Sergeant Barrett stepped forward. "Let's move on," he said, ignoring her question. "These are shields," he pointed to an astounding array stacked along the wall, each more ornate than the next. Some had crests with winged dragons and others were decorated with serpents and crossed swords, lions, stylized crosses, falcons and *fleur-de-lis*.

"You won't be using these. They're kept here in case we are attacked and need them for defense. But come here and pick a sword," he indicated a wooden block that reminded Makka of her mom's knife holder.

"The longest are heaviest so I suggest Makka and Rose stick with the smaller ones."

As they stepped forward and grasped the hilts, five young soldiers entered the chamber and approached the group. Each wore tattered camo rags and a knit hat pulled down to the ears.

"You'll practice here for a few hours with Khana, Whit, Tajari, Tor and Modie."

The baby-faced soldiers saluted. Then Khana stepped in front of Makka and Tajari moved to Rose's side. Tor and Modie faced off against Brian.

"Hey," shouted Rose, always ready to protect her brother. "Two against one isn't fair."

"Life isn't fair," said the Captain. "Tor will act as our third instructor today. We'll each work with one of you to perfect your skills in the art of self-defense. This morning we'll work on the self-protective moves and later this afternoon we'll switch it up to taking the offense."

Sergeant Barrett stepped forward. "If everybody is ready, let's begin."

Makka's arm ached from lifting the heavy sword. "This is too heavy," she complained.

Ignoring her, Khana swung her dangerous weapon over Makka's head, the whoosh cutting the thick air like butter. Suddenly, the athletic teen was alert and on the defense.

Studying the way Khana held the sword, she placed both hands on the hilt. She drew the blade aloft and felt a thrill of victory as she staved off the next blow, metal clanging and sparks flying.

"Nice," exclaimed Khana. "Now watch carefully, I'm going lower, protect your knees. Without them, you can't run."

A few feet away, Rose was struggling against Tajari who leaped and pranced like a gazelle. Poor Rose was flushed with exertion, her cheeks red, her body soaked with perspiration. She was no match for Tajari and finally dropped the weapon and sank to her knees.

Sergeant Barrett strode over and helped her up, brought her to the corner—like a boxer's manager might do—gave her some water to drink, wiped her brow and sent her back with a lighter foil with a thin blade that could inflict deadly damage.

The rest of the afternoon was lost in a haze of war drills, jabs, thrusts, parries and feints. This was not for the faint of heart with the constant heat, noise, commotion and assault on the senses.

Brian held his own against Tor and Modie. Makka managed a fleeting glance and was impressed that he held both of them at bay. She felt as though they were in a remake of *The Three Musketeers*. Could this really be a movie set? If she was being pranked it wasn't funny.

Then, without warning, she felt the flat part of the blade hit her squarely between the shoulder blades, toppling her forward into the dust. Khana stood over her. Makka turned her dirt-covered face upward. "What the?"

"You took your eyes off the enemy. That's how you get killed my friend." Khana held out her hand and pulled Makka up. Back on her feet, they shook hands.

"Lesson learned," said Makka. "Thanks."

By late in the day they were too drained to continue and Captain Lourdes ordered everyone to the mat for exercises: crunches, sit-ups, pushups, squats and jumping jacks. Rose swooned, lying beet-faced in a puddle of sweat. Tajari went to fetch a cup of water and tossed it over her, soaking the pink shirt. Makka felt awful for her friend as Khana urged her to do ten more sit-ups.

Brian had taken off his shirt at some point and his hairless back was drenched in sweat. But she couldn't think of anything even remotely romantic when her head was pounding like a herd of wild horses and her muscles screamed for mercy. Rose howled in pain. Her long hair was plastered to her head and her face was dangerously flushed. They both needed to cool down immediately—if not sooner.

As though reading their thoughts, Khana and Tajari led the two friends to adjoining small rooms each with a large wooden tub filled with bubbles. On the edge of each was a bar of balsam-scented soap; fresh cloths to dry off were laid nearby and a clean set of dry clothing, fragrant and perfectly pressed, hung from a nearby hook embedded in the dirt wall.

In the privacy of their respective chambers, Makka and Rose each climbed into a tub and slid down under the soapy water, relishing the luxury of the moment. Makka stayed in until the water turned cold and she began to shiver and the bubbles dissolved, leaving a filmy scum. Stepping out, she toweled off and dressed in her new clothes, laughing at the cotton broadcloth granny pantie. As she buttoned the shirt, something caught her attention.

Turning her head, looking at the tub she had just exited, Makka leaped with fright and backed against the wall trembling with shock. Snakes slithered in the water—brown, black, green and coppery colored in all sizes, from small to lethally large. The water roiled as they tried to leap out, only to fall back splashing and writhing.

Horrified, she pulled her clothes over her wet body and yanked open the door, fleeing down the corridor toward her assigned bedroom, growing more alarmed by the second. When she saw the familiar coverlet, she leaped into the room, slammed the door shut and threw herself on the hard mattress curling into a ball.

Something sinister was going on here. She needed a plan to climb out of this pit of despair before she was pulled into something even darker and more menacing.

Makka knew that danger is part of a teenager's life: getting caught up in the peer pressure to smoke, drink, and try drugs. But this—*this was light years beyond danger. This was insanity!*

~ 22 ~

THE QUEST

Makka lay in bed unable to move. Every muscle screamed for mercy. Khana knocked lightly and entered the room, quiet as a whisper, holding a clay jar of cream. "Sore?" she asked sympathetically.

"Does a cat have whiskers?"

"Here," she said. "rub some of this on your sore muscles, you'll feel better in a few minutes."

With Khana standing over her, Makka smeared some on her thighs, arms and shoulders. It tingled hot, cold and suddenly she felt back to normal. She slid out of bed, bending down into a squat and rising with a huge grin.

"That's amazing. Do you have some to spare?"

"If you need it, send us a message and the Grizzards will bring it."

"The Grizzards?"

"They run important errands as needed. They've been well-trained, which is a good thing because if they weren't they could tear us to bits and then feast on our flesh."

A shiver went down Makka's back. "Does Rose have some, and Brian?"

Khana nodded. "They're already up at breakfast."

Makka grabbed her clothes feeling put out. "Why didn't you wake me?"

"I did."

"Earlier, I mean. I *hate* to be last."

"You're up now," Khana said, biting her lower lip. She had only been following orders, allowing the special guest a few extra minutes to sleep.

Moments later, Makka dressed and ready, sat at the breakfast table and poured a dollop of honey into a mug of steaming tea. She dug into a sweet roll and grabbed a few pieces of bacon. "How do you feel?" Brian asked.

"I was really sore, but now—thanks to some magic muscle relaxer—I feel great."

Rose piped up, her mouth full. "We got some too. Good thing because I was so stiff I couldn't even move."

"That was quite a workout," said Brian, smothering a roll with red jam. "I think we learned a few tricks that'll hopefully help should we need to defend ourselves."

"When you're finished eating, please join us in the Throne Room. Thio the Fair has some parting gifts and so do I," said Captain Lourdes.

The three friends threw glances at each other, scarfed down the rest of their food, washed it all down with a few gulps of tea and apple cider and followed Sergeant Barrett down the long corridor.

Once again they stood awestruck at the stunning pearly-complexioned greenish-white leader of the Moss People. She was dazzling in her simplicity and yet complex at the same time. "The time has come for you to leave us," she said. "You have an extraordinary mission ahead of you."

Then she turned to Sergeant Barnett who stepped forward. "On behalf of our people, I'd like to present these short swords and scabbards. They will come in handy if you are in need of defending yourselves."

With the assistance of the Captain, they showed Makka, Rose and Brian the hammered metal swords, measuring about eight inches, with bone handles and worn leather scabbards to hold them safely to their belts. The two men helped each visitor slide the loop over the buckle and around to the back where the scabbards rested.

"This way it won't be in your way on horseback and you just have to reach behind you to be armed immediately. Try pulling the blade out now."

Makka and Brian had their swords out and in position in a split second while Rose fumbled with the scabbard. "You'll need some practice," said the Captain. "But you'll get it. Remember, you will be relying on speed and secrecy while traveling."

Then Thio slid off her Burl Wood Throne and walked over to Makka holding a cream colored quilted vest. It was sleeveless with a fur collar and chain splints running down the front. "These have been custom-made for you. We need to keep you safe at all costs. Only the finest virgin materials have been used and if you note, they have not only the chain splints to keep swords from slicing through you, they also have a thin layer of metal inside."

She flipped one open and under the silk lining, Makka could feel the hard suppleness of the chain mail. There were two large pockets outside and leather ties to hold it together in cold weather. There were no sleeves, which would have made it too bulky to move rapidly and with ease.

Captain Lourdes and Sergeant Barrett helped Brian and Rose slip into theirs. The vests were all identical except for the color: Makka's being lightest, Rose's a tawny hue and Brian's was loden green.

"We wish you the very best on your journey," said Thio, pressing her palms together and bowing. She made no attempt to embrace any of them, especially Makka. Nobody in Etrunia had the right to lay a hand on her—she was something special, sent by the forces of good and meant to lead them into the future.

They followed the Sergeant and Captain up the ramp and outside into the muted light of early dawn. The sky above them was streaked with gold and pink infused by shades of lavender and tangerine.

Three horses snorted and pawed the ground. Sergeant Barrett held the reins of a powerful white horse with green mane and tail, which swooshed back and forth flicking away pesky flies. They shuffled, as though eager to be on their way. Brian was already mounted on a gray mare and Rose sat astride a chestnut and Makka sat astride a white horse.

The army of ragtag teens waited until everyone was settled. Makka said a prayer of thanks for the pants, riding in a skirt would have been a tremendous challenge.

In addition to the short swords, Brian had a bow with a quiver of arrows, Rose had a long, thin sword attached to her saddle and Makka had a slightly heavier one with a flat, hammered surface that looked sharp enough to sever an arm. She shivered at the thought, as fear scurried up her spine and her stomach churned with anticipation.

"I'm excited," said Brian, beaming with a warrior's fierce pride.

With a series of whistles, the party of fifty armed warriors moved forward under a cloudless sky on an absolutely gorgeous day. Birds swirled in the sky, diving and looping as though doing a ballet routine for her amusement.

The magical dance almost made Makka forget that she was on a secret mission and that danger lurked everywhere. Thio's words of warning buzzed in her ears along with swarms of flying insects as they rode on.

Brian, who seemed as comfortable on a horse as he was on a speed bike, trotted up to her and asked how she was feeling. Makka nodded and forced a smile even as her face clouded with concern.

They rode for endless hours as the day heated up and their legs began to burn with the exertion of holding on tight around the saddles. After stopping for a mid-morning snack and a water break, their party of soldiers, officers and the elite three, continued on for another couple of hours. Then Captain Lourdes and Sergeant Bennett trotted up to the front.

"We've reached the end of the Morass," explained the Captain. "We must turn back here."

"Can't you come with us a little further, until we get to the Tower at least?"

"We've escorted you as far as we can. Nideon's Tower is two days ride. Once you get to the heat shield you know you're close."

They'd been advised about an invisible heat force and an invisible tower. It was a lot to think about.

"Just remember this," added the Captain. "Time in Etrunia has no meaning. A second can seem like an hour, an hour can be a day; a day may only be one minute. And always: Today is yesterday, yesterday is tomorrow and tomorrow is today."

The three American teenagers were shocked with disbelief. They were strangers in a stranger-than-strange land where time apparently had no meaning.

~ 23 ~

ON THE ROAD

"I think I zoned out back there while Thio was explaining how things work here," Makka said, grinding her teeth; her legs screamed with protest as she clamped them tight to avoid falling off as her horse trotted along.

"It was a lot to take in," Brian agreed. "Which part do I need to fill you in on?

"Okay, so we're going to get the Vector…"

"Cvector," he corrected.

"Right, and then what? I didn't get the part about the Ancients. What the heck is that?"

Brian pulled his horse closer so they were shoulder-to-shoulder. He didn't want to talk any louder than necessary. Ears were everywhere, not all of them on the side of good.

"At one time the Great Pharmakeus and Lady Eyrie—brother and sister you remember?"

"Yes, I got that part."

"They lived in the city of Missilium, which is located on the eastern border of Etrunia. But that left the north and south unguarded."

"Okay. I'm with you."

"They decided to split up. He went to Northgate, over the mountains to the very top of the land and built Aragantha, an imposing castle-fortress. From there, he could detect any invading forces from the north.

"Lady Eyrie went in the other direction to Southistle and built Blackwater Castle. There, in secret she took up the practice of sorcery under the tutelage of the Grand Wizard Archite."

"But what about Miss…Miss…what was that?"

"Missilium. According to legend, it was an impressive city, complete with the grand palace where Lady Eyrie and The Great Pharmakeus grew up. Supposedly there was a treasury brimming with gold and silver and gems of every kind."

Makka nodded.

"Then, when the sister and brother went in opposite directions to better rule Etrunia, the ornate buildings—and in fact the entire city—was covered over by sand."

"Sand?"

"Yes. People still live there, but here's what's important: The Master Grand Wizard Archite created an object called the Cvector, which was shaped like a round locket elaborately decorated and very useful. Once opened, it would guide the bearer back to the entrance in the sand covering Missilium. Only a rightful heir to the throne of Etrunia would be able to use the

Cvector. If anyone else tried to open and use the Cvector to find the lost city, the glow from the Cvector would burn their eyes until they were blind."

"And our mission is to get this so-called Cvector? What if it burns our eyes out?"

"It won't. Trust me."

Makka gritted her teeth. "I hate that phrase. Why should I trust anybody? This is positively crazy. How can people still manage to live and thrive even though tons and tons of sand blot out the sky?"

Brian rode for a while not talking, wondering how much to reveal to Makka. Finally, he said, "I imagine they must have a water source and a way of growing crops and raising livestock. Anyway, from what I've heard through the grapevine..."

"Grapevine? Brian, what the heck are you talking about? I thought you were just here to rescue me and now I feel that you're into this whole adventure for a different reason. Are we here to save Etrunia because I absolutely *have* to get home."

Brian raked his fingers through his hair pulling it away from his handsome face. "It's not as simple as that."

"So who are The Ancients?" asked Makka. It seemed that everyone was treating this utter nonsense as reality.

"According to the history books, the Ancients who were first people to make it into the country of Etrunia, but they slowly disappeared over time without any explanation. All that's left from their reign is the ancient capital of Etrunia, now called the White City. There, we'll find the magnificent castle named

Lovenfell. I hear it's made of the finest marble and it has a hundred rooms or more. Supposedly, after the Ancients departed, a spell was placed on it and only a true descendant of the Ancients can enter. There, the entire history of Etrunia will be revealed."

Forcing a smile, although she was scared out of her mind, Makka managed to reply: "I feel as though I've fallen into the land of the Hobbits with wizards, crystal balls, cities buried under sand and the mysterious Cvector that can zap a person's eyeballs out. Are you pulling my leg, Brian?"

"Yeah, I know it seems like that, but this is as real as it gets."

"Pinch me!" Brian reached over and poked her in the ribs.

"I was only kidding, but seriously, what's the deal with the invisible tower?"

"That's where the Cvector is. That's where we're going now."

They rode in silence for a while as Rose trotted alongside, her cheeks apple red. "I'm so hot."

"I was just explaining about The Ancients to Makka."

"It's complicated, but all will be revealed in time."

"Great, just what I need." Makka wiped her brow with her shirt sleeve.

"What we really need is ice—which, of course, we don't have—because we've come to the heat shield.," announced Brian.

"By the way, the Tower of Nideon is invisible as it's painted with a powder made from mica, one of the minerals that is plentiful here, and mixed with a little black magic."

Makka's mouth fell open. "Then how will we know that we've found it?"

"We're coming to the heat shield now. We must tread carefully, we are surrounded by danger."

~ 24 ~

BRIAN'S CONFESSION

The sun began its western descent as the assembly moved closer to the invisible Tower of Nideon. Makka guzzled water to quench her thirst, nearly draining their meager supply, but she was still super thirsty. She was also weary and irritable, wondering when this nightmare would end and why she was even here.

Brian pulled up alongside her. "We're getting close to the grasslands; it's going to be extremely hot."

"Hotter than this?"

"Much. But there's nothing we can do except to get through it as quickly as possible."

They rode along in silence for a few minutes as Brian shifted uncomfortably in his saddle.

Makka waited impatiently for Brian to explain more but secretly she hoped he'd ask her for a date when they got back to Granite Falls. That would be too cool. The steady clip-clop of the hooves on the dirt path lulled her into a fantasy of wildly romantic proportions.

At last he spoke up. "I have something to confess.

He's in love with me. No, wait, I'm too young to think about things like that.

"Makka," Brian's voice broke through her fantasy.

"Yes, Brian?" She tried to keep her voice steady, but it went up a notch despite her best attempts to remain calm and cool. *Was she kidding?* She was roasting in the fur-collared vest.

"It's about the heat," he confessed.

"No big deal, Brian. I can handle it."

"The heat shield was put in place by my father's wizards to deter the enemy from discovering Nideon's Tower."

"What are you talking about? Your father's wizards? I think the heat has gotten to you."

"My father is the Great Pharmakeus." He hung his head for a second as the air crackled with the truth.

"Good one, Brian, very funny. I wasn't born yesterday. Your dad is Mr. Abadon and your mom is Augusta. They seem a bit strange to me but what do I know? She paused for a heartbeat.

"I have to admit your house seems very odd, decorated like a castle with hidden staircases and underground tunnels."

If Brian was telling the truth about being the son of Pharmakeus, she prayed that meant they were protected by a higher power.

At last they called it a day. They were all hot and tired, and their legs ached from hours on the horses. Brian helped the girls unpack their saddlebags and set out some food and water for the horses.

"Go easy," cautioned Rose, "we have a long way to go."

Makka nodded and sank down onto the brittle yellow grass, grateful to rest for a while as the horses munched contentedly.

As they settled in for their first night alone as far off the grid as possible, with no grownups to offer protection, no roof over their heads, and only some simple vests made with chainmail to protect them, Makka said: "I think you owe me a great big explanation."

"We do," Brian agreed. "So here it goes."

Makka sucked in a mouthful of hot, dry air, wiped the sweat from her upper lip and tried to ready herself for whatever truth was about to spill out.

"We are the children of the Great Pharmakeus and Lady Augusta," said Rose. "Meeting you on our bikes the other day was no accident. It was preordained."

"Preordained?"

"Set in motion long before any of us were born," Brian added. "I don't know all the particulars but your mom and dad were also part of Etrunia."

Makka leaped to her feet, furious at their insinuation, her hands curled into fists of fury. "You're lying. They were not!"

Brian and Rose were taken aback at her outburst. "Sit down and keep quiet," commanded Brian. "We can't be loud or we'll be detected by the enemy."

Rose leaned in toward her. "Listen carefully and try to accept what we tell you. More will be revealed as we go along. You didn't end up going through the portal by accident. Think about it. What were the chances of a gnome stealing your cell phone anyway?"

Makka sat in stunned silence, her hand gently stroking the fur collar for comfort, the way she often petted Sasha, as Rose and Brian took turns explaining the past and the present.

"Rose has the power of ESP," said Brian. "She can sense the future and she's usually right."

"Not always, but I feel the power now that we're here. And Brian also has powers," added Rose. "He can sense if someone is good or evil and, like some superhero, his strength increases tenfold when he's attacked."

Brian's cheeks flushed. Makka wasn't sure if it was from the heat or embarrassment at being compared to a superhero.

"It's likely that you also have powers," added Brian. "We just don't know what they are yet."

The three fell silent. The only sounds were crickets chirping, the horses munching and owls hooting as the sun fell below the horizon casting salmon-hued rays into the sky. It was too dangerous to light a fire and, besides, the heat from the force shield was already more than they could bear.

They ate some bread and cheese, bit into mushy apples, drank sweet fruit cider and then spread their blankets on the ground. Brian unsaddled the three horses. They were sticky, stinky and icky as the day faded to night.

The rustle of leaves plus the overpowering heat of the invisible shield made sleep impossible.

Makka said a prayer to her guardian angels to keep them all safe and to send a message to her parents letting them know she was alive and well.

~ 25 ~

THE HEAT SHIELD

Before the rooster crowed—just before dawn—they were up and on their way, horses rested and fed. "Did you hear that?" Makka cocked her head and listened intently.

"What?" asked Rose.

"The screeching."

"A screech owl most likely," Brian explained. "I guess you don't get a lot of those in Florida, but we have them all around our house on Apple Tree Lane. Anyway, no need to concern yourself when we have bigger issues to contend with today."

"Like what?" Makka's stomach started to hurt and her hands trembled as she settled herself in the saddle and gripped the reins.

"We're in enemy territory, we might be attacked any moment, so have your short swords ready."

As instructed, Makka unsnapped the scabbard—just in case. By mid-morning the heat was unbearable and their water supply was dwindling drastically. Rose's tongue stuck to the roof of her mouth and Makka couldn't swallow. They rode in silence, sweaty and anxious along a trail that dipped, turned and zigzagging off into the trees now and then. Despite their discomfort, their determination to retrieve the Cvector and accomplish their mission flowed through their veins like a powerful elixir.

"I feel like someone is watching us," said Makka.

"You could be right." Brian shifted in his saddle, turning to look backward for any signs of Lady Eyrie's devious scouts. "We have a long day ahead of us before we arrive at the Tower. "Hopefully we'll be able to sneak in undetected."

As the sun moved through the cerulean sky east to west, disappearing through clouds that stretched to the heavens, they passed by well-tended fields and meadows and over rutted roads past farmlands. Sad looking pups stayed cool in the shade of spreading maple trees or under the thatched roofs of the farmers' huts.

They stopped at one settlement in the middle of nowhere to refresh themselves with clean water, fruit, meat pies and buckle berry pastries, supplied at no cost by the friendly but poor residents. Everyone was cheerful and welcoming; she was surprised and sort of happy to find that life was perfectly ordinary without the benefit of cars or fast-food restaurants.

The trail continued lazily up small hills and past fields of golden wheat that almost seemed to burn in the overwhelming heat. A winding dark blue ribbon in the distance was a lifesaving stream of cool clear water. They filled up on water, and they drank greedily and let the horses have their fill. Fortunately, the sun remained hidden behind clouds for most of the day as they trotted and until night began to fall—again—and Brian called a halt to the day. He unsaddled the horses while the girls prepared for the evening meal, fortified with the provisions they picked up on the way.

Makka awoke before the first streaks of pink lit up the sky in a shallow shelter of leaves. They were saddled and ready to leave in less than an hour and yet, despite the slightly cool, clear morning, fear rose up Makka's spine as they rode on. Before long they felt the shift in temperature; it became hotter and hotter every minute while all around was sun and heat, heat and sun— the smell rank and stale, of burned grass and rot.

By midday, the air was so dense that just staying upright in the saddle took tremendous effort. Their eyeballs burned, their throats were parched—as if they were drying up from the inside out.

"We've got to turn the horses loose," said Brian, slipping to the hot earth and helping Makka and Rose dismount. With a sharp smack on the hind quarters, he sent them back to the Morass. They would die in this heat waiting while the three of them were in the Tower.

Breathing was nearly impossible; they felt dizzy and yet they kept going, feeling alive and acutely alert. An eagle swooped low in search of prey as Makka's stomach churned and her vest felt like a million pounds in this unbearable heat. The protective chain metal vest was just too hot, it seem as though they were baking in a furnace.

Just as the sun kissed the horizon, at the very moment Makka felt she couldn't take it anymore without passing out, Rose called out, "I sense it!"

"Sense what?" asked Brian and Makka in unison.

"The Tower."

"I don't see anything," Makka and Brian echoed in sync. With hands outstretched, they shuffled through the high grass like blind people.

"Keep your weapons handy," Brian cautioned. "Anybody or anything could be lurking."

Exhausted, Rose yearned for a chocolate bar, Makka for a hug from her mom—*could she really have been involved here?* Makka's hands felt something warm. "Here! Over here. This is it, I think."

Six hands felt up and down, their excitement contagious. They wanted to hug each other or jump for joy but were too exhausted. Following Rose, they felt their way around the hot stone blocks looking for an entrance.

"From what I understand, once we get inside, there is a double staircase," Rose explained. "One goes up and one down. If we go in the wrong direction, we'll be quickly discovered.

The Sentry Falcon that perches atop the roof will fly off to notify Lady Eyrie. The warning system was set into place long before we knew that she was pure evil. And our father vanished so suddenly, he didn't have time to do anything about it."

Brian said: "She wants the Cvector in the worst way, but she doesn't know where the Tower is located. However, if the Falcon flies to her, she'll know someone has come and she'll stop at nothing to destroy us and take the Cvector. We must not draw attention to ourselves, no matter what. Understand?"

Makka nodded and remained silent. Then, suddenly, her hands ran over the rough wood of the invisible door and she pointed to it nodding. Brian whispered: "I'm opening it now. Is everyone ready?"

They quickly shed their heavy vests, numb with fear, and terrified that the Falcon would fly to Lady Eyrie. Makka, was ready to strike, even though she was dizzy with fear.

She promised herself that when she got home, IF she got home, she'd make her parents move back to Florida where ocean breezes blew and cool surf lapped the shore, where girls wore bikinis and boys surfed and everyone laughed and had fun.

~ 26 ~

THE CVECTOR

Although it was dark outside, as they entered through a small wooden door, a soft glow illuminated intricate carvings. Quickly, they slipped inside feeling the ancient history of Etrunia. Without a doubt, the tower was full of mystical intrigue. Makka held her breath until she felt faint.

She could hear a pin-drop as their eyes slowly adjusted to the lack of light. They listened intently, but heard only the scratching of rodents along with the soft meowing of a cat somewhere nearby. Makka hoped her allergy to cats wouldn't cause her to sneeze and give away their presence.

With shuffling feet she moved forward, dust rising from the stone floor until her foot hit the riser of the first step. She moved aside to let Rose lead the way as they searched for the right staircase.

She acted bravely, but an irrationally intense fear that something would befall them made her body tremble. She could not allow herself to become immobilized, not here, not now.

On their journey to the Tower, Brian had explained that a man, not much bigger than one of their garden gnomes, lived upstairs.

His name was Nideon and he possessed the precious Cvector, the highly-coveted amulet that could find the ancient city of Missilium that lay hidden under the hot sands of the Desert of Lost Souls. This was their ultimate quest, or so she thought. Little did she know that this was only the beginning.

"We cannot fail," Brian whispered. "We cannot leave without the Cvector, no matter what!"

Rose added ominously, "it's do-or-die time."

Makka's knees trembled as they climbed the circular stairway, her fingers tracing a path on the cool stone wall as her heart beat like a drum. Slivers of pale dusky light began to spill down, illuminating the way as the Tower staircase narrowed to shoulder-width. They prayed that Nideon was asleep so that they could snatch the Cvector undetected and make a fast, clean getaway.

Brian turned back to the others and put a finger over his lips. Silence was critical. Even breathing was risky. This had to be a surprise attack, or the consequences could be deadly. They would get no second chances.

Finally, up at a landing, they faced a thick oak door, again intricately carved with mystical designs. It stood ever so slightly ajar. Slowly, cautiously, they slipped through. The round room was surprisingly spacious considering the narrow width of the staircase.

It had numerous small slats for windows. In the dusky air, Makka shivered as she scanned the cluttered space filled with bits and pieces of rubbish strewn on the floor. Two wooden chairs were overturned and a cot had been placed along one wall, the pillow tossed over the side, a moth-eaten olive blanket dangling over the side. Dried flowers hung upside down from hooks embedded in the stone walls made a half-hearted attempt to give it a homey appearance. A large, dark wooden desk dominated the very center of the room but her attention was quickly diverted to Nideon himself.

He was a small man, dozing in a tall chair. He looked like a discarded doll, head lolling to the side, his short legs propped on the edge of the desk. On his feet were handmade leather shoes, scuffed from years of wear, with holes in the soles.

Green-gray striped socks covered his short legs from ankles to knees. He wore brown shredding tweed pants with a rough-spun tan cloth shirt, stained by grass and wine. Nideon!

Her eyes traveled over the leather vest and the very thing they had come for—the Cvector. It was attached to a heavy metal chain that hung around his neck.

That presented a huge challenge.

Nideon had sparse gray hair that stuck out like straw around his large ears and a bulbous nose that quivered when he snored. His mouth was agape and, as Makka took a closer look, she realized his eyes were open! *Open and yet not seeing.* Was he blind? She could only assume so and it creeped her out.

She became aware that Rose was poking her arm, pointing to the ornate medallion hanging around the little man's neck. Although he was sound asleep, Makka was fearful of leaning in for a closer look. What if he awoke and grabbed her by the throat? After all, his eyes were staring right at her.

"He's blind," whispered Rose. "Don't be such a weasel."

Upon closer inspection, Makka realized the Cvector was a work of art—a stunning hand-crafted silver ornament with gold inlay around the rim and intersecting gold lines forming an X. At the intersection was a ruby, glistening crimson in the fading light. Small pearls spanned the perimeter and in each of the spaces created by the X was a star, surrounded by elaborate enamel designs.

It was truly spectacular, the most unusual, eye-catching adornment she'd ever seen. But although the outside was dazzling, Makka did not know that it would change her life forever.

Brian reached for it, pulling it ever so slowly over the man's head while trying not to wake him. But his fingers trembled and the chain caught on Nideon's large ear.

He awoke with a start.

"Eeeeehhhh, who's there? Who dare take the Cvector from me? Be prepared to die!" He yanked his short legs off the desk and jumped unsteadily to his feet, twisting his body around to find the source of his disturbance.

"Run! Run now!" Brian commanded as the little man continued to rant.

"I am the guardian of the Cvector. It was given to me by The Great Pharmakeus."

Brian stopped and turned, facing Nideon. "I am the son of Pharmakeus. I have returned to restore order to Etrunia."

Nideon shuffled unsteadily toward Brian, arms stretched in front of him.

"How dare you? You are nobody! An imposter! Prove it, if you can."

Brian retorted easily: "Ask me anything."

Nideon rubbed his eyes and yawned. "You interrupt my sleep, try to steal my Cvector and now you want to play guessing games? I'll report you to Lady Eyrie. You'll never leave Etrunia alive."

"Just ask," Brian whispered. "Ask me anything."

"What is the favorite meal of the Great Pharmakeus?"

"Roasted pheasant wrapped in bacon."

Nideon jumped up and down. "No way!"

"Yes," said Rose, her voice trembling. "I'm his daughter and, yes, that's his favorite meal."

Nideon stumbled backward reaching out for the chair, knocking it over in the process. It clattered to the stone floor with a terrible crash that echoed off the walls as dust rose into the air and Makka sneezed.

"Even if you are who you say you are, you have come too late. I will never give up the Cvector. I will have you all killed!"

Brian's face turned red with anger. "You promised long ago to protect and serve our family, now we learn that you are nothing but a traitor."

"How dare you?" Nideon screamed, punching the air with his tiny fists. "Do not expect that you will escape in one piece— any of you!"

As Nideon stumbled around blindly, Makka reached over his head and pulled the chain up, finally bringing the Cvector over Nideon's head. Now it was theirs!

Brian grabbed Makka's hand, yanking her back toward the spiral stone staircase.

The Cvector was tucked safely in her pocket. But as Makka turned to look back at Nideon, she spotted something on the desk—it was hot pink.

"Wait, Brian." She tried to wrench free, but he held her with an iron grip.

"We can't stop. He's calling the guards."

"It's my cell phone. It's on his desk! How did it get there?"

With Rose pushing and Brian pulling her forward, Makka had no choice. But she couldn't wrap her head around the fact that her precious phone was here, in a blind man's tower in the middle of nowhere.

Reluctantly, she allowed herself to be dragged out of the room— but in a daring move that surprised everyone and put all of them risk—she darted back and snatched the pink object, shoving it into her pants pocket before racing down the steps until she was dizzy and her knees rubbery.

A few seconds later, they heard the loud bang of a trapdoor being shut above their heads. They were on their own, caught between two worlds—lost in time and space and at a loss to explain how it had all started—or how it would play out.

~ 27 ~

NO WAY OUT

They sped down the stairs at breakneck speed. Their lives depended on getting away as quickly as possible. Although the stone steps were firm, it felt like they were running through quicksand—being sucked down into a bottomless pit.

Breathlessly, Rose gripped Brian's shirt and whispered urgently, "Remember, we have to descend the right stairs or the Falcon will warn Lady Eyrie."

Makka was three steps ahead, now secure in the knowledge that she could summon help with her precious phone.

"Stop!" Brian froze three paces behind them. "I think Nideon is trying to trick us somehow. We should be at the bottom door by now. This stairway is not leading us back to where we entered. We must proceed quickly, but with great caution."

Rose held up a hand and they all froze. "There must be a passageway that leads out."

Makka pulled out her cell phone. The battery was almost gone, but once Makka switched on the flashlight app, they saw dozens of stairways suspended in air going all over in different directions, a labyrinth of staircases going up and down—sometimes, and quite impossibly, at the same time.

"I don't know how we'll get out of here," she whimpered.

Brian was suddenly next to her, his body sending out powerful vibrations that calmed Makka's nerves. "Now what? Which way Rose?"

"If we continue down this stairway we're probably doomed," she reasoned. "It's the natural way so we must outsmart Nideon. Here, let me see the phone."

She held the flashlight up in each direction; then, using it like a torch high over her head, she led the way, looking for a connecting stairway. As they scurried along, Brian remained the voice of reason.

"Listen, Nideon doesn't want to send the Falcon to Lady Eyrie. She'd be furious that the Cvector has been stolen. He'll keep that secret as long as he can."

"I agree," Rose chimed in. "But even if she does find out, we'll be long gone from here—at least I hope so."

"What if there's no way out?" Makka asked, thankful for the cool moist air that circulated through the staircase. Then, suddenly, she realized a breeze was wafting her ponytail.

She turned to Rose. "Find the source of this draft, it might be our way out."

Rose led them up and around, down and through ever-narrowing corridors, ramps and spiraling stairs. It was suffocating and claustrophobic as they fought down the rising emotions of uncertainty. Finding the way out of the Tower was like wrestling with an octopus.

She turned off the flashlight and sniffed the musty, mold-filled air. When she turned it back on, they realized they'd reached a fork.

"Try the left," said Brian, sprinting past her and taking the lead, heading down, down and even further as the air became cooler and clammier, smelling of ages past. And then, in a soft glow ahead, they saw it.

A door.

Light sipped through the bottom indicating something on the other side. Help maybe?

They skidded to a stop, nearly tumbling over themselves in their haste to get out of the narrow, cramped passageway.

"Makka, you have the Cvector?"

She grabbed the gorgeous pendant which hung around her neck from the heavy chain. As she wrapped her fingers wrapped around it, she felt calm and certain they would make a clean getaway. "Yes. Right here."

"Good, that's the only thing that will help us find Missilium to fulfill the destiny of restoring the Great Pharmakeus and Lady Augusta."

"Your mom and dad, right?"

The air hung in silence for a while. Both Brian and Rose heard the sarcasm in her voice. They could pick a fight or ignore it. Now was not the time for a confrontation.

"Yes, our parents who once ruled Etrunia. But they were not alone, Makka. They had help."

"I'm *sure* they did."

Rose spoke up. "You don't understand. Your parents were involved as well."

Makka took a step back shouting, "No way! I don't believe you. You're lying." Hot tears sprang to her eyes. "Why would you say something like that to me? My mother's a school principal and my dad is a programmer. They'd never be involved in something as crazy—as this. Don't lie to me, please. Let's just get out of here alive and back to Granite Falls as soon as possible. They must be sick with worry."

Brian and Rose glanced at each other and nodded imperceptibly. "Okay sure Makka. No more silly talk. The truth will be revealed in time. Let's see where this door leads."

The door was smaller than usual, worn from centuries of use.

"Take out your short swords," Brian commanded in a harsh whisper.

"Could it be a trap?" Rose asked as she fumbled with her weapon. It clattered noisily to the floor.

"Klutz!" Brian was a powder keg of raw emotion. "Quiet or all hell will break loose."

Makka held tight to her dagger, which quivered unsteadily. Could she really use it? Would she be able to stab someone? Her doubts threatened to overcome her resolve.

"It might be a trap, so get ready." Brian pushed down on the handle just as Makka put her hand on his hand to stop him from opening it.

"Stop! We don't have to guess where this leads or if it's an ambush. You said the Cvector will lead us so let's try it now, see what it shows us."

She held up the Cvector and stroked the inlaid metalwork and gem encrusted cover. "Let's open it."

Brian watched intently as Makka lifted the cover ever so slightly, holding his breath as the interior neon green glow slipped out. As Makka fully opened it, an arrow in the middle began spinning and when it stopped, it pointed back in the direction they'd come from.

"Good call," Brian whispered. "That was a trap that could've gotten us all killed."

Quickly they reversed direction, retracing their way down the stairs again, and down yet another staircase as the air grew heavy in the vault. They stopped, gasping for breath.

Rose said, "My mouth is as dry as a desert."

Then come quickly," said Makka, taking the lead. "The Cvector is pointing this way."

Again, they groped along the damp walls as footsteps could be heard in the distance behind them in the direction of the door that they hadn't opened.

"Faster, go. Go. GO!" With the green light providing illumination and the arrow pointing to the left, she hissed,

"Stop!" Brian and Rose slammed into her back, nearly knocking her over.

"What?" they asked in unison.

"There." She pointed to a solid wall.

"No way," Rose exclaimed. "That can't be right. We're dead."

Brian and Makka ran their hands over the cool, moist blocks of stone

Suddenly, as though guided by divine providence—or in this case the inexplicable power of the Cvector—one of the stones swung back revealing a narrow passage.

Brian and Rose squeezed through as Makka stood riveted, mouth agape, her heart hammering in her chest like a frightened rabbit.

Then Rose grabbed her sleeve and yanked her through just as the door slid shut and locked in place with a muffled click.

~ 28 ~

SECRETS & LIES

The silence was deafening. It was darker and scarier than anything they'd yet experienced in their short lives. "Open the Cvector" Rose whispered. "We can't see a thing."

Makka pulled it out and opened it. It glowed softly and gave out enough light for them to forge ahead. Being stuck in this place was like being buried alive. Nobody would ever find them.

"Let's go," Brian said, as he moved forward quickly, turning to the right and the left as the passageway twisted and turned. This was a real life horror movie, not something fake like on TV.

Rose asked, "What time do you think it is? My stomach's growling like crazy."

"How can you be concerned with food?" Brian's voice was hard.

Fighting to control her hunger and her emotions, Makka trailed behind, running her hands against the cool stones, trying to keep her bearings in the dark, convoluted and confined space. Her legs felt like rubber, as though she'd been walking forever, although it had just been since morning—through the heat shield, up and down the Tower staircases, grabbing the Cvector and then racing down the stairs and through the wall—a dizzying ride that threatened to swallow them whole.

Things had gone from bad to worse, but on the upside, she had her precious phone and the highly coveted Cvector. Although they were not safe here—or anywhere for that matter—their senses tingled with anticipation. Every nerve in their bodies was on high alert as the ceiling began to close in on them.

Ducking their heads, the stones gave way to dirt. They were down on hands and knees as the passage narrowed even more, barely wide enough for their shoulders. Every few feet they touched the wooden braces keeping the tons of dirt from crashing down and burying them alive; it was a small comfort in the terrifying journey that had befallen them.

Then Brian's voice ricocheted back. "It's a dead end. Makka you have to turn around."

Was he joking? There was no way she could move, squeezed in so tight she felt she was being born again—not that she remembered being born at all. "I can't, I can't move at all."

In the near darkness, Brian spotted a tree root that, amazingly, looked like a door handle.

"Wait. Hold tight. I think I found something." He grasped it and pulled. With an unearthly groan, the heavy stone door slid open.

A throaty voice boomed out from beyond: "It's about time. What took you so long?"

"Come in, come in," said another with a slightly higher pitch, as Brian rolled into the narrow space and tried to stand upright on cramped legs. Rose tumbled in, brushing dirt from her hair and

Makka followed, not even bothering to stand but simply collapsing onto the floor. She had tucked the Cvector into her shirt so nothing was visible.

As they pulled themselves into upright positions, they noticed they were in a cozy room with a pint-sized hearth aglow with hot embers and a hanging cauldron with something that smelled amazing. They were all starving, thirsty and beyond exhausted. They prayed these were friendly folks and not weirdos who'd boil them up for dinner.

The ceiling was low, held up by thick worm-eaten wooden beams, but Brian had an inch of headroom. As their eyes swept the space, they noticed a long table with two benches near the rudimentary kitchen. A few pots hung from chains attached to another beam. Luckily, the men who welcomed them had neither fangs nor claws, but they were certainly odd.

They were short, dressed in loose moss-green breeches, threadbare and stained cotton knit sweaters and waist-length leather deer-hide aprons. Their heads were covered by stocking caps knitted in shades of buttercup and tangerine. On their feet were heavy leather boots reaching up to their ankles. In turn, they each stepped forward, bowed and introduced themselves to the stunned visitors.

"I'm Thorvi," said the most grizzled of the three, bowing from the waist, balancing on his left leg. His right one was missing below the knee and he walked with the aid of a wooden crutch.

"I'm Agmar," said the most youthful one, adjusting a black patch over his missing right eye, and then stroking his long brown beard.

"Last but not least, I'm Melker," said the stoutest of all, holding his right arm behind his back to hide the fact that his hand was missing. But the three visitors had already seen that his shirt sleeve had been pulled over the stump and tied in a knot.

"Welcome to our humble home," said Thorvi, offering up the three straight-backed chairs. "You are the first visitors we've had in forever."

"Forever and a day," chimed Agmar.

"Forever and a century," added Melker.

"I thought time had no meaning here," said Brian grinning. "But more important, what happened to you? Not to appear rude, but it looks like you've been through a war."

The three compact men glanced at each other and nodded in agreement. "We will reveal the truth—but only because of her."

Melker pointed to Makka with his left hand. "She is the reason we look like this."

Makka was stunned. They *all* were. Were they blaming her for this catastrophe? *No way!*

"I don't even know you," she sputtered. "I've never seen you before."

Agmar pulled at the hairs on his chin, his bushy eyebrows knit together. "That's true. But we know who you are and why you're here."

"You do?" asked Rose, incredulous.

"Of course," said Brian. "I get it. You're part of the Resistance. Am I right?"

The three men nodded silently. "Please have a seat while Melker and I get you something to eat," said Agmar.

Rose wanted to melt into a puddle of gratitude on the floor. She was beyond famished. Makka placed her hand over her stomach to stop the rumbling and Brian was so starved he couldn't talk. From a nook around the corner, they heard plates and cups being moved around and water being poured.

"Did you notice their accent?" asked Rose.

"Sounds like Snow Valley to me." Brian's eyes wandered around the room.

"Where's that?" asked Makka.

Before he could reply, Thorvi cleared his throat. "I hope you don't mind if I ask."

"Ask away, just bring us something to drink first," Brian joked.

They motioned to the table which the visitors now realized had been set with bread, fruit, pies, some kind of dried meat which looked disgusting but smelled marvelous, plus tubs of puddings, roasted root vegetables, jams and other unidentifiable edibles. The goblets were filled with honeyed beet wine and they all sat down—the war veterans on one side, the Americans on the other. The visitors all drank greedily and dug in without being asked.

"So," said Melker, glancing around. "You have the Cvector?"

Brian wasn't eager to share the information with anybody. "Why do you ask?"

"We know who you are and why you're here." They all stared at Makka. "If you have it, we'll tell you why Nideon is blind."

"Brian?" she looked to him for a final decision.

"It's fine. They were ready to lay down their lives for Etrunia."

Makka slid the Cvector up from under her shirt and held it by the chain as Agmar, Thorvi and Melker whispered eagerly among themselves in a language none of the others understood—a secret code perhaps?

Quickly, she let it drop back into her shirt and took another few bites of food, feeling her energy return.

Then Thorvi, who seemed to be their one-legged leader, told them the story of Nideon and the Cvector and how he lost his sight.

~ 29 ~

NIDEON'S CURSE

Agmar began the story of Nideon.

"We knew that Pharmakeus and his sister, Lady Eyrie, once lived in the great city of Missilium, on the far eastern edge of Etrunia. But that left the north and south unguarded. She moved to Southistle and built Blackwater Castle, which was surrounded by massive briar hedges.

Pharmakeus moved to the land beyond the mountains to Northgate where he built the fortified fortress known as Argantha. It was a masterpiece of modern architecture."

Melker adjusted his eye patch. "At one time we lived up north, in Snowmass which is in Snow Valley, near the mountains around the castle of the Great Pharmakeus. Although we labored in the mines, we knew there was trouble brewing between our leader and his sister, Lady Eyrie, who'd taken up wizardry."

Thorvi took over the narrative. "We could hear sounds down under the earth, voices and the yelling. If we pressed our ears to the walls, we could even hear Lady Augusta crying at night. Don't get me wrong, the castle was not built in a hurry. It was solid stone, each block precisely cut to fit together seamlessly and able to withstand a siege with hundreds of trebuchets."

He stopped looking at their quizzical expressions. "Trebuchets were large stones hurled at the walls to break through. But this was a fortress. Of course there was a moat and bridge, as well as a towering citadel for the gate keep and a solarium for sewing and weaving as well as a chapel, prison tower, great hall, and two kitchens. It had everything—even lavatories with water!"

He paused. "Still, sound travels to the strangest places."

The three men took turns explaining the sequence of events. Over time, Pharmakeus knew that a civil war was inevitable and he covered the city of Missilium with a ceiling of sand and it became known as the Desert of Lost Souls. Many of the inhabitants stayed behind to keep watch over the treasures and the secrets of the olden days, including the ornate throne he once sat upon to rule Etrunia.

"The people are in a trance-like state. They don't hear or see anyone and walk around like they are the living dead," added Melker.

It was Thorvi's turn. "The throne was all-powerful. It's said that anyone who sits in it will become our new ruler." It is also said that the throne is able to bring Pharmakeus and his family back to Etrunia.

Brian interjected without even thinking. "But Nideon, the greedy little toad, wanted to be the one."

They nodded and their faces fell. "Sadly," said Melker, "The Great Pharmakeus made one fatal mistake. He left the Cvector, which he had specially made by his finest craftsmen and most powerful wizard, in care of Nideon, his specially appointed confident."

"So he wasn't always blind?" asked Rose.

"Nae, but he was sly as a fox." Agmar continued. "Just as Pharmakeus left on his ill-fated journey south, to see his sister at Blackwater Castle, he entrusted the Cvector to Nideon, the worm."

"So that's how he got hold of it?" Makka found this history lesson fascinating. Much more intriguing than any lesson she'd had in all her years at school.

Melker nodded. "It was given willingly. But when Pharmakeus disappeared in a cloud of smoke and his fortress was left empty, thanks to the treachery of Lady Eyrie and the Grand Wizard Archite, Nideon seized the opportunity to try to claim the throne and crown himself the supreme ruler of Etrunia."

"I think I see what's happening here. It's a case of..."

"Yes, payback is harsh sometimes," Thorvi interjected. "His lesson in disloyalty was learned the hard way."

Agmar finished the story. "He opened the Cvector to see where the arrow was pointing so he could find the Desert of Lost Souls and the city of Missilium that lay beneath the sand, but the light burned through his eyes and destroyed them. He must live every day with the memory of his treason."

"But," added Thorvi, "he has developed powers of a much higher level with his other senses. He can hear things from afar and can feel the presence of people."

They thought back to their encounter earlier and how he had woken from a dead sleep, somehow aware someone was in his chamber.

Makka spoke slowly, putting the pieces of this disturbing puzzle together. "So he guarded it, trying to keep it from Lady Eyrie because he didn't want her to rule either. Most likely, she would've had him murdered, since he couldn't be trusted any longer."

The three nodded. "We moved here so we could keep a closer eye on him, monitor his coming and going and keep track of the falcon," added Melker.

"And now that I have it, everything is up in the air," Makka remarked, fingering the Cvector that lay on her chest under her shirt and vest.

Brian stared at her, mouth agape. So what they had been told about the Cvector was indeed true.

"Makka, you looked directly at it and didn't have your eyes burned to a crisp."

Rose put her hand over her mouth and gasped. "You could have been blinded."

"But I wasn't. That makes me wonder...."

They glanced at one other warily.

"Listen," said Melker. "We know this is only a humble hole in the ground, but you should spend the night in the beds we have to offer and get some rest, and in the morning we'll give you food and directions to the White City where you'll find answers to all your questions."

Brian cleared his throat, shifting uncomfortably in his seat. "I have a few questions—if you don't mind." The three small men glanced at each other and nodded. "What's going on, besides the usual sorcery?"

Agmar's good eye wandered around the room before he answered. "We are part of the underground Resistance. It's a secret collection of people from all around Etrunia who are against the taxes Lady Eyrie has imposed and her lack of concern about any of us."

Thorvi joined in, banging his crutch on the dirt floor for emphasis. "It's worse than that. Lady Eyrie and the wicked Lord Hviti are conscripting the children to become an army of ghouls."

"Ghouls?" Rose sat forward, frightened and worried. "What do you mean?"

"Five children are taken from every village each year to build his evil army," replied Melker. "They want to suppress all of us, steal our hard-earned money, leave us nothing to live on and make sure that we have to rely on them just to live and breathe."

"They'd tax the air we breathe if they could," added Agmar. "It's outrageous. What happened to the right of happiness and basic human rights?"

Makka nodded and her eyes met Brian's. She felt a tingle of something she couldn't identify creep down her back. "I wish we could help."

Melker, Agmar and Thorvi glanced at each other again, their lips curling into smiles. "You can," they said in unison. "That's why you're going to the White City. The answers lie there."

"The White City?" she asked.

"It's not far—only a day and a half from here," Agmar explained. "We'll pack your provisions and draw out a little map. It'll take no time at all."

The thought of more walking made Makka so sleepy she could barely keep her eyes open. She soon curled up on the only comfortable chair in the place and was out cold in minutes.

The little men fussed around her, covering her weary body with soft blankets and kneeling in front of her, hands clasped in prayer.

"We have waited ages for you Dear One, Davina of Saragon. Our lives depend on your strength, cunning and courage. We hope we have helped you to understand the need for your purpose here and we give you our humble blessings for your ultimate success."

Brian and Rose, who both knew why Makka was brought to Etrunia, joined them with a soft chant:

"To us you are a blessing
Sent from another world to bring peace
To end our strife and rivalry
And make Etrunia whole again."

But she slept through the chorus, which was murmured late into the night with fervent hearts.

~ 30 ~

THE WHITE CITY

They awoke to the fragrant aroma of cinnamon and hot brewing tea. After pouring fresh water into earthenware basins, the visitors washed up and joined Agmar, Thorvi, and Melker for breakfast of whole grain bread and yellow cream with fresh honeycomb, cheese, ripe berries and the ever-present bowls of oatmeal.

Travel packs had been prepared for their journey. After their meal, the three hosts walked the visitors down a long corridor on the opposite side of their underground home from where the American teenagers had entered the night before.

"We will bring you past the heat shield in this passageway and up on the other side," said Agmar who was leading the way with his one good eye.

"It is just about one-and-a-half days by foot to the White City and quite a nice stroll," added Thorvi, clumping on his crutch. "We've done it many times."

Twenty minutes later the ground sloped upward and Melker, who brought up the rear, tapped Brian on the shoulder with his

147

good—his only hand—and said, "Take care of her, she's our salvation."

Brian nodded. *He knew.* They all knew—except Makka.

Agmar pushed open a trap door hidden under a meadow. It was a glorious day with a clear blue sky sprinkled with white clouds. Below, fields of green grass stretched like a stunning patchwork quilt.

"Freedom is a beautiful thing," said Melker, optimism flowing into his veins like oxygen. "Someday, with your help, we hope to be a united Etrunia. We pray you can make that happen."

"I'm all in," Brian replied, shaking the hands of the small men.

Makka let the upbeat feeling wash over her. *They were in it to win it.* Etrunia would be saved and evil vanquished. How, she hadn't a clue. But she was going to give it her best shot. The cell phone in her pocket and the Cvector around her neck gave her the courage she needed to remain positive.

They set out with high hopes, passing strands of pine, oak, and eucalyptus, leaves hanging thick and heavy on stout branches. Birds chirped and woodpeckers hammered their red heads. The morning passed in a delightful haze of wonderment. Eagles soared overhead in search of prey and pretty gray and white doves chirped from swaying cypresses.

They followed the slips and dips and, as they crested a small hill, Rose stopped to admire the incredible tapestry of green, golden, and tawny farmlands spread out below them. A brook ran nearby with sandy banks and smooth stones washed by the water for centuries.

The scene was hyper real, as though they were watching themselves from above as they stopped for a picnic lunch, washing their hands and faces in the ice cold water, polishing off the sandwiches and golden berry juice provided by the hosts. The day wore on and the sun began setting in the west casting rays on fields of barley, rye and wheat and lighting them with an unearthly glow—a dazzling display of Mother Nature at her finest.

"Wow, look at that!" exclaimed Rose pointing to the glowing pink-hued shadows. "Gorgeous."

"I've never seen anything like it," Makka agreed.

As the sun sank below the horizon, the heavens glowed with shades of tangerine, persimmon and pinky-lemon.

Makka piped up again. "When are we going home? I need to get ready for school."

"Time has no meaning here," said Brian. "Maybe we'll be home in an hour—or maybe in ten years."

"Ten years?" exclaimed Makka. "I can't wait ten years. This is crazy. Get me home now."

Brian and Rose exchanged knowing glances as Makka wiped away a tear.

"Soon," said Brian, putting an arm around her shoulders. "As soon as possible. We're doing our best."

Makka nodded wearily as the light began fading. As dusk deepened, they came to another small stream. Gallantly, Brian offered to carry Makka across. She refused, so instead he grabbed her by the waist and swung her over like a sack of potatoes.

"You'll be happier with dry shoes than wet ones," he said as she felt her body tingle with electricity. No boy had ever wrapped his hands around her that way. She wouldn't have let them. But Brian was different. *Special. Magnetic.*

After helping his sister to the other side, Brian called the day to a halt. They found a comfortable, safe and snug hollow among the roots of an old oak tree. Cozy and hidden from view they listened as moths and night bugs flittered above their small apple wood campfire. Around them, the dark devoured the land. After eating again and rinsing their mouths, they settled down in cozy nests of fern and moss. Owls hooted overhead and rodents scurried through the underbrush.

They slept close together, Makka in the middle like a precious gem set in a valuable ring with Brian and Rose on either side. Although they couldn't see to the treetops in the dark, the Grizzards settled comfortably onto stout branches and watched over them.

~ 31 ~

LOVENFELL

Day two of their journey to the White City was an easy three-hour hike. They were well rested, well fed, and eager to see what lay ahead.

"We're getting close," said Brian, pointing to cottages with russet thatched roofs and pens of livestock. There were cows in the nearby pastures and sheep bleated, their dirty white woolen coats in need of shearing. Lambs followed close on the heels of the ewes and rams butted heads as dogs barked. Further ahead they spotted what appeared to be small village shops and stalls.

"I'm starving," Rose said. "Let's grab a bite to eat."

"You're always hungry," taunted her brother.

"I'm hungry too," Makka chimed in. Girls had to stick together.

The aroma of freshly baked goods drew them like magnets. Makka felt as though she had stepped back four hundred years and pinched her cheek to see if she was dreaming. She wasn't.

In fact, the Cvector that lay on her chest felt hot on her skin. She wondered what that was about and touched it lightly. It made her feel grounded.

At the first stall, which stood right outside a bakery, they met a short, heavyset woman with a blue kerchief tied over her head. Her rosy cheeks and bright hazel eyes drew them in as they surveyed the assortment of puddings, tarts, wafers, marzipan cakes, and cheese pies.

"I want one of each," Rose said eagerly. They selected three, but when Brian reached into his pocket he realized they had no money.

Frantically, his eyes darted from Rose to Makka, but they shook their heads and stared forlornly at the treats so near and yet so far.

"Don't you worry now," said the vendor. "I wouldn't let you leave hungry." She pushed the food toward them with a smile and a chuckle. "Go on now. You have important work to do."

A few steps away, Makka turned to Brian and asked, "What did she mean by that?"

"Beats me, but she's right. We're here for a reason. Let's find out why."

As they ate, they moved through the town, marveling at the level of activity, like a busy flea market with numerous vendors in outdoor stalls, a mosaic of colors, shapes and sizes offering fruit and vegetables, clothing, stinky fish, spices and sweet-baked breads.

A florid-faced man was crafting reins from a leather hide and another was plucking feathers from a freshly-killed chicken. The commotion and excitement was refreshing after so many days of stress.

Veering off the street to a road running behind the town, Makka was surprised to find that the dirt path had become a marble cobblestone road. As they glanced around, they realized they must have come to the edge of the White City.

The grandeur of once stately buildings began to line the cobble stone road they had stumbled upon, although windows were missing and wooden doors had fallen off their hinges and some of those that were somewhat still intact stood ajar as mice and other vermin scurried in and out. The roofs had caved in making them appear like marble ghosts palaces.

Grass and other weeds poked out between the stone walls like lace trim. Marble palaces, once so proud and gleaming, were now covered with moss and streaked with grimy mold. Many were overgrown by bushes and vines.

Their heads swiveled left and right as they tried to figure out what had happened here. Agmar, Thorvi and Melker hadn't said anything. Could this be the result of Lady Eyrie's evil intention to destroy anything good?

Suddenly and without warning, they heard the distinct sound of hooves thumping on the hard cobblestones echoing off the stone walls and getting louder. Careening around a corner, Brian spotted two huge, black stallions galloping toward them at a furious pace, ridden by figures in dark, hooded cloaks, their faces completely covered. Stout boots laced to the knee protected their legs and lethal-looking swords hung from long scabbards.

Brian, Rose and Makka searched frantically for a place to hide, pressing back against a thorny hedge and finally scrunched down far enough where they could get under and behind the hedge.

Hidden, but still able see the horsemen riding by through the leaves, branches and thorns, the air was suddenly pierced by shrieks. Lightning sparked from branched forks striking suddenly from a clear sky—as though the gods were furious.

"Be very quiet!" commanded Rose with fierce authority, her ESP on high alert. "This is no accidental meeting. I feel violence and hate. Something awful has happened but I can't tell what."

Makka also felt the spooks were a sinister omen as they raced by in a fury, hoods slipping off revealing dark grimaces, angry black eyes and unbridled hate.

"Someone doesn't want us here," said Brian. "That's for sure."

When the riders had passed and the sound of hoof beats had died away, they pulled themselves out of the bushes and raced in the opposite direction, down one lane and up another until they were on the outskirts of the deteriorating city facing a huge hedge covered with thorns and purple blooms wilting in the sun.

Breathless, they pulled up short and wondered if they were still in the White City. This seemed to be the outskirts with just a few white marble buildings that once stood dazzling proud but now appeared sad and forlorn. At one time, it had been inhabited by people that must have been very wealthy, but now each building was in dreadful shape: dingy, crumbling and covered with moss. Moving along, listening intently for sounds of galloping horses and trying to find some peace in these unfamiliar surroundings, they walked slowly along the road until each of them stopped and stared gasping for air.

"What the...?" asked Rose as they crept closer.

"It's…it's just like the one we have at home," said Brian, fingering the iron gate that was attached to a high wall hidden under the dense shrubbery.

"Look," said Makka. "Yours has an A, but this has an L. What does that mean?"

"Let's find out," said Brian, stepping up to the plate. "Where's the buzzer?"

"There isn't one." Rose pushed the metal gate lightly and it swung open.

Before them stretched a very long, smooth marble cobblestone pathway leading to what appeared to be a large palace with a tall tower made entirely of gleaming white marble. The large palace, standing four stories high, had turrets and balconies, numerous doors and over one hundred windows, many of them made with stained glass, still intact. The façade was breathtaking in its opulence. The tall tower had large oblong windows and ornate spires that rose to the blue sky above. The front door seemed to beg them to get closer.

"I feel as though I've been here before," Makka said, walking slowly, as though in a trance. "I need to get inside."

"What if it's locked or if someone lives there?" Rose grabbed at Makka's hand, but she was in forward motion, moving toward the heavy wooden front door.

Suddenly, a rail-thin figure, tall as a sapling, leaped out from behind a pillar. He wore dirty, moth-eaten pants that were held up by a frayed cord. His leather vest covered a grimy shirt. His eyes were hollow, his teeth rotten and his hands gnarled. He pointed a twisted finger at Brian.

"Who might you be?" he asked in a raspy voice.

Brian gallantly stepped between the unsightly figure and the girls, holding out his arms to protect them while unsheathing his scabbard for easy access to the short sword. "And just who might YOU be?" He stepped toward the man, forcing him back.

"G...G...Gareth Woodenwood," he stammered. "Gate Master."

"Gate Master?"

"Yes, the Gate Master. I've been waiting forever for you to arrive."

"Us?" asked Rose. "Why us?"

"Not you," he said, pointing a crooked finger with long yellow nail. "HER."

Brian protectively stepped next to Makka and wrapped his arm around her, sending a quiver of electricity throughout her body. "And what do you want with her? Who are you?"

"G...G...Gareth Woodenwood, I...I...told you that."

"What is this place?" Makka asked gently, not wanting to upset him. The old guy looked as though he'd blow over in a breeze.

"Lovenfell."

"Lovenfell? Is that the name of the family who lived here?"

Woodenwood shook his head. "We've been waiting for you. Go inside. You'll see."

"Do you have a key?" asked Brian. "Can you let us in?"

"Maybe."

Makka pointed to a huge, white obelisk that stood in the center of the lawn."

"What's that?"

"All will be revealed in time." The Gate Master said, walking toward the front door as they followed unsteadily, feeling insecure and totally vulnerable even though the old man himself looked harmless.

Brian suspected he knew more than he was letting on. Up the front steps they all went and stopped in front of the huge timbered double doors. The knocker was in the shape of a lion's head. Without speaking, Rose pointed to it. Brian nodded. Makka got it, too. It was the same as the Abadon home.

"Does anyone live here?" Rose asked. "It looks deserted."

Before Woodenwood could utter a reply, the doors swung open revealing a dark interior. Brian put out his arm to prevent the others from entering. Rose closed her eyes and stood completely still.

"I don't think danger lurks here, but something even more disturbing is going on—I'm getting some really odd vibes, like nothing I've ever felt before."

Gareth Woodenwood opened his mouth to speak, but before any words were spoken, Makka—as if pulled by an invisible rope—marched straight through the door and into the murky hallway.

"Wait Makka!" Brian called out. "Wait for us."

Rose and Brian each took a step forward, but as they moved forward the doors slammed shut with a resounding clang. Brian and Rose desperately tried the handle in turn, banging their fists on the door, and pounding the metal knocker while shaking the metal grip with all their combined strength. It was useless. The door had mysteriously locked!

From the inside they heard Makka's voice calling out for them, but she sounded a million miles away. They wanted to help; they knew they had to get in. But for the moment at least, there was nothing they could do.

"Are there other entrances?" Brian demanded grabbing Gareth's shirt. "Let us in. Where are the keys? I'm going to have to break a window."

At that moment, in front of their astonished eyes, Gareth Woodenwood turned to dust and crumbled into a pile of sawdust at their feet. A sudden gust of wind blew what was left of him away and they stared at each other in shocked silence and total amazement.

Had he been hanging on just to make sure Makka got into Lovenfell? No matter how or why, she was now all alone with the ghosts and spirits that inhabited the huge palace named Lovenfell in the White City somewhere in Etrunia.

~ 32 ~

HALL OF MIRRORS

Makka spun around in terror and grabbed the huge brass handle from the inside, shaking it violently. She pushed and pulled with every ounce of strength she could muster, finally unsheathing the short sword and wiggling the tip into the lock, but nothing worked. She was alone, trapped inside as Brian and Rose shouted frantically from the other side, calling her name and banging with their fists.

But the building seemed to want her unaccompanied. She was exhausted and afraid, sobbing quietly for a few minutes before drying her eyes and looking for a solution to her immediate problem.

She stood up and studied her surroundings. The massive building was stunning and majestic—not menacing or spooky—with bright, high ceilings and a floor inlaid with magnificent black-and-white marble tiles in a harlequin pattern. The beige walls were decorated with colorful banners. Was she crazy or did they hang exactly the same way as in the Abadon house back in Granite Falls? She shook her head in confusion.

The banners had colorful crests, falcons, lions, flowers, and criss-crossing stripes reminding her of the shields in Thio the Fair's armory. The different shields and patterns must have represented a number of families that once inhabited Lovenfell over the centuries. But who had built this magnificent structure and who were the people that had lived here?

It seemed to be as fresh and untouched as the day it was built, colors still vibrant, no dust or mildew—as though time had stood still. And yet Makka felt an eerie familiarity. The mystery of the White City and its inhabitants and this puzzling place with its legendary history was more than Makka could digest.

She wrapped her fingers around the cell phone in her pocket as she walked down the center aisle of the great hallway that seemed to stretch forever. It didn't, of course; still, it was the most massive building she'd ever been in.

Makka felt her knees begin to tremble and she willed her heartbeat to slow down as she followed the harlequin tiles to a grand staircase. Up she went, as though drawn by a magnetic force.

She stopped to unlace her shoes. If someone was waiting to ambush her, she didn't want to give her presence away by clumping around—not that anyone could have missed the slamming door and her sobs a few minutes ago. But if anyone *was* there, a surprise attack was best. She carried the short sword in her right hand. She marveled that the stunning pictures and gilded mirrors could have withstood the ravages of time.

As she traveled down the hallways, she noticed doors on either side and although she was tempted to open them, she dared not. She felt as though a thousand eyes were watching her. She was outnumbered, that was certain. Turning around, she found a door ajar and peeked in. There were mirrors and chairs but no beds or other furniture and no signs of life. Feeling emboldened—and, surprisingly—as though she belonged here, she opened door after door with the same results. Empty. Empty. Emptier. Some chambers were devoid of any furniture; as though the residents left in the middle of decorating.

She sat down and slipped back into her shoes before heading down another long hallway on the main floor. She felt alone and vulnerable and yet completely at peace; she forced herself to remain calm, focused and strong. Eventually, she'd find an exit and would be reunited with her friends, or they would burst in and save her—not that she seemed to be in imminent danger.

Although it was darker down this passage than the main hall, enough light spilled in through mullioned stained glass windows that soared from the patterned floor to the high ceiling above—as if to heaven itself—creating purple, gold, scarlet and sapphire shadows on the floor and walls as the light shone through. She thought briefly about trying to break out, but the windows depicting scenes of battles and knights, flowers and pastoral villages in equal measure were too gorgeous to touch.

Standing in admiration of the fine craftsmanship in the perfect stillness, she noticed another staircase that ran up the far end of the hallway. As she climbed the stairs, she saw a mural that ran the length of the wall dotted by dozens—no, hundreds—of mirrors. In fact, the entire huge palace or mansion or whatever it was called, was basically a collection of murals and mirrors. The story of Etrunia was here and she, Makka Sinclair was in the middle of it.

She moved closer to study the painted scene, expertly drawn by an artist of amazing talent many years—or possibly centuries—before. It depicted people with crowns on proud, saddled horses, displaying colorful shields and lethal weapons.

The joyful panorama turned ugly and bloody with battles, fallen soldiers and dying horses. Dark castles and menacing ghouls in dark capes took over the landscape, turning it ugly shades of brown, charcoal and blood red. She stopped in her tracks, staring at the face of a man who was a dead ringer for Mr. Abadon and a general who looked astonishingly like her dad lying on the ground, a sword through his chest!

Was that crimson smudge blood dripping down the wall—or just paint? She leaned in and sniffed, jerking back and nearly toppling down the steps as the odor of copper hit her nostrils. Glancing down, she noticed that it had formed a puddle on the floor not only here, but in other places as well. Tears sprung from her eyes.

The violence, the treachery and treason along with the horrifying agony of the gory battles reminded her of Agmar, Thorvi, and Melker with their missing limbs and their woeful story of a country under siege. Could her parents really have been part of this? How was it even possible?

Only if time had no meaning, as Brian had said!

With her body prickling, she climbed even higher and saw her own image in one mirror as it morphed into her sister, Ann. No, that cannot be; this is too much. She sank down on the step and put her face in her hands, wishing she was back at home—anywhere but here. Without Brian and Rose, she couldn't even begin to know what was going on.

She pulled out her cell phone and snapped a few photos. The battery was dangerously low, but she had to show it to them, ask for their advice, figure it out and make some kind of sense of it— or at least put it in historical perspective and understand how it affected her and what part she played in this.

Obviously, this was not happening by chance.

In the silence, alone but now feeling calm and resolved, wanting to deal with it—even without her friends—she moved toward an ornate mirror at the top of the staircase, feeling drawn by a mysterious force. It was rectangular; in it she saw an unblemished reflection of herself surrounded by a gilded frame lovingly carved by some craftsperson somewhere back in time. She stared with mounting dismay.

Her face was grimy and her eyes red-rimmed. Her hair was a holy mess with brambles and leaves, her lips were cracked and she had a bloody scratch on her cheek. Suddenly the hairs on her arms and neck prickled as the pieces of the puzzle begin to drop into place. Her parents were definitely somehow tied up with the Abadons!

Just then, her face morphed into something blurry and ghostlike and she moved away quickly, stepping over to the next one where a man with heavy black brows and dark scornful eyes appeared. Picking up steam, she scooted along the circular hallway, noting that every face was different. They had chubby cheeks and fat lips, yellow eyes and splotchy skin, green eyes and bushy brows, some had pale faces with angry scars or disheveled hair and blank orbs filled with the cold gleam of evil.

There were sour faces, ugly and pretty ones, warty and heavy lidded and some with huge bulging eyes and wild expressions.

There were shrewd faces, gorgeous faces and leering ones with hair in every color—on their heads and coming out of noses and ears—and some with no hair at all.

She shivered in their presence feeling they were alive. "How can I get out?" she asked one of them. "What's going on; who are you?"

She expected at least one of them to answer, but all she heard was her own heavy breathing.

Following the hallway with the mural and mirrors, she faced a door that was slightly ajar. She slowly pushed it open on creaky hinges. The room was lit up in royal blue, ruby and ochre, rich garnet and gleaming gold, the light streamed in through more stained glass.

The round domed ceiling glowed with gilded detail work and below her feet was a thick carpet in deep red. Completely encircling the room were even more mirrors in all shapes and sizes—all in gorgeously carved gilded frames. So many of them!

She walked around the room in amazement as they began to talk, their voices coming from every direction into her subconscious mind—or were they actually speaking aloud?

~ 33 ~

DAVINA OF SARAGON

As she moved slowly around the room, the voices in the mirrors began to repeat parts of the epic tale she'd heard at Thio the Fair's underground fortress.

The Ancients had mysteriously appeared long ago, creating a country they named Etrunia. It was a peaceful land that prospered for many centuries. As time passed, fierce warriors infringed, claimed the lands and created the kingdoms around Etrunia, until the wars broke out. After years of combat, the Ancients slowly disappeared and left the White City and Lovenfell as their legacy.

She heard the words Davina of Saragon and whipped around. *Who'd said that?* It sounded so familiar, as though she'd dreamed about it. More voices poked through the fog in her head.

After the Ancients, there was a succession of Lords and wannabe Kings and others who tried to rule, but no one was strong enough to stay in power and rule. Time passed and after a long period of unrest, the Great Pharmakeus, son of Lord Percival, who was cruelly assassinated, took charge. He was only seventeen at the time and his sister, Lady Eyrie, was fourteen. Together, they ruled Etrunia fairly and with love. There was finally peace and prosperity in the land.

Another mirror, a wise old face with bushy brows and wild gray hair, spoke through her thoughts.

Eventually, Pharmakeus married the beautiful Augusta, daughter of King Stefan of Savea. It was an arranged marriage but the two fell deeply in love, and the countries were aligned in a solid pact of peace. Lady Eyrie never married and became cold and cruel as she aged.

A chorus of voices called out as she swept from that room, down the stairway and up the steps again as a steady stream of information assaulted her—far more than she could process, especially while watching the gruesome murals.

Great unrest developed once again and they fought hard to keep the enemy out. Pharmakeus lived in the stronghold city of Missilium to the east. But that left the north and south unprotected. In a smart, preemptive move, he relocated to Northgate and Lady Eyrie went to Southistle.

The wizards cast a spell over Missilium to cover it with sand. A flat sand dome protected the city under the desert and the few remaining inhabitants went about their business, unaware of any turmoil above ground. They were simply spirits living beneath the sand dome named Desert of Lost Souls.

Makka returned to the main hall near the front door as the old tale continued, spilling into her brain from more strange and frightening faces.

And now Lady Eyrie is in charge, having vanquished her brother and Lady Augusta and some of their servants in a cloud of black smoke. She is aligned with the most evil of them all, Lord Hviti who dwells in Valgard, the Dark Fortress, in the middle of a lake. He is all powerful, flanked by an army of ghouls and it's said that he collects souls—especially those of children and teens. God help anyone who gets caught by his army. They will simply vanish, never to be seen again.

Makka fingered the Cvector under her shirt. This was too much information for her to process. *And what did they expect her to do?* She couldn't change the past or stop the madness. She was only fourteen for goodness sake! Suddenly, the mirror closest to her lit up in a soothing pink-orange glow and a woman, who looked exactly like her mom, appeared.

Her image was stronger, more defined than the others. She wore a netted lace headpiece of gems over her straight blonde hair and her flawless face seemed happy and proud. Her beautiful familiar voice filled Makka's heart with hope and happiness.

And so you've found our secret, Makka.

"What? What did you say?" she asked aloud.

The face in the mirror smiled benignly. Yes, it's me. I'm so happy to see that you are alive and well. My heart was filled with tears and sadness when we found out that you slid through the portal without telling us. But this is where you belong. Soon we'll all be reunited and peace will rule again my darling girl.

"Mom, I miss you so much. I miss Dad and Sasha and Eddie and my sister. I want to come home now. I have to be at school soon."

No worries came the telepathic reply. We all miss you, too. But you're there for a reason and remember: time has no meaning. I love you Davina. Now go back to the round room and see the future.

Makka recoiled at hearing the name Davina. This was the third time. What the heck was happening?

She quickly retraced her steps to the domed room and noticed a pedestal in the center. Certainly it hadn't been there before. An object was on it covered with a golden damask cloth. Slow as a snail, she inched toward it, her arm reaching out as though pushed by an unseen hand. Her fingers grasped the edge and the cloth slid off revealing a stunning clear quartz crystal ball.

Stepping closer, she peered into it, studying the whitish veins that ran through the interior, marveling at the small rainbows that appeared. Then, suddenly, it clouded and began swirling, smoke circling inside.

As the smoke cleared, she stared into it and asked, "Am I safe?" The ball pulsed green. "Please tell me that I'll be home soon. Please let me know Rose and Brian haven't abandoned me."

The crystal glowed blue. Not knowing what that meant, tears leaked down her smudged cheeks, her shoulders sagged and she felt ten thousand years old. When did this adventure begin, when would it end—and, most importantly, would she survive?

As she turned away the crystal began to glow and an image appeared. Makka prayed it would show her the way out; perhaps she could snap her fingers and find this was all just a crazy dream.

Suddenly her phone vibrated in her pocket. Hopeful that someone had located her and was calling to say help was on the way—or that there was enough juice left to call 911—she pulled it out. The screen lit dimly and her brother, Eddie, appeared with his unruly mop of auburn hair and his bright green eyes. His image faded in and out.

"Stay strong Makka. You have a hard road ahead, but I have your back. I'll never abandon you."

"Eddie, Eddie, help me get home. Tell Mom and Dad, call the police."

As the phone faded to black she heard him say: "You'll be fine. We all love you."

Makka dissolved into a puddle of gloom as the sun dropped below the horizon and long shadows fell upon Lovenfell. Outside, her friends fretted with worry. Brian pushed the door for the thousandth time and, amazingly, this time it creaked open.

The story had been told.

Makka Sinclair, aka Davina of Saragon, had heard the long and bitter saga and knew she would not be returning home anytime soon.

In fact, she had no idea what lay in store for the future.

No clue at all.

PART FOUR: VALGARD & THE DARK FORTRESS

~ 34 ~

SOUTHISTLE

Unlike the northern section of Etrunia which was mountainous, cool and dry, Southistle to the south was warmer and densely populated. When Lady Eyrie moved there many years earlier, she hated the humid climate and the endless summer. But she found that crops were abundant and with the seaport and all the trading under her domain, she soon had everything she needed to rule in splendor.

Large wooden sailing ships brought silk cloths, the finest brocade and spices from afar, diamonds, precious gems and metal ore from the Dark Continent. There were exotic rugs and more, and all this incredible wealth was hers for the taking.

The people under her rule would have been happy with the multitude of goods and with a ruler who turned their once sleepy city into a bustling and thriving center of commerce. The problem was that Lady Eyrie was cold as a winter storm, as ruthless as Genghis Kahn, and bitter as lemons.

The people were taxed to the point of starvation while she had more riches than anybody could imagine—more than she could spend in a lifetime—or even ten. She lived splendidly in

Blackwater Castle, a fitting name for a woman with a heart made of evil. Her trusted confidant was Councilor Simeon whose discretion and opinion she valued, even if she didn't always follow his advice. The person who held most sway over the wicked ruler was Lord Archite, the Grand Wizard, whose heart was almost as frozen as hers.

The seaport and town of Southistle wasn't the only busy place. The kitchen in the huge walled castle was bustling with activity as the Cook barked orders at Dottir Dumbledale, a tall auburn-haired teenager who rolled her blue eyes at the Cook—who she called the Troll—told her to work faster and harder.

"You're nothing but a spoiled rotten child," she spat out. Dottir didn't turn around, but she could picture the petty tyrant who was as wide in the beam as she was tall, picking at a scab on her chin. She was a dour woman, fat as a tub of lard with cheeks red as berries. Her apron was stained with juice and her hands were raw from scrubbing vegetables.

Dottir didn't even know her real name. She was just Cook—an old bat with bad teeth and foul breath who bullied the help without remorse, especially Dottir.

The stone kitchen was large enough for a small herd of cows to wander around comfortably. Along one wall were two openings: one was an oven for baking bread, the other was a hearth with a long iron arm to hang a cauldron—large enough to cook an entire boar.

Shelves ran along another wall with an assortment of urns, bowls, pitchers and assorted crockery. Rows of drying herbs gave off a wonderful mixture of aromas. Along a small alcove hooks had been embedded in the stone to hold pheasants and rabbits and the occasional goose for special festivities. There were chopping blocks, bins for vegetables and piles of split wood for stoking the flames.

Dottir tried to work as far away from the Cook as possible. She stank of garlic and body odor. She had seven moles on her chin, each with a long black hair sprouting from the center. One day the moles, hairs, and her nasty smelling sweat would fall into the food served to Lady Eyrie and her henchmen. It would serve them all right.

Dottir hated the kitchen but she had been obligated to work there for five years. After that she could apprentice to the head housekeeper. Yet she felt lucky, considering some of the other options that could have befallen her—like raking out the stalls. Her younger brother, Bodie, had chosen that as his term of servitude.

There were rumors in the town that Lady Eyrie was involved in black magic and that she was in constant contact with someone or something even more evil, if that was possible. Lord Hviti ruled Valgard, also known as the Dark Fortress in the middle of a lake. People spoke of ghouls, dark spirits and unimaginable horrors that took place at Valgard in the middle of the night.

It was even said that slimy sea creatures lurked in the lake and anyone unlucky enough to step into the brackish water would be torn apart.

Nobody knew what to believe and nobody was willing to uncover the truth. Some things are best left alone, hidden in the mind of one's wild imagination.

"What are you doing?" Cook screamed from across the vast room, her face the color of boiled beet juice. Dottir was slicing carrots and nicked her finger at the sudden interruption. She put her finger in her mouth and sucked the salty tasting blood. She carefully wiped it on her apron and used the back of her wrist to swipe a tear from her cheek. It stung like heck but she would never show the Troll that she was careless. There were worse jobs for girls like her—like cleaning the chamber pots or washing sheets and Lady Eyrie's undergarments, gross.

"Yes, ma'am," Dottir said, curtsying, "what can I do?"

The Cook placed tea and biscuits on a tray, adding a small silver spoon for the sugar and placed a linen napkin over the top. "Take these upstairs to Lady Eyrie. She's in the Throne Room with her advisors."

Dottir scooped up the tray and left the kitchen. She had never been to the Throne Room before and she trembled with anticipation and fear. The other two young helpers, Pim and Meg, looked at each other with fear, happy they were not the ones being sent to the Throne Room and Lady Eyrie.

As she traveled down hallways and up stone staircases she couldn't help noticing how lacking of warmth the castle was. It seemed a strange contradiction to the wealth Lady Eyrie was reputed to have. The Throne Room was located on the second floor, up a winding flight of steps lit by torch sconces. A mouse scurried out of the way as Dottir took each step slowly, careful not to slosh the tea from the pot or rattle the cups.

Outside the Throne Room, she found two guards. "Tea for Milady," she said, her knees knocking. The guard to the right picked up the linen napkin to make sure there was no weapon and then threw open the door, nearly causing her to drop her precious cargo. She curtsied again.

"For the Lady," she said. The guard stepped back to allow her entrance.

As she stepped in she didn't know where to look first—at the gilded walls and throne or at the circle of guards, each holding a sword and circling the Lady of the Castle protectively. They wore dark blue capes and boots. It seemed to Dottir that all of Lady Eyrie's wealth was concentrated in this wondrous room of colorful silk banners and brocade wall tapestries, golden furniture and pedestals with precious crystals.

Lady Eyrie wore a fortune on her head in the form of an elaborate diadem and a dress of black velvet studded with gemstones. On each of her bony fingers was a golden ring with a different colored stone: ruby, sapphire, opal, amethyst, emerald, and a few Dottir could not identify.

"Who are you?" demanded Lady Eyrie. "I've not seen you before."

Feeling as though she'd faint from fear, Dottir's hands shook violently. "I'm Cook's helper. Your regular servant is sick and she asked me to bring this to you."

"Put that tray down before you drop it and make a mess!" Lady Eyrie barked.

Dottir searched frantically for a table but didn't see any where to set it down until the guard nearest her stepped aside. She quickly set the tray down and began to back out of the room. She tried not to think of all the stories she'd heard about people disappearing after meeting with Lady Eyrie in the Throne Room. In all her short life, she'd never been so frightened.

As she neared the door, a small man stumbled into the room. He looked like a garden gnome wearing green pants and hat with a belly that hung over his belt. He was weird alright and yet everybody stepped back to let him pass. Dottir felt her legs turn to jelly. She froze as he blurted out, "The Cvector has been stolen from Nideon! Whoever took it has vanished without a trace."

From the doorway, Dottir noticed Lady Eyrie's fists ball into hard knots, the rings cutting into her thin flesh. Her face was grim—an ugly mask of vengeance.

"Who's the traitor?" she shrieked through clenched teeth, her venomous rage filling the spacious room. "Tell me right now Jesper. Is it Nideon? Is he trying to deceive me?"

Jesper looked down. He knew the truth and could get his head lopped off before he had a chance to explain the foul-up to his advantage. His foot scuffed the black and white marble floor.

"Well?" Her voice was pitched high enough to shatter glass.

"It was stolen from his neck while he slept."

"He's not paid to sleep," said Councilor Simeon. "He is paid to keep the Cvector from falling into the wrong hands."

"I know, I know. It was all a mistake."

Jesper could hardly admit it was HIS mistake. If he hadn't stolen Makka's cell phone and allowed her to chase him through the portal, none of this would have happened. He wouldn't be here being grilled and fearing for his life. His knees trembled so hard he thought he'd tumble down into a heap. Though he also knew this was preordained and bound to happen.

Lady Eyrie's voice sliced through him like a sharpened sword.

"And whose mistake would that be, you little good-for-nothing worthless turnip."

Jesper cleared his throat. "Technically…"

"Yes?" prompted Lady Eyrie, her irises black laser-like pinpoints.

"Technically, I suppose it was just a cluster of inexplicable events that began back in Granite Falls."

She leaned back smirking. "Yes, Granite Falls, where you were sent to keep an eye on my brother. What does he call himself now?"

"Mr. Abadon."

"Yes, now I recall. Royal Abadon and his wife, Augusta. How pretentious."

Jesper smiled thinking she would begin reminiscing. But he was wrong. She leaned forward, nearly toppling off the throne as she wagged a bony finger in his face. "So you allowed a perfect stranger into our land and now, as a result of your supreme stupidity, we have lost the Cvector."

Jesper didn't dare tell her that Makka's friends Rose and Brian—the son and daughter of Royal Abadon—were also in Etrunia and that all three of them had possession of the priceless Cvector. He would be shredded to pieces if he confessed that sin. So he simply nodded and knelt down on one knee, his hands pressed together as if praying for mercy.

"The Cvector holds the key to the Lost City of Missilium. Nobody may enter there but me," Lady Eyrie shrieked. That has been the plan since the beginning. Only the Grand Wizard Archite knows how to use it so it's of no value to anybody else, but I MUST have it. Immediately!"

She turned her gaze back to Jesper. "As for you, it's into the dungeon until I decide what to do with you."

Although Lady Eyrie was known throughout Etrunia as a great beauty in her youth, she had grown ugly with greed and hate over time. Now with her face darkened in rage, Dottir feared she would vanish in a puff of black smoke.

Two guards picked up Jesper by his elbows and carried him out, legs churning as though he were riding a bicycle. Councilor Simeon bowed and backed out of the door.

"I will see to it Milady," he said, ushering her out. After years of lying and cheating to reach his coveted position, Simeon now had great influence over the Lady of the land. Still, he had to be careful since five of his predecessors had mysteriously disappeared. He did not want to be the sixth.

~ 35 ~

ORN WITTENBERG

Back in his chambers, Councilor Simeon closed the heavy wooden door and leaned his back against it. He enjoyed the power he had, but it came at a very high price and now his nerves were frayed. If he didn't deliver the missing Cvector to Lady Eyrie, his head would be on the chopping block. He had to retrieve the lost amulet. Was that even possible? Who had it? Where was it? No matter what, the burden was upon him to produce it.

He picked up a small bell and immediately a guard came into the room. He needed to be extremely careful about who was chosen for this dangerous mission. The guard came in as silently as a cat, his face covered with a dark hood, which unnerved Simeon.

It was rumored that some of the looming figures that came and went in the darkened hallways were shadows from the past and not real. Nobody knew for sure and nobody wanted to be the first to find out. Many believed they had been created by the Grand Wizard Archite to Lady Eyrie's specifications. Others thought they were sent over by Lord Hviti from the Dark Fortress where they trained. No matter what, they were to be dreaded.

Councilor Simeon whispered to the hooded figure, "Go to the stables. Bring a messenger."

Orn Wittenberg had, like all the other teenagers, been conscripted to serve Lady Eyrie. He had been assigned to the stable to rake the muck and had graduated over the years to positions of more responsibility. He had a way with the huge animals, speaking in low tones and soothing their restless spirits. He calmed feisty steeds and kept the stables running smoothly. Now, at eighteen, he was paid a small and steady wage, meaning that he was at Lady Eyrie's beck and call.

The guard appeared and Orn followed.

"Bodie, I'm putting you in charge," he said to Dottir's little brother. "I'll be back soon."

"Really? Me? Okay, great. What should I do?"

"Give all the horses apples and watch out for robbers."

"Robbers? Really?" Bodie's eyes opened wide.

"Kidding. Just carry on."

The hooded figure led Orn through the kitchen where Cook was grumbling about Dottir and what a lazy wench she was. "I sent her up with a tray an hour ago," she complained—although only fifteen minutes had passed. "Tell her to get her lazy arse down here will ya?"

Orn smiled, turning away so she didn't see him grin. But she was too busy to notice that he stuck his tongue out at her. Pim and Meg giggled quietly. Up the stairs they went, straight to Councilor Simeon's chambers. He was standing behind his desk, extremely serious. All business.

Orn bowed slightly. "I am at your service."

Simeon came around the desk and stood in front of Orn. "I have a mission for you. But first, come with me to see Lady Eyrie.

"Lady...Lady...E...Eyrie?" Orn's knees trembled. "Can't you tell me?"

But the Councilor was already out the door and the hooded figure loomed behind Orn. Slowly, he pivoted and left the chamber, his heart hammering in his chest, his throat dry with fear, his mind racing to determine if he'd done something that required punishment. He couldn't think of a thing, except perhaps joking with Dottir that morning at breakfast.

Orn was tall, six feet and sturdily built, his head was a mop of curly blond locks and deep-set brown eyes seemed to melt the hearts of all the girls he met but as he followed Simeon, all the air was sucked from his lungs.

He had been lucky to get an apprenticeship at the stables from the Councilor. It was an opportunity for his family to live in relative peace and under protection. If he had turned it down, they would have been punished. To his surprise, he enjoyed his job, but he never expected to be called upon for a mission of any importance. Mucking horse dung was not glamorous in any way. Councilor Simeon must have felt his anxiety because he suddenly grabbed Orn's elbow and whispered, "Steady boy, get a grip on yourself. You have been chosen specially for this mission."

Orn was sick with fear; his heart thumped like a kettle drum in his chest. Please let me not perish in the line of duty, he prayed. I'm too young to die like my brother who'd been killed in a battle. They entered the Throne Room. Orn didn't know which way to look first. He knelt in front of Lady Eyrie, surrounded by her guards. Simeon stood at his side, his meaty hand firmly on Orn's shoulder. Lady Eyrie handed a letter to Councilor Simeon who, in turn, handed it to Orn.

"You must ride to Valgard and deliver this letter to Lord Hviti. It's a message from Lady Eyrie and that's all you need to know." Simeon flipped the parchment envelope, over so Orn could see it was sealed with wax. "Take the fastest horse and get this delivered as quickly as possible."

Orn stood dumbstruck.

"Speed and discretion are of the utmost importance. You are the only one I trust," said Simeon.

Somehow he stumbled down the hallways and staircases, passed through the kitchen in a daze. Dottir asked, "Where are you going in such a hurry?"

"On a mission," he said, smiling in spite of his fear.

"Want company?"

"Sorry, not today."

Cook wheeled around. "Get upstairs you brazen wench and fetch the tea tray from the Throne Room. You ain't goin' nowhere."

Dottir smiled ruefully, but Orn had already left the kitchen and was trotting through the courtyard halfway to the stable. He found Big Gray, a huge dappled steed with hindquarters made for racing. It took a few minutes for Orn to get him ready. The letter was stowed safely in the pouch attached to the saddle and the broadsword secured in the leather loop. Bodie asked where he was going but Orn was swinging up onto the saddle and didn't hear him—nor could he tell his destination since it was top secret.

"I'll be back in two days. You're in charge."

"Me?" Bodie was flabbergasted.

"Yes, you. Remember to feed them in the morning and evening, water too, only one apple a day and no more than that."

"Don't worry. I know what to do."

On his way through the courtyard heading for the tall metal gate, he heard Dottir calling his name and saw her holding up a sack of food. She ran toward Big Gray, her cheeks flushed, her hair frizzy and her white cap falling off. He thought she was the most beautiful girl he'd ever met. She smiled and tossed the burlap bag to him. He caught it, winked, smiled and said, "Thanks. See you soon."

As he headed out of Southistle toward the Trail of Fears, which, in turn, led to the Forest of the Damned, he knew nothing of the terrible things that would befall him. The land outside was fraught with danger.

He patted is sword and urged Big Gray into a gallop.

~ 36 ~

DOTTIR DUMBLEDALE

Back in the kitchen, Cook waddled around, hunting for a special pot to cook up rabbit stew. "Where's the cauldron?" she asked Dottir, as though the girl had it hidden under her skirt.

Dottir shook her head, her long brown hair bouncing. "It should be around here somewhere."

"Somewhere doesn't help me. Here," she thrust the rabbit at Dottir. "Skin it—and where is the tea tray?"

If there was anything Dottir detested more than the Cook, it was cutting up rabbits. She'd cry if she had to do it and vowed to find some way out of it.

"I'll go upstairs and fetch the tea tray," she offered. "I'll cut the carrots and onions and run down to the root cellar for more vegetables." Nobody was going to make her do such a hideous thing to the poor dead creature. Even plucking feathers from a chicken gave her the creeps.

"Be quick about it," said the Cook, making clucking sounds with her tongue.

Without wasting a second, Dottir dashed from the kitchen toward the Throne Room in the tower. She took a deep breath as she approached the tall double doors. Two guards stood on either side, covered head to toe in dark capes. Their eyes were blank, like coals stuck in a skull; hands holding heavy metal swords that pointed downward. Both swords rose immediately upon her approach, barring her way and making a metallic clunk as they smacked together.

She curtsied to one and then the other. "I need to get the tray and tea cups, if you please."

Solemnly, the guard to the right pushed the door open and allowed her access. She slipped in quietly and spotted the tray where she left it, napkin still on top of the biscuits as though nobody had touched anything. She inched toward it, hands shaking, knees wobbling as she picked it up and swiveled back toward the door intending to wrap all the leftovers in the napkin for later.

As she made her way back to the doorway, the conversation she accidentally overheard between Lady Eyrie and Councilor Simeon made her blood run cold.

"Was the message sent?" Lady Eyrie asked.

"Yes, the messenger is on his way" said Councilor Simeon. "He should arrive tomorrow, but I don't expect that he'll return."

"What does that mean?"

"Lord Hviti kills the messenger, just in case they've stuck their noses where they don't belong. He'll send one of his own men with the reply."

The room was silent, save for the slight tremor in Dottir's hand that caused the teacups to rattle.

Lady Eyrie's eyes clouded. "I don't like that news. What right does he have to kill my messenger, that's unacceptable!"

Simeon's eyes dropped and his shoulders drooped. "I might have made a mistake."

His words shot like a hot arrow into Dottir's heart as Lady Eyrie asked: "Mistake? You are not paid to make mistakes Councilor."

"I'm terribly sorry. I forgot to give Orn the password what will save his life."

She drummed her fingers on the throne, the only sound in the room. Finally, she spoke. "It doesn't matter," she sniffed. "We have others to take his place." She swept her arm dramatically around the room. "We have an endless supply of messengers and more where these came from."

Nobody spoke. Nobody wanted to run an errand and never come back.

"By the way," she snorted, "what is the secret password?"

Councilor Simeon leaned in toward Lady Eyrie as Dottir held her breath and tuned out all other noises. She absolutely *had* to hear the password. Orn's life depended on it. Without it, he would surely die and she could never allow that to happen. She would give up her own life a hundred times to save his.

"Hail Lady Eyrie," Simeon said in a low voice. Dottir couldn't make out the words and wanted to cry. Tears stung her eyes as Lady Eyrie sat up straight on the throne and repeated the password clear as a bell on a Sunday morning: "Hail Lady Eyrie. I think that has a nice ring to it."

Without waiting to hear more—or waste another precious minute—Dottir sprang through the open doorway and raced down the steps, cups falling and breaking on the stones as she grabbed the napkin and wrapped the biscuits, tucking them in her apron the three precious words that would save Orn ringing in her hears: The messenger would be killed if he didn't know the password. Orn would die! His life was in mortal danger. She had to stop him from delivering the letter—or warn him that something awful would befall him—or better yet, give him the password and return home with him safe and sound.

Dottir hurried down the hall, slowing down before she reached the landing. She needed to walk, remain calm—or at least appear that everything was normal. No way she could allow panic to creep in. She had to pretend everything was all right, grab her brother, Bodie, from the stable and get on the road to Valgard as quickly as possible. As she passed through the kitchen, she tossed the tray onto the wooden butcher block and tore off her apron.

"You stupid little girl," the Cook yelled. "You've broken the teapot. That'll cost your family dearly. How could you be so clumsy? And where's the cauldron?" With her face twisted in a grimace, she tossed the dead rabbit at Dottir. "I'll find the pot, you skin this by the time I get back or you'll spend the rest of the day in the pigsty. I promise you that. Don't make me tell the Lady that you've..."

Dottir didn't wait for the rest of the threat. She ran from the kitchen into the courtyard, tripping to the stable and grabbing her brother by the collar. "Saddle two horses now! We're leaving."

"What? No. I'm in charge."

"Now listen to me little brother," she pushed her flushed face into his. "Saddle two fast horses and do it NOW. If you don't Orn…" She didn't finish. Instead, she raced to the closest stall and unhooked a tall roan mare. She backed the horse out of the wooden enclosure and looked around for a blanket to throw over its back. "Get the saddle on," she barked at her brother.

"But…" He stood bewildered.

"GET GOING!" The horse whinnied and shied away. She patted its nose and held out a biscuit. "Sorry."

She let go of the reins and backed out a smaller black horse, found a blanket and then grabbed two short swords from hooks on the wall and handed them to Bodie to affix to the saddle horns.

"Hurry," she urged. "Hurry Bodie. I'll tell you everything once we're on our way. They'll be looking for us soon. We've got to leave now or we'll never see Orn again."

Within minutes, the two siblings were up on their steeds and tearing across the courtyard toward the portcullis gate. "Open up!" cried Dottir as the guards looked up with startled faces. "Raise it now, be quick, Lady Eyrie is sending us on a special mission."

"*Are* we going on a special mission?"

"Quiet little brother. All will be explained in good time."

Within minutes they were beyond the gates of Blackwater Castle, heading toward the Trail of Fears. But first a quick stop at home to tell Mama Dumbledale they had an errand to run, a special undertaking for Lady Eyrie.

It would not be the truth exactly, but close enough for them to make a clean getaway and without getting their mom in trouble. The less she knew the better.

Even the walls at Blackwater Castle had ears.

~ 37 ~

IN HOT PURSUIT

With their saddlebags full of bread, cheese, and slices of cooked ham, and with their goat bladders filled with water, the siblings picked up the Trail of Fears and trotted as fast as possible without looking suspicious. This was a busy road with travelers on foot with donkeys, and astride horses. Merchants had carts laden with produce and goods while dogs ran to and fro jumping over the ruts in the dirt road.

Etrunia had spies everywhere and citizens had to be mindful of what they did and said. People disappeared all the time, never to be seen again. Nobody knew anything more than their sad, oppressive reality.

The future was bleak, but Orn had a mission to carry out and Dottir. along with her brother Bodie had one, too. All three felt energized and in forward motion, but not all of them would return to Southistle.

Since it was considered treason to say anything negative about Lady Eyrie or talk about the glories of the past when Pharmakeus was ruler, people rarely mentioned it, or talked only in whispers with close family members. Even friends were suspect. One never knew who was a spy.

As they reached the first bridge, a voice shouted out: "Halt! Halt! The two of you. Stop right now."

Dottir and Bodie reined in the horses at the wooden guard house that sat to the right of the Bamberg Bridge. Their hearts hammered with fear.

"Where were you going in such a hurry?" asked the caped guard, adjusting his woolen hat. The broadsword slapped against his black leather boots as he approached the trembling teens.

"We're going hunting, just for the afternoon," said Bodie, putting on a bravado that his sister found endearing.

"Then what's the rush?"

Dottir leaned down and batted her eyelashes. "It's getting late and our mom said to hurry. Our larders are empty and we'll go to bed hungry if we can't catch anything. You wouldn't want that, would you?"

The guard walked closer and eyed them up and down. Dottir thought she'd faint and fall right into his arms. But the guard reached out and patted the horse's neck. "That's a fine looking animal. Where did you get it?"

Dottir's brain scrambled for an explanation. Most common folk had old nags or mules, not fine stallions and certainly they wouldn't have two. Or perhaps he recognized it from the stock kept in the stables. Either way, she had to pull another lie from under her skirt.

"My father served Lady Eyrie for years," she lied. "He was injured, lost a leg in battle and since he couldn't walk, Councilor Simeon gave one to him with her blessing."

The guard took a step back. "Then how did you get two?" He eyed Bodie up and down, running his hand over the horse's leg. "This fella looks princely."

"Well…well…" Dottir's brain couldn't think of one more untruth.

Suddenly, Bodie blurted out: "I work in the stables of Lady Eyrie and one of my duties is to exercise them. We'll be back before the sun drops."

The guard had no recourse but to let them pass. "All right then, be on your way. Catch an extra rabbit or pheasant for me too." He laughed, showing bad teeth and winked at Dottir. She shivered with disgust.

When they were safely out of earshot she said to Bodie: "That was close. It's been a crazy awful day."

"What the heck is happening and why did you lie? You know Dad is fine."

"Think about it dummy. What was I going to say? That we stole two horses and we're committing treason?"

"Treason?"

"Don't worry about that. Keep your mouth shut and your eyes open. Be on guard. Now let's hurry. Orn's has at least a three-hour head start and he has a speedy horse. He'll cover more ground faster than we ever can."

They rode in silence for a while as traffic on the road thinned out. The trot became a cantor as the sun began its descent toward the horizon. So far the day had been perfect—perfectly awful and wonderful at the same time. They were out of Blackwater Castle on their way to save a life.

"What if something happens to you?"

"Just worry about yourself little one."

"I'm not little, I'm twelve."

"Good, then hang on. We're speeding up. We have a lot of road to travel before we reach the Forest of the Damned."

"That's a terrible name."

"And a terrible place," said Dottir solemnly. "Or so I hear."

Sunset was unremarkable, no red streaks in the sky or brilliant rays of sunlight lighting up the clouds. The overcast day simply became a gray evening. The forest loomed up ahead filled with holly trees with gray-green trunks, dark pointed leaves gleaming in the fading light. Birds called out to each other overhead; it was time to hunker down and stay safe from predators.

Dottir patted the saddlebags that held their supplies: spare clothes, a rabbit vest, and broad-bladed axe, a box of salt, plus flint and tinder for making fires. They stuck to the shadows as much as possible as the moon rose and unseen creatures hissed through the heather.

As they entered the forest, Dottir knew that there were treacherous swamps and dangerous roots that could trip a horse and break his leg. Then what? They'd be done.

Jagged clouds raced overhead and the wind whipped through her skirt and thin cotton jacket. The air was filled with darning needles, wasps, buzzing insects, and pine branches caused an unearthly howl. The woods were fraught with danger as they followed the narrow path that wound under a small granite cliff.

The horses plodded onward and she prayed they didn't encounter any black wolves, the most ferocious of all.

~ 38 ~

TO VALGARD

As soon as Orn had mounted his horse and started on the long and arduous journey to Valgard, he stopped and let his family know that he would return soon.

"Don't worry about me," he said, but he knew his mother would fret constantly until he was back in the stable at Blackwater Castle. His mom hovered around him like a vapor cloud pushing bundles of food into his hands.

"I have to go," he said impatiently. This was the most important mission of his life so far—the beginning of something special. If he could pull this off, then he'd rise quickly through the ranks and join the Lady Eyrie's elite inner circle, perhaps one day become her advisor.

Poor Orn had no idea how wicked she was or that his dream would never come true. If only he had galloped north as fast as possible and found the army of the Resistance on the eastern edge of the woods, his life would have turned out quite differently. He urged Big Gray down the Trail of Fears as fast as possible and shortly before dusk he entered the Forest of the Damned.

He consulted the hand-drawn map given to him by Councilor Simeon before he left the castle gates and saw that the fastest route was along the western edge of the forest which would bring him to the southern end of Lake Valgard where he'd catch the ferry to the Dark Fortress. It seemed simple enough as he urged Big Gray into a copse of stunted alder trees under a dusky sky. In this fairly sheltered corner of the forest, long black treetops moaned and dark wings flapped above. He heard the rush of water and saw shadowy figures darting in and out as he plunged further into the undergrowth. As darkness descended, the cold increased and shrill cries rang out from spooky shadows. Orn put on a brave face, patting the horse's neck and trying to quell his mounting fear that something dreadful would befall him before he could successfully deliver the letter to Lord Hviti.

He'd heard awful stories about what went on in Valgard and whatever fears he'd held in check began to fester. He knew that's where they trained sorcerers and dark knights. Horrible rumors of torture and brutality were spoken in whispers, as though the town of Southistle was filled with spies. In fact, it was.

In the glimmer of the rising moon, Orn noted that if he cut across the marshes he would arrive sooner. The marsh had standing water and enough mosquitoes and gnats to suck all of his blood. But the water in the bog was not deep and he urged Big Gray off the pinecone laden path and into the muck. They hadn't gone very far when second doubts began creeping in, along with ghastly feelings about the whole thing. Although he appeared eager when Simeon ordered him to deliver the letter, now the sinking feeling in the pit of his stomach was getting worse with every squishy step.

The dark dense forest canopy made it seem hours later. Whispering branches sounded like a small army following him and the air was thick with vapors rising from the stagnant water. Terrifying things lived in the tree trunks that were said to gobble people. As he rode slowly, Orn watched each one of the tree trunks; some were straight and tall and others gnarled with greenish brown moss. He felt torn about going this slowly through the shortcut and thought if he could find dry ground, or maybe a well-worn path that ran through the woods, he'd save hours.

As the moon rose overhead, he found dryer ground and picked up speed, urging the horse into a gallop, ducking branches and swerving around boulders. Fox, rabbits, hedgehogs and moles scurried out of his way. As they approached a dark winding ribbon of water, Orn—totally and completely exhausted—slid off the saddle, rubbed his legs and stretched his back. Then he knelt down and drank deeply using his hands to scoop the water. Big Gray slurped as though he hadn't had water for ages.

"Might as well camp here," he said, gathering dry fir-wood and moss to make a fire. Soon he had a warm resin-scented blaze making a merry crackle. He ate some more bread and a slice of dry ham for dinner, tethered the horse to a tree, unstrapped the saddle and used the horse's blanket to make a nest for himself in the hollow of a giant elm. Through the canopy of leaves above, he could see a clear and starry night. Wisps of mist crept from the damp marsh like wraiths. It was creepy, yet comforting, and soon Orn was lulled to sleep by the hooting owls and the soft munching of Big Gray as he devoured all the grass in sight and any leaves he could reach. With luck, they would arrive at the ferry to the Dark Fortress around sundown the following day.

~ 39 ~

FOREST OF THE DAMNED

Dottir pulled her horse to a stop and stared at the forest in front of them. Twilight had come and soon darkness would fall, not something she was looking forward to. She did not want to go in and she had a bad feeling about Bodie. Taking him on this perilous journey was a tremendous burden. If anything happened...no, she couldn't allow herself to go there.

She never imagined that she'd ever have a reason to go through this sinister wood that was rumored to have strange and terrible things happening in here. This was the last place on earth she wanted to be.

Her greatest desire was to board one of the huge sailing ships that came into the harbor and sailed out into the world. She'd spent hours at the wharf and knew they came from exotic places she could only dream about. She promised to fulfill that dream after she rescued Orn. Hopefully, he would come with her, but if not she refused to be held back by a man—even a good looking one that seemed to like her. She'd swab the decks—do just about anything to get out of Etrunia

"Come little brother, let's go. We've got no choice."

They moved forward cautiously as she searched the ground for signs of Big Gray's huge hooves, but saw nothing; nothing to prove this was where Orn entered. She scanned the line of trees that stretched as far as she could see and realized with dismay that any chance of catching up with him in this vast and overpowering tangle of trees, roots, and vines was impossible. Her only hope was to reach the ferry to the Dark Fortress in time to warn him.

"What's in there?" asked Bodie as he pointed into the forest, "do you know?" Bodie sounded small and frightened. Dottir felt the same way, but put on a brave face.

"There's a couple of small villages along the edge, but in there nothing but trees, rocks, small rodents, and the bog. But we're not going anywhere near that. I don't want to breathe the swamp gases." What she didn't say was that the place reeked of death.

"Do we have to continue?" Bodie asked in a little-boy voice.

"I'm afraid so. Believe it or not, Valgard was once a place of good wizardry. But Lady Eyrie turned it into a fortress of dark magic and then got Lord Hviti to rule over it. Every year children are plucked from all over Etrunia to study the dark arts and turned into evil beings. Be thankful you're not one of them. Now let's get going. We must catch Orn. He's in mortal danger."

"You like him, don't you?"

"Shut up Bodie, you don't know what you're talking about."

Bodie kept silent, but he knew he was right. His sister wouldn't risk her life for someone she didn't love—or at least liked a whole lot.

They entered the woods as the last rays of light dimmed. They were engulfed by darkness as the trees shut them in. The horses instinctively moved closer together as the trees with old and twisted branches formed a canopy above them. The siblings traveled along a path of pine wood, moss and broken dreams. Deeper they went as a light rain began to fall and the wind blew steadily from the west as they slogged along chilled to the bone.

Anything could go wrong, she had no doubt about it and she had to keep a watchful eye over her brother—the apple of their mother's eye. If anything happened to him, she would never forgive herself. And neither would anybody else.

Trusting her instincts, she began to hum an old song that her mother used to sing to her; Bodie began to sing along and soon the horses were trotting in rhythm to the tune.

She stopped suddenly, pulling up on the reins as her horse reared up and a fox scurried in front of them. "I've heard there are boardwalks built by the ancient swamp people," she said, urging the animals on slowly. "It's said they're hidden in the trees. If we could find that, we'd make better time."

"Yes, perfect," Bodie chirped. "The sooner we're outta here, the better. This is creepy."

"There's just one problem."

"You're funny. I can see ten problems right from here."

Dottir smiled despite her anxiety. "Legend has it that it's inhabited by dark and dangerous creatures. I'm wondering how long it would take to go around the forest instead of through it."

"It'd take too long," Bodie answered, a boy wise for his years. "Orn wouldn't stand a chance."

"Then let's get going. We have at least an hour or two before we need to bed down and if the old stories are true, the boardwalk should start not far from here."

Deeper and deeper into the forest the siblings went, surrounded by dark shadows and red eyes glinting from behind gnarled tree stumps; high above in branches dense with leaves, owls peered down and watched every move of the cautious travelers.

She didn't want to know what might be lurking in the underbrush as she hunched forward, keeping her head down. Trees groaned and unseen creatures made eerie night noises. Dottir didn't want to hazard a guess as to what was watching them or how this grand adventure would end.

But only a miracle could make it end well.

~ 40 ~

BEWARE THE COCOONS

Dottir and Bodie moved swiftly, they had no time to waste. Traveling alone on a powerful steed, Orn must be far ahead. Perhaps he knew a shortcut, perhaps not; in any case, he had a few hours' lead time.

As they slipped into the shadows of the deep forest, they felt as though the horses were carrying them into a cave with no end in sight and suddenly realized they were, indeed, in a tunnel. Dottir turned her head from side to side as the stone floor echoed noisily under them, reverberating off the walls.

The feeling was like being swallowed whole, but before she had a chance to think about an alternative, her face was entangled by an enormous spider web. She felt sticky strands wrap around her eyes and nose as she ripped it away, praying it didn't hold a deadly red-and-black spider or one of the hairy monsters she often saw crawling through the kitchen. One bite and she wouldn't last through the night.

She dared not open her mouth but she had to warn Bodie to be careful. Whipping out her sword, she held it up to cut through any other sticky traps along the passageway; with her forearm, she wiped away the remnants of the web until she felt reasonably certain that it was gone. Then she turned around and said one word: "Spiders!"

The passage twisted around a few turns and then began to rise steadily until it evened out again. The air was dense and muggy with a foul stench of skunk. Dottir held her sleeve over her nose as she caught brief glimpses of narrow offshoots too small for their horses to pass. Bodie asked, "Where do those tunnels go?" But she had no answer and didn't want to open her mouth in case the spider was still lurking somewhere in her clothing.

As their eyes grew accustomed to the absence of light, they were able to make out gaps in the stones, allowing small bits of moonlight to shine in. She had no idea who built this or why. Perhaps the Forest People she'd heard about from her parents— or some grand wizard from long ago. It seemed stranger-than-strange to have a stone tunnel in the middle of a forest. Then again, she was ignorant of most things having to do with the Ancients of Etrunia.

Anyway, she had more important things to think about—like sailing around the world and getting the attention of Orn Wittenberg.

At last she felt a fresh breeze blow through and the sound of the hooves on stone diminished, replaced by the soft sucking noise of the squishy ground as they exited the man-made passageway and into the open.

Travel was slow and tedious through the forest. It would take a stroke of extraordinary luck to find the mythical boardwalk and yet a few minutes later Bodie called out, "Over there, I think that's a path."

At that moment, the howling of wolves filled the air and the horses reared up with apprehension. Dottir and Bodie stroked their necks and talked steadily in soft voices as the sound of hooves on wood rang in their ears. "Hooray," shouted Bodie. "We found it. Let's gallop."

Dottir smiled, her teeth gleaming. "Hold on little brother. We're not sure how sturdy this is. I mean, it's been here since ancient times. What if the wood is rotten and your horse falls through and breaks a leg—then what? We have to proceed with caution. Okay?"

Bodie knew his sister was right and whined, "I'm hungry."

"Me, too. Okay, since we found the boardwalk, let's celebrate with a little food." They dismounted and Dottir dug in the bags while the horses nibbled on the plentiful grass that grew between the planks. Brother and sister sat on the boardwalk and shared what would ultimately become their last meal together. As they took their first bite, an ungodly howl pierced the air.

"Yipes," said Dottir, placing her hand over her heart. "That scared me. Get your dagger ready. Anything could be lurking out there."

"I feel as though I'm being watched."

"No doubt we are. So let's finish up quickly and be on our way."

The horses looked up, their liquid brown eyes wide with fright and it took a good deal of soothing and an apple for each of them until Dottir and Bodie had them back under control. They were now riding on top of a narrow path elevated from the water-logged ground. The clip-clop of the hooves was reassuring and provided a sensation of comfort, even as a cool updraft of air mixed with the smell of rotting vegetation made Dottir sick to her stomach. More danger lay ahead, but she refused to acknowledge it or think about what might happen.

The woods were alive, that was for sure, and she fought hard to control her emotions, which were on the brink of erupting. She wanted to scream and race back to the safety of the kitchen. For once she wished Cook was here to scare off the ghosts. Just one look at her face and they'd go running in the opposite direction! And yet within minutes, the steady hoof beats on the boards lulled both of them into a stupor. The horses skillfully stepped over the empty spaces where boards had rotted away and soon Dottir felt her eyes closing. Time ceased to have meaning and the night swallowed them up.

Dottir didn't know how long she slept or if she even slept at all. But suddenly she was wide awake, aware that the air was filled only by buzzing insects, owls hooting and cries of small rodents as they became prey. She turned around in her saddle to see Bodie behind her grinning.

"We've traveled the whole boardwalk," he said. "We're almost there."

"Maybe or maybe not," she answered. "I'm exhausted."

"Not me. I'm wide awake." He stared hard at something to his left, a dark shape hanging from a tree branch. Without much light, it was hard to determine what it was so they both moved closer, slowly and cautiously.

"It's a bat," said Bodie.

"No, it's too big for a bat. It looks like a person in a cloak."

He snorted. "That's ridiculous. Why would a person hang upside down from a tree in the middle of the forest wrapped in a hood?"

"I don't like it. Let's go."

"No, not yet. Look, it's moving."

"It's creepy," she warned sternly. "Don't get any closer."

But Bodie was in motion, he had dismounted his horse and was walking slowly up to it. He picked up a branch and held it out like a sword. As he got closer, he poked at it.

"Don't!" his sister hissed. "Be a good listener. Come on, let's go, right now. It could be dangerous."

"You're just a scaredy cat," said Bodie, but no sooner were the words out of his mouth than two green eyes began to glow and the cocoon started to unfurl. Before she could grab him back, Bodie thrust the stick at the cocoon and was snatched forward and into the dark gray folds. It happened so quickly he didn't have a chance to cry for help and Dottir had no opportunity to react. As she rushed forward screaming his name, Bodie vanished completely into the cocoon-like creature. "No, NO, NO! Bodie where are you?"

She grabbed the stick he'd dropped and swatted it with all her might. Then she raced back to the horse and grabbed her sword from the saddle horn and thrust it toward the cocoon, horrified to see it bulging and shrinking, wiggling, filled to bursting—as though digesting something. Muffled cries came from within the undulating form becoming weaker and more desperate as tears streamed down Dottir's face and she screamed until her throat ached.

"Let him out, let him go!" She stabbed it. "He's my brother; he's just a little boy. Stop it, STOP RIGHT NOW!"

Liquid spilled from the bottom of what she now realized was a Flesh-eating Cocoon—a myth that was written into children's books to frighten them into listening to their parents. But it was REAL. It was ALIVE. And Bodie was in its grasp. Dottir couldn't bear to look at the thing, which shook violently.

She heard the horses whinnying and stomping their hooves, pawing the earth as though they were just as horrified. Every molecule of her body was on fire with rage and at the same time filled with a despair so deep it was impossible to fathom. There was no doubt that Bodie had picked the wrong thing to investigate—that his insatiable curiosity had caused this horrible situation. She sank to the ground on her knees wondering if he would come out alive, and if so, what he'd look like. She couldn't bear to imagine what was happening as his pitiful cries for help faded and the sword fell from her hand. She didn't have the strength to hold it. She was inconsolable and there was nobody anywhere nearby to offer words of comfort.

Suddenly, the cloak split open and a pile of bones and yellow slime spilled out, nearly landing splat on top of her. Dottir scrabbled back in horror. Bodie had been devoured!

The Flesh-eating Cocoon swayed back and forth as she used a forked branch to sweep the bones from the gory mess toward her. She couldn't leave them here. This was her sibling and he needed a proper burial—what was left of him. She didn't know anything about anatomy but that looked like a leg bone and tiny pieces that she assumed was the spine sat atop a pile that included slender curved ribs and miniscule fragments of toes and fingers.

She picked each one up with reverence, stifling her revulsion until she could no longer contain her horror.

Scrambling a few feet away, she threw up her dinner and everything else until she was exhausted. Then she returned to her neat little pile of bones wondering where the skull was. It was probably still inside the Thing, but she couldn't wait for it to spill out; she had to get away swiftly. Perhaps she'd find it on her return trip she thought, while tears were running down her cheeks.

She pulled a blanket from the saddle bag and carefully wrapped up what was left of Bodie. His black horse shied away from her as she tried to place the blanket back in the saddlebag—as though to say, no, not poor Bodie. He was a good kid.

So many emotions swirled through her body that Dottir didn't know how to react: shock, surprise, loathing, fear and guilt. She tumbled into a sorrow so deep and profound she didn't think she would ever recover. Traumatized to the core, she wiped her tears with the hem of her skirt and in a trance she walked to her horse and climbed wearily into the saddle. With the reins of Bodie's horse in her trembling hand, she began the long trek alone through the forest towards Valgard.

Although nothing could save Bodie, she could still save Orn. Bodie was gone and his death was on her shoulders. *If only I'd been a better sister*, she thought. But all the internal chatter didn't change a single thing. She pulled the hood of her cape over her head and moved forward. The little joy she had in life was sucked dry. She'd never forget his muffled cries for help, or the wriggling, bulging cocoon dripping with Bodie's blood.

~ 41 ~

THE FERRY TO VALGARD

After stopping for a few hours to sleep and eat, Orn was back on the path, consulting Councilor Simeon's rough-drawn map. He wasn't far from his destination—the ferry to Valgard that would shuttle him across the lake to Lord Hviti's castle where he would deliver the message, bow with respect, and then ride on Big Gray like the wind until he was back at Blackwater Castle's stable again. That was the plan. He was weary and frightened and yet excited by the knowledge that he was almost finished with his mission.

As he approached the dock, two guards wrapped in black hooded cloaks, stepped out from behind two trees and blocked his path to the dock. They reminded him of the cocoon-like figures he'd seen hanging upside down in the forest surrounding the marsh. He shivered with disgust but squared his shoulders as he slid off Big Gray. While holding the reins tightly in his left hand, he spoke with all the authority he could muster.

"I'm here on official business from Lady Eyrie," he said, trying to keep his voice calm so it would not betray the fear coursing through his veins. "I have a message for Lord Hviti. Please allow me access to the ferry so I can complete this journey and be on my way."

Neither of the guards spoke. After a few tense moments, they stepped aside. Orn tied Big Gray's reins to a sturdy fir tree, patted his neck and then reached into the saddlebag for an apple and the precious letter from Lady Eyrie.

He stroked the horse's velvety nose and whispered, "Be a good boy. Eat your fill and be ready to make haste home as soon as I return."

Then he made his way along the wooden structure to the ferry, which was tied to the pier with a strong hemp rope.

The ferry was not much more than a raft with railings and oar locks. Two shrouded figures covered in tatters sat on hard benches, one on each side their bony fingers wrapped around the oars. The ferryman, another hooded figure that Orn assumed was a human, untied the mooring rope and cracked a whip over the two beggars. Slowly, the craft began to glide away from the shore. There was no turning back as they traveled quickly over the choppy water.

Orn wanted to believe this would be over quickly, although a nagging voice inside told him otherwise. Still, he had to squash all negative thoughts and picture himself with his friends Bodie and Dottir at home with his mom or grooming the horses in the Blackwater stable. He had to remain positive at all costs and not allow fear or uncertainty to overwhelm him; he'd get back alive. Somehow.

The air was damp and he shivered as the flat-bottomed ferry quickly moved across the vast lake. Orn gazed out at the ever diminishing figures of the guard and Big Gray munching contentedly—without a fear in the world while Orn wondered if he might ever return. After all, how long did it take to hand over a message and be on his way—perhaps only a few minutes? If they offered him food, he would refuse. If they asked him to stay overnight, he would politely decline.

While his mind wandered, he thought he saw something dark and slimy wiggle in the waves. He shuddered. Orn knew nothing about underwater creatures, except the tall tales the sailors told— stories he figured were made up by lonely and homesick men. But no, there WAS definitely something out there. Suddenly, just above the surface there was a large eyeball starting in his direction. Quickly, Orn sat down on the bottom of the craft. He dared not ask about it and muttered under his breath, *don't think about it, don't think about it.*

I'm probably so tired my mind is playing tricks on me, he thought to himself. Nothing is out there, just don't fall overboard. He turned his back to the wind and clasped his hands together in prayer muttering under his breath. "Almost there and then I'm headed home. Just a little more time. Hang in there, Orn, hang in there. Dottir is waiting back in the kitchen with a freshly baked blackberry pie just for you."

The ferry hit the dock at Valgard with a hard bump, nearly toppling Orn onto his back. He looked up and sucked in a lungful of damp air. The castle was massive and oppressive. Older, uglier, and darker than anything he had ever seen before, surrounded completely by a wall that looked twenty feet high. It occupied nearly the entire island in the middle of the lake, with numerous towers of different sizes and a few small windows at the top.

He had arrived at the Dark Fortress in Valgard!

A group of black-clad soldiers marched across the narrow road that led from the dock to the castle wall. Each had a white star in the center of his cap. They stopped in a formidable line and watched, holding their swords and waiting for one false move. A Sentry stopped Orn.

"Who goes there?"

Orn fought to keep his voice from betraying his rising terror. "I'm a messenger with an important document for Lord Hviti from Lady Eyrie."

His skin crawled at the prospect of entering the gates and ultimately the castle. Why had he agreed to this? What choice did he have? *Obey or die.* Or maybe he'd die anyway. The gate opened and he crossed the drawbridge, the sound of his steps and the soldiers following him echoing in the damp and cloudy morning air. The height and breadth of the fortress was beyond understanding.

He could be lost for a thousand years in there. Even if he wanted to escape, how could he find a way out? Impossible. He shivered at the prospect.

The massive wooden front doors were decorated with secret symbols and guarded by two additional sentries. Again, Orn explained his purpose, this time reaching into his cloak and pulling out the sealed document. "For Lord Hviti from Lady Eyrie." The guard stepped closer to inspect it and Orn smelled an awful stench, an odor so disgusting he tried not to breathe until he was waved through.

~ 42 ~

ERIC & ANDERS

Dottir rode through the dense forest throughout the night. She dared not stop or dismount. Every sound, every snapping twig and whispering branch sent her heart into overdrive. Sweat dripped down her back even though the temperature had dropped and a chilly wind whistled through the trees. At some point she dozed off, but she awakened with a start as a barn owl screeched while swooping down on a helpless rodent.

As dawn broke, the horse under her slowed to a stop and Bodie's smaller black stallion nudged her leg. She reached down and patted it, feeling the overwhelming ache and pain of Bodie's untimely demise. She prayed it was just a nightmare, but the bulging saddlebag was a grim reminder that it was real.

Astonished to be free and clear of the trees, she watched clouds scudding across the pink early morning sky, shimmering off Lake Valgard spreading like a mirage in front of her.

A snort caught her attention. Not far away she could see Big Gray tied up. That meant Orn had already taken the ferry to the Dark Fortress and she had no time to waste. The horse seemed nervous, skittish and Dottir didn't blame him one bit. She felt sorry for Orn. He didn't know that death was just around the corner. Kill the messenger was Lord Hviti's motto. Orn was in grave danger and she could not bear another death—Bodie was already more than she could handle. She shuddered and pointed to the saddlebag containing his bones that had been sucked clean by the horrid moth creature.

Suddenly, she spotted a guard—then another. She dared not wave or make a sound as her stomach lurched. This was the land of the enemy, an unfriendly and alien land where people could be gobbled up in the blink of an eye and she alone could save Orn. She had to. As she scanned the surrounding area, she noticed two boys down by the water, hiding in the tall grass behind some thick trees far enough away from the dock so the guards wouldn't notice them. They appeared to be about her age, maybe a bit older. They waved at her.

She led the two horses toward them while avoiding being seen by the guards. From behind the thick trees, she smiled cautiously. They appeared harmless, but she couldn't be sure. Everything was creepy about this place, from the marsh to the noises and especially the things hanging from tree branches.

"Who are you?" asked the younger teen, a pink-cheeked lad with dirty brown pants, dark curly hair that reached down to his shoulders, and stubble on his smooth cheeks.

"You're not from around here," chimed the other one who looked like an older version of the first with green pants and dirty cream colored shirt, light brown hair, and a jagged pink scar on one cheek. She assumed they were brothers with their incredible hazel eyes, glinting like gold in morning sun.

"True enough. I'm Dottir Dumbledale from Southistle and I've come…" She let her voice trail off. The less said the better. They could be spies for Lord Hviti.

"I'm Eric, I'm seventeen, and this is my brother Anders."

"I'm fifteen," Anders offered. "We come here to catch fish for dinner and keep an eye on Valgard. That's a strange and forbidden place. What are you doing here? We don't get many visitors."

"I have some business to attend." Dottir twisted the hem of her cloak in her hands. She needed help but didn't know if they were trustworthy.

Anders spoke up sharply. "Why do you have two horses? Where's the other rider?"

Dottir dodged the question. "How could I get over there—to the castle—without being seen?"

The boys stared at her and then at each other. "Why do you want to go over there?" asked Eric. "That's crazy! Nobody goes there voluntarily."

"Usually they're dragged kicking and screaming," added his brother.

"Is your friend there? The one whose horse you're holding?"

Dottir marveled at their astute questions. "Let's just say it's a matter of life and death. I'll give you both these horses if you help me."

The boys stared at each other and grinned broadly. A horse was as valuable as a bag of gold to people who had nothing. And two was the prize of a lifetime and definitely worth risking their lives for.

"But you'll have to keep this a secret," added Dottir. "You can't even tell your parents."

"How will we explain the horses?"

"You wait until my friend and I are safely away and then you say you found them wandering in the woods. They won't ask too many questions."

"Yeah," said Eric. "The less they know the better it is for all of us."

"Are you taking that big gray one over there?"

Dottir nodded. "Yes, he belongs to my friend who's in the Dark Fortress. I need to get him out and we'll both ride him back home."

Anders and Eric nodded to each other. They didn't say that they had an ulterior reason to help her. A while ago their father, a blacksmith, had been fishing for dinner when he was captured by the two guards at the ferry entry and sent to Lord Hviti as a prisoner. That meant he would never return alive—unless they could rescue him. The three of them stood a better chance of accomplishing their respective missions together as a team.

"But how do we get over there?" asked Dottir. "I don't suppose we can ride the ferry and walk up to the front gate."

"Not on your life. But we have a plan we've been working on for a while," said Eric. "Meet us here at midnight and we'll tell you." We can't do this during daytime, we need the cover of night. She had no clue how many hours it would be until midnight but it seemed much too long to wait—practically an entire day in which she would be helpless to do anything productive. Not moving forward with her plan was not an option. She had to do something. HAD TO.

"How will I know when you're coming?"

"We'll hoot four times, like owls. We'll meet right here so get some sleep and eat something. It will be a long and dangerous night."

If she wasn't so worried about doing something stupid with all the idle hours she had to wait, Dottir would have kissed them with gratitude. Instead, she nodded and rummaged in the saddlebag for something to eat. She took the reins off so the horses could graze and rest. She waved goodbye to Eric and Anders and said a prayer of thanks for her good luck in meeting them. She hoped it would hold fast for at least another day—until she and Orn were on their way home safe and sound.

She realized how tired she really was. The horror of the sleepless night was catching up as her eyelids closed.

"Patience," she said to herself. "Have patience and everything will work out." Of course she didn't believe it for an instant. Orn was inside the Dark Fortress; perhaps he was being murdered right now. But getting herself killed wouldn't help matters at all. It would only compound the problem. She had to bide her time, nearly twelve hours, without going stark raving crazy.

~ 43 ~

LORD HVITI'S EVIL SECRET

Orn hated leaving Big Gray. He felt lost and alone as he was escorted into the castle by the two guards with a sinking feeling in the pit of his stomach—as though he were tumbling back in time. How ancient was this Dark Fortress?

How many people had lived and died here? Who built it? He'd heard rumors of a dark castle that once existed in the Forest of the Damned. Apparently it had been ravaged by angry mobs that put an end to the evil that went on there. Then they rebuilt it in the middle of Lake Valgard to prevent it from ever happening again was supposed to be used for white magic to help people , but now it was fully back into the depth of darkness once again. Never in a million years did he ever believe he'd see it, much less BE in it! He could not wrap his brain around the fact that he'd have so many incredible stories to tell when he got home. He'd be a hero, the toast of the town. Everybody would be talking about his amazing adventure.

Although he had not seen even a fraction of it, the entire structure appeared to be one giant accumulation of interconnected buildings, added on over the ages without rhyme or reason. Some walkways were enclosed; others were open to

218

the elements. None of it made any sense and he was quickly lost in the labyrinth of hallways, turning right and left and right again, going up stairs and down and catching glimpses into rooms filled with dark carved wooden furniture—or empty, save for a single chair or broken piece of pottery.

Unlike Blackwater Castle, which was filled with colorful banners and torches to light up the dark passages, this was startlingly barebones. At one point, he glimpsed into what appeared to be a library with tall wooden shelves and heavy tomes, dusty with age, and ladders leaning up against them. He also saw rows upon rows of triangular glass flasks with cork stoppers. It was only a quick glimpse as he passed, but they seemed to be filled with a haze that resembled human faces. Each was different, but all were grimacing—as if the end had come suddenly, without warning.

He shuddered. Was it some macabre joke? Who would keep something as grisly as that on display—and there were so many—thousands he estimated.

He wondered if the guards were deliberately trying to disorient him so he could not find his way out again. If so, they'd succeeded. Orn was totally and completely lost. Without someone to guide him, he would remain in here forever. A shiver of fear raced down his spine.

As they passed through one open corridor, he peered over a walkway and saw soldiers training, swords flashing in the sunlight and arrows hitting the mark on archery targets set up for practice. It was late morning and he wondered how quickly he would be done with his mission and if he could make it back through the Forest of the Damned before night fell again. Back inside, he saw figures skulking and scurrying around and wondered if these were the sorcerers he'd heard so much about.

Rumor was that they were all empty souls whose bodies were taken over by wizards—the living dead. There was certainly something extremely unsettling about them, not the least of which their faces were completely shrouded and hidden from view. They could be hideous creatures for all he knew. When he was good and lost, they came to the first sentry point inside the fortress.

The guards who had been escorting him turned and left him with the new set of weirdoes. Orn pulled out the sealed letter and said: "Message from Lady Eyrie for Lord Hviti." Did they even speak his language? He couldn't tell, but every fiber in his body screamed that he had to deliver the message and get the heck out as quickly and painlessly as possible.

Without a word, the second set of doors swung open and, accompanied by one of the sentries, Orn proceeded along yet another corridor, this time leading to three sets of stairs. Not a ray of sunshine pierced the gloom. Torches lit the way and every few steps he passed another cloaked figure. It was more frightening than his worst nightmare and his mind scrambled to remember which direction he had come from, while trying to recall landmarks places he'd passed.

Completely lost, he followed like a robot as everything around him appeared the same: dark, cold stone stairs, long hallways and rows of torches. Who lived like this? At least Lady Eyrie had windows and tapestries.

His boots echoed in the narrow confines as he was escorted to a short set of steps going down and around. The sentry made a quick right, quick left and up another passageway—not steps but an incline which opened into a vast chamber with white marble floors and exquisite carved columns stretching up to the vaulted ceiling. He wondered if they had finally arrived when a procession of caped figures chanting in deep voices passed him. Orn lost count at twenty-three. Bizarre. Totally off the charts.

His hand clutched the hilt of his sword and he was surprised they hadn't confiscated it when he entered. If he reached for it, he knew he would be surrounded and killed instantly so he left it alone, finding comfort as it bumped against his leg with every step. As the footsteps faded away, a door slid open and a figure appeared. It could only be one person: Lord Hviti himself.

The figure standing in front of Orn was tall, over six feet, with heavy black eyebrows, dark scornful eyes set wide apart with a cold gleam of malice. His face was thin and his lips appeared to have been sucked into his mouth; his sunken cheeks were an unhealthy shade of grayish green.

He wore a dark velvet cape lined with blue and tight-fitting black pants and a tunic over it. An ornate medallion on a silver chain hung around his neck. The cape had a hood which was up, covering his hair and ears, leaving only his frightening visage and bony, blue-veined hands exposed. The hairs on Orn's arms stood up, giving him the feeling of goose flesh.

The voice of the Evil One rose up as though from the floor, deep and filled with malicious secrets, rolling toward Orn like cart wheels crunching over gravel.

"You've brought me something?"

Suddenly, Orn felt the weight of two hands pressing on his shoulders. He knelt and bowed his head, praying a sword wouldn't sever it from his trembling body. "Yes. I have it right here." He reached under his cape.

"Do not move!" Lord Hviti commanded. As the words tumbled out, Orn felt a hand yank his arm behind him. Of course, he could have been reaching for a dagger to throw. Now the same hand was fishing in the secret pocket and extracting the official letter, handing it to Lord Hviti.

"You may rise."

Orn stood, grateful to still be in one piece. In only a few minutes they'd bring him back to the ferry and he'd be on his way home with the story to end all stories. He bowled his head in respect and mumbled, "Thank you sire."

As Orn turned to leave, he heard the voice boom once again. "But wait, didn't you forget something?"

"I have given you the letter. That's all I brought."

"Not exactly." Lord Hviti's eyes, cold as steel, pierced Orn's soul and he knew that he was in deep trouble. He smelled his own fear.

"It is our tradition that visitors must have a password to exit Valgard. Or, I'm afraid to say, you are here to stay. The password please."

Orn was bewildered. His knees buckled. Nobody had said anything about a password—an exit password no less. His mind raced back to his interview with Lady Eyrie and Councilor Simeon. Perhaps it was on the back of the map.

"If you don't mind, I would like to reach into my pocket. I have a note from Councilor Simeon. Perhaps it's written on there."

With his face frozen in a frown, Lord Hviti nodded and gripped the message with Lady Eyrie's seal, his knuckles white with tension. Another hapless soul stood before him as a smirk began to play around the corners of his ugly mouth.

Orn awkwardly fumbled for the map, drawing it out and checking front and back. There was the crude rendering of the forest and lake and the place where the ferry was moored. He flipped the paper back and forth, back and forth. Finally he handed it to Lord Hviti. "This is all I have."

Without touching it, Lord Hviti nodded at the guards and Orn felt two arms tighten around him and a sword point to his chest. The paper fluttered to the stone floor.

"Such a shame," Lord Hviti cackled. "Away with him."

"No, please! Please there's been a mistake. I'm sure I just forgot it. I'm sure they gave me the password."

But Lord Hviti had already turned away. Over his shoulder he growled, "Perhaps the rats in the prison will help you remember."

~ 44 ~

TO THE RESCUE

Crickets filled the night air. Dottir was wide awake when she heard an owl hooting. She had spent the last few hours watching the place where Orn had ferried across from their hiding place. Every time the clouds parted to reveal the moonlit lake, she shivered with fear. From a distance everything looked like a dark fog. She assumed the guards were dressed in black clothing and the castle wall was chiseled stone covered with black mold. Her eyes ached from straining to see. Suddenly, she heard a rustling behind her. Leaping up, she held the sword in front of her body.

"Stop or I'll use this. Just because I'm a girl doesn't mean I won't kill you."

"Easy there, easy. It's just us, Anders and Eric.

Dottir's shoulders slumped. A real owl hooted and a fox scurried between the trees. "I'm a nervous wreck," she said.

"You have every right to be. The rumor is that strangers who visit Valgard usually don't leave—at least not in one piece. The truth is that we've never seen the ferry bring anybody back from the island."

She shuddered. "Jeez, why would you say that? Now I'm really freaking out."

"No worries," said Anders. "I'll be right back."

He disappeared into the forest and came back with three dark capes, exactly like the kind the guards wore.

"Where did you get these?" Dottir asked, holding one up and examining it. Suddenly, it reminded her of the moth creature and she dropped it. She had to ask them about that, but not now. They had a mission.

Eric piped up: "Mom and dad would kill us if they knew we had them. We keep them for emergencies."

"What emergencies?" Dottir was frightened beyond measure.

"Like this one."

"We've never really had an emergency, so now we get to test them out," added Anders with a sly grin.

"Wait a second, boys. You've never used these capes and you've never gone over to the castle? I'm your guinea pig, is this some kind of weird experiment?"

The brothers grinned at each other. "You promised us those horses, isn't that right?" She nodded. "Then we'll do whatever we need to."

"Even if it means risking your lives?"

"Yes, one horse is worth its weight in gold here and we'll have two. We will be rich."

"The truth is, our dad disappeared a while ago while fishing in this very lake and we're certain that he's a prisoner at the fortress, too," said Eric. "We've been planning to break in but wasn't sure when to do it until today. It seems as we were meant to meet and do this together, everything has a reason for happening."

"Put the cloaks on," Anders said. "Then follow me."

"Where are we going?"

"To the island."

"Are we swimming?"

"No, we have a boat hidden under the trees."

Silently, the cape-clad trio traipsed through the trees to a heavy willow tree that dipped into the lake; Anders grabbed the edge of a green piece of fabric and pulled it off, revealing a rowboat.

Dottir gasped. "You boys really are clever little devils, aren't you?"

"More clever than you can imagine."

They quietly shoved the craft into the water and climbed in.

"Be quiet," warned Eric. "Voices can be heard a long way over water."

Gingerly, Dottir moved to the bow, trying not to rock the boat. If she fell in, she'd drown. Not only didn't she know how to swim, the heavy cape and her boots would drag her down to the bottom of the murky water. Her lungs would fill with water as she'd gasp for air. It was one of the most awful deaths she could think of—except Bodie's. But there were so many other unpleasant ways to leave the earth and Lord Hviti knew them all.

Each boy took an oar and silently they slid over the black lake, bow pointed at the dark castle. The surface rippled from the wind—and also from the creatures that lay in the murky depths. "Don't put your hands in the water," warned Anders. "And keep a lookout for anything strange that sticks its head out."

"Or tentacle," added Eric.

"Shut up you two," Dottir hissed. "I'm scared enough as it is." But only a minute later, she heard a swish and a bubble as great rippling rings formed nearby. "I hate this place!"

"They call the creature Mordir," explained Anders. "At least that's our name for it. It has six long arms that can reach right into this boat and snatch us out."

Even as the words tumbled from his mouth, the ripples came closer, some overlapping the gunwale and sloshed around her feet. The lake was seething, as if hundreds of snakes were slithering just under the black shiny surface. Suddenly, a long sinuous arm, pale green and dripping wet, broke the surface and reached toward the boat. Eric pulled out a knife and slashed the tip off. A geyser of brackish water rose into the air and the surface boiled as more arms reached out, accompanied by a hideous stench.

Anders rowed furiously, even as something tugged the oar from his grasp. Eric reached over and pulled the oar back, both boys gasping as they beat Mordir until the rippling stopped and the water lay calm once again. Their hearts all hammered like drums until they had caught their breath and set the oars back in the locks. When things calmed down they continued the journey toward the Dark Fortress.

"It happened to my friend Darvis," said Eric.

"What happened?" asked Dottir, not really wanting to know.

"He was gone in a flash when one of those hideous creatures pulled him overboard. His mom never got over it."

"That's enough," commanded Dottir sternly, thinking about her brother and how his passing would break her mother's heart. "I've got stories of my own."

"What?" asked both boys in sync.

"Not now. We've got to get Orn out in one piece."

"And our dad, too." She nodded solemnly.

The rescuers made good time getting across the lake. On the other side, they stopped in shallow water and Eric silently jumped out, pulling the craft ashore. They left it near a pine tree and covered it with the green cloth and tossed some branches on top until it looked like a mound of debris and nothing more.

Anders whispered: "We walk single file. Nobody talks. Keep your hand on the shoulder of the person in front. Capes on, hoods up, hide your faces." They obeyed their leader as Dottir noticed a few small huts in front of the castle wall. She hoped they wouldn't encounter any guards living there. She was pale and faint with fear.

"The fortress look like it's ready for an attack," she whispered.

Anders stopped. "We can't talk now because this is where Lady Eyrie trains her evil sorcerers and soldiers. We don't know what, or from how far they can hear us. They use the dark magic that they've learned since they were mere children."

"Why didn't you join them?"

Anders stared at her as if she had said the craziest thing. "Did you ever look into their eyes? They're empty, like two pieces of coal that absorb all the light. They never talk or laugh, they are shells. Even the food, I mean the mush they eat is gray. They don't even seem human."

"Shhhh," warned Eric. "They'll hear us."

Silently, they moved forward as one unit under cover of the dark night in a line, as everyone else at Valgard seemed to do. They walked steadily, but not too fast so they didn't attract any unwanted attention. They stayed near the shoreline until Anders veered to the left and took them up a grassy path toward the foreboding outer wall and the hideous gargoyles that stared down at them. She tugged Anders' sleeve. "What's that sound?" she whispered urgently.

"That's the sound from the Gargoyle rain spouts. Ugly aren't they? Don't let them bother you. We have more important things to think about."

Dottir nodded: Get Orn out in one piece and get the heck back into the boat, untie Big Gray, and ride like the wind home again.

She stopped short and Eric bumped into her. Even if they got Orn and their dad out, five people could never—not in a hundred years—fit into that boat without it sinking. They would have to hijack the ferry to get back. Maybe she could return with Orn and leave Eric and Anders to take the boat with their father. She began sweating, thinking about abandoning the boys who'd risked their lives to help her. As they passed a group of figures in capes, she felt her knees buckle.

What if Anders and Eric were scouts for the evil ones, bringing her as a sacrifice? What if she was a lamb being brought to slaughter? She stumbled into Anders' back and fell, pulled herself backup and continued to walk single-file through the front gate—without being stopped.

That's when she knew her worst fears were about to come true. Although there were armed guards, they were able to walk into the courtyard under their own steam, without being questioned as to their intention. Either security was alarmingly relaxed or they were expected. And if they were expected, she knew for certain that they had lured her ever so cunningly into their trap.

Dottir was a goner. So was Orn. They were both going to die in the Dark Fortress. They would never see their friends or parents again. Her foolish desire to help him had backfired so astoundingly that her knees finally gave way and she dropped to the ground. As Eric and Anders begged her in urgent whispers to get up, she simply could not move. She was overwhelmed with dread. She was too young to die. They hooked an arm into each of her elbows and pulled her to her feet.

Anders hissed in her ear, "Get a grip Dottir. Get your spine up and your feet moving."

She did as she was told, her heart racing; sweat was dripping down her sides. The guards allowed them to pass under the two most hideous gargoyles, full-sized monsters hunched over the main entrance as though to say, *beware!*

The trio walked towards the inner wall and then made their way down the first staircase they saw which lead them inside a kind of deep prison cylinder shaped building, very dark with lit torches. It made perfect sense that prisoners were held underground—or perhaps they were held in a tower and they were going in the wrong direction entirely.

Suddenly, they pressed themselves against the wall as they heard a voice echoing off the stone walls: "Two new prisoners the last couple of weeks. A fine catch. A fisherman worth nothing and the messenger—a special treat. I relish putting him in a flask; one more thing to make Lady Eyrie bend to my will. I will have complete power over all of Etrunia, not just Valgard."

He burst out in a raucous howl, an unearthly sound that made their blood curdle. "Come," he said to his henchmen, "let's go check the library and count our new additions."

With the coast clear, the three were on the move again—making their way through twisting corridors and up cobblestone steps. In a small area, lit only by a single flickering torch, Eric suddenly disappeared.

"Where is he?" Dottir whispered urgently. "Where did he go?" She clutched Anders' arm. With his other, he lifted a tapestry so dark that Dottir didn't notice it. He pulled it aside and there she saw Eric already peering through one of two peepholes in the stone.

Anders whispered, "It's Lord Hviti's chamber. We found it by accident a few months ago. Yes, we've been here before, exploring at night under the cover of darkness."

She put her eye to the hole and saw a tall, swarthy man dressed in black, his eyes burning like glowing embers. She cringed. This was pure wickedness. She watched as he sat down on an elevated burgundy velvet throne and two sorcerers carrying flasks stood in front of him.

"Your orders, Lord?"

"Take both flasks to the Library of the Silent then deliver the book and the messenger's flask to my chamber before sending a message back to Lady Eyrie.

"I wish she could see this—maybe I should send it to her. I'm sure she would appreciate the artistry it takes to suck a person's soul from its body. This will be a valuable lesson for her."

Dottir stared wild-eyed at the flask on the desk. It looked like Orn but all smashed up in a bottle with a stopper, eyes wide with astonishment, his beautiful mouth twisted with horror. The world suddenly turned black and her legs buckled. With a tiny gasp, she fell backwards in a heap.

Anders was so fixated on the other flask, the one he now recognized as his father, that he didn't even notice that Dottir had fainted. Eric shoved his fist into his mouth to keep from calling out in anguish.

When they had finally collected themselves, they huddled in their hiding place behind the tapestry, sitting on the ground in complete darkness.

"What's going on?" asked Dottir. "Is Orn dead?"

Eric spoke in whispers. "No, not dead, just an empty vessel."

"If we can get his body—and our father's—we can bring them back to life," added Anders. "But only if we get the flasks with their souls and someone with the knowledge of how to undo the spell and reconnect the pieces."

"White magic," said Eric. "We need someone versed in white magic and we need to find their physical bodies and grab the flasks."

"Yes, but how can we get them?" asked Anders.

"And where are their bodies and the Library of the Silent?" Eric wanted to know.

Anders, the oldest and wisest of the three, said: "Here's what we have to do: We need to grab the flask with Orn, locate the Library of the Silent, somehow find their soulless bodies, and then hijack the ferry to take us all back to the other side of the lake."

Dottir and Eric stared at him as if he were crazy. That was an impossible task.

"And we have to do this before the sun rises," he added. "Or none of us will live to see another day."

~ 45 ~

LOST SOULS

The next few hours flew by in a haze of frantic activity. As they huddled together, they made a plan.

Dottir said, "Eric, you go and find the library, get the flasks of Orn and your dad. Orn has a black ribbon tied around his. I suppose they want to deliver it to Lady Eyrie as a warning. Anders, you go down to the dungeon and see if they are in there and I'll race up to the tower and check there. We all meet back here. Okay?"

The brothers nodded. Eric reached into his cape and pulled out three pieces of limestone. He handed them around. "Mark the walls of the staircases you take, top and bottom, so you can find your way back here. It will be dark. Make a thunderbolt so it will look like a scratch, not an X which would be easily noticed."

They clasped hands and bowed their heads. "I'm sorry to say this," whispered Anders. "But anybody that gets taken is on his own—or her own. It's too dangerous to attempt any kind of rescue right now. We have a mission and we must stick to the plan. Agreed?"

All three solemnly nodded. Then they scurried off, each with a heavy heart.

Dottir had to assume that the others knew what they were doing since they were familiar with the Dark Fortress as she took off on her own and quickly found an upward staircase, leaping up the steps two at a time. It was well past midnight and that left only a few hours until daybreak. She tucked her unruly long hair under the hood and marked the wall when she reached the top.

With no tower in sight, she followed the hallway until she came to another set of steps leading up. At the bottom and again at the top of, she marked thunderbolts. At least Anders would be able to find her if the dungeon held nothing more than straw and skeletons.

She shivered. This was creepy beyond words. For a Dark Fortress, she was impressed with the carvings and columns, which were artistic and fanciful in some places—glowing in the light of flickering torches. A few alcoves made perfect hiding places in case guards were patrolling. But it was late and she didn't think anybody would be around. She held her breath and listened for cries of help. But all was silent.

After finally getting to the Library of the Silent, Eric stepped in and peered around. A huge carved wooden table dominated the room. He spotted an oblong, red leather-bound book on it, fingerprints smudging the dust that had accumulated on it over time. Right next to it was the flask with Orn, but where was his dad's flask?

As his head swiveled, he was startled to see shelves stretching from the floor to far above his head. Extremely tall ladders rested against the warped wood. But most startling of all were row upon row of glass flagons or flasks with cork stoppers. They looked as though they were filled with smoke. It seemed weird. But as he stared, he realized he was looking at faces. Faces of the people who'd disappeared since Lord Hviti had been ruling Valgard—from long before he was born until this exact moment.

His legs buckled and he fell to the cold slate floor and ducked under the table as the steady beat of footsteps echoed from down the hall. Shrinking into a little ball, wrapped in his black cloak, Eric prayed they left quickly.

From his hiding place, he could see the flagons and figured, correctly, that his father would be one of the last additions and, therefore, toward the end of the row. But which row? There were so many! And then, there he was—the careworn and familiar face of his dad Pieter, the blacksmith. He almost yelped with joy, but caught himself just in time. He heard the book slide off the table and whoever took it groaned with the weight.

When the footsteps receded, he stood up, swept Pieter's flagon off the shelf and turned to get the black-ribboned flask containing Orn only to find it had been taken, along with the book. This complicated his mission and, for a few brief moments he felt he would fail. But he absolutely could not go back to Dottir without Orn's flask so he crept along after the guard down cold, stone hallways, following the sounds of his footsteps.

Anders carefully marked the top of each staircase as he descended into the belly of the fortress. He marked the bottom as well so he could find his way back up. At last he saw flickering light from far down the passageway and followed it to find the dungeon covered with straw. Leg and wrist irons hung from the wall with two partial skeletons still attached.

As he peered around in the gloom, he noticed a heap of something like ivory in the corner. Approaching it cautiously, he realized it was a pile of old bones. Reeling back in repulsion, he fell against the wall.

Anders said a quick prayer for the lost souls. But Orn and his father hadn't been here long enough to be gnawed clean. That meant they had to be in the tower. Without wasting a second, he turned and raced back up the steps, following the marks he'd made. He had to give his brother credit, the limestone chalk was brilliant.

Panting, he reached the tower and found three bodies, two more dead than alive and the third, Dottir, holding what he assumed was Orn and sobbing silently. He went over to her and gently placed his hands on her trembling shoulders.

"It's okay, Dottir. He's alive," he said, walking over to his dad who was curled up on the ground in the corner and hugged him with tears in his eyes. "Come, we must go quickly."

She nodded as she held Orn's limp body, his eyes staring at her blankly, unknowing, perhaps even unseeing. She wasn't sure how much damage had been done. Could he walk or talk? Did he recall anything from his past and how could they put his soul back into his body? The questions formed a tornado that threatened to make her mind explode. She felt Anders pull her up.

"I can lift my dad, he's not that heavy. But you'll never be able to carry Orn. So stand here. I'm going to put him on your back and you'll drag him along. When you feel his weight, grab his forearms and hold on."

"I'm not strong enough."

"We're going downstairs, so it'll be fine. Thank goodness they weren't in the dungeon."

Soon she felt Orn being draped over her, like a cloak. She smelled his warm breath and smiled. At least he was still alive. Score one for the good guys.

As instructed, she grabbed his arms. It was like hauling a very big sack of heavy potatoes. But she'd done that for Cook. They were heavy, too. She watched as Anders expertly hoisted his father up over his shoulders and they were off, moving as fast as they dared toward the thunderbolt design that marked the first passage down to safety and freedom.

Meanwhile, Eric, with Pieter's flagon in hand, snuck after the guard who carried the heavy red book and Orn's soul.

~ 46 ~

ESCAPE

Progress down the hallway was slow and treacherous. Orn was heavy, one-hundred and seventy pounds of muscle. Dottir wasn't used to the weird position and soon her back was screaming for mercy. But there was no stopping now. They took the first marked stairway down and she heard his boots thump on each step, praying that it wouldn't echo so loudly that the guards would come running and put them all back in the tower—or worse, the dungeon.

When they reached the first landing, Anders whispered, "Go left." For a moment, she forgot which was which and turned the wrong way. "No," he hissed. "This way!" Every few steps she had to stop and catch her breath. Progress was painstakingly slow and the difficult escape was full of danger.

Meanwhile Eric was on the heels of the guard who'd taken the flask with Orn's soul and the mysterious book. Instead of hiding, he marched in plain sight right behind him. After all, he was wearing the uniform and it made perfect sense that he would be there. But his heart raced with fear of discovery. He was an imposter, an imposter trying to pass as a soulless guard in the army of the most dangerous and wicked man in all of Etrunia.

But their mission was righteous—returning the souls of his father and the messenger named Orn, who'd done nothing to deserve this. Rivers of sweat dribbled down his back under the heavy cloak although the night was chilly. The guard suddenly entered a chamber through an arched doorway and Eric, having no choice, followed quietly pretending to be part of it all.

The room was dimly lit with candles, but he could see sturdy wooden chairs lining the room. Two more hooded figures emerged from a side entrance and he barely dared to breathe. Nobody spoke as Eric willed his heart to stop thundering, least somebody hear it. A large table sat in the middle and here the guard placed the book and the flask with Orn's grimacing visage. They turned on their heels and left. Eric followed them out, then abruptly turned and stealthily crept back into the room.

He peered into the smoky jar and saw Orn's face, eyes open wide with fear and pain. The silence was overpowering and Eric feared that it wouldn't last. Or would it? They were in the small hours of the morning. Everybody must be asleep, but he had no idea where his brother or Dottir were, or if they had found the bodies that matched the flasks. Perhaps they, too, had been taken prisoner.

Eric shook the idea from his head and without wasting another second, he scooped up the flask and the book and made his way quietly as a mouse out of the room and down a narrow staircase toward a battlement that ran around the fortress, exposed to the elements. He sucked in the sweet night air, smelling the scent from Lake Valgard with the slimy Mordir. They had to take the sturdier ferry back to the other side. There was no other way.

He hooted four times, but no answer was returned. Deep within the confines of the Dark Fortress, Dottir and Anders made slow and steady progress toward the front gate as the sky began to turn pink and the sun made its inevitable ascent to the heavens.

Time was running out. The three rescuers had a very short time to complete their daring escape, overpower the ferryman, and return to the other side of the lake.

Frantic with worry, Eric scurried back to the space under the tapestry outside Lord Hviti's chambers, the place they had agreed to meet if things went sour. Now, as he crouched with his heart thudding, he worried that something had happened to his brother and Dottir. For a fleeting second, he considered leaving the flask and book on the floor and quickly running out of this horrid foreboding place of death and doom. Time was of the essence. Soon the sky would be light and any chance of escape would be out of the question. He decided to count to one hundred before bolting to the front gate and safety.

But by the time he'd counted to twenty, he heard the deep raspy baritone of Lord Hviti calling to his guard. "Get me the book and the flask with the messenger," he commanded.

Eric held his breath. This wasn't happening! If he found them missing, then nobody would come out of the fortress alive. The front gates would close tighter than a tomb and they would all be at Lord Hviti's mercy. Crouching down, he peeked from under the tapestry and made sure the coast was clear. Then he snatched up the flask and book and tiptoed to the staircase marked with a thunderbolt and flew down at breakneck speed.

He held the book tight against his body with his elbow, hidden from sight under his cloak fearful that it would fall and alert the guards. But his heart nearly leaped out of his chest as he rounded the corner and saw the dead souls filing in, walking like zombies, eyes blank, mouths agape, fists balled into knots, their swords clanking against their belts, and boot heels clumping against cold, hard stone. Eric pressed himself into one of the small alcoves and allowed the hollow husks to pass. When the coast was clear he was in forward motion again, hooting for Anders as daylight approached.

Anders heard his brother's call and knew it meant he was heading out toward the front gate. Dottir was using her last reserves. She hadn't eaten in hours and hadn't really slept at all for at least a day—or more. But she couldn't drop Orn, couldn't slow down, and had to find her way out and onto the ferry before the same fate befell all of them.

They felt the cool night air and Anders, still carrying his father and breathing hard, swiveled to his right and hooted back. Eric returned the call and within minutes all three were through the massive front doors, scurrying over the drawbridge as fast as possible to the ferry.

They found the rope that moored the ferry to the dock. The guards that usually tended it were nowhere to be seen. The trio had caught a very lucky break. Eric placed the flasks and book on a seat and then helped Dottir drag Orn over to the wooden flat-bottom boat. They laid him on his side and Dottir tenderly rubbed her hand over his face and hair, murmuring that everything would be okay although she didn't believe a word of what she was saying.

Eric helped Anders lay their father, Pieter, next to Orn and smoothed his thinning gray hair. Then they untied the rope and each grabbed an oar. By the time the light had burned through the night haze, they were far out onto the lake. A barrage of angry shouts assailed them, followed by a blitz of arrows fired by the guards from the parapet. Anders and Eric rowed faster, their faces bright red with the exertion.

Dottir grabbed the book and held it on her lap, opening the pages to reveal yellowed parchment written with black and red ink. They seemed to be spells mixed in with weird symbols like runes. There were pages with names, too. She assumed they were the real names of the men who had lost their souls. Quickly, she scanned the pages and dates and sure enough, there was Orn, listed only as Eyrie's messenger #12. They didn't even know his name.

The thud of an arrow landing near Orn's leg brought her back to the moment. "Faster," she cried, "faster or we'll all die!"

The boys slowed down when they were well out of reach of the arrows, some tipped with fire which fizzled into the lake with a hiss and a plume of steam. Pieter and Orn had eyes hollow and empty, saliva dribbling from the corner of their mouths. They all needed water and a week's worth of sleep but they had no time.

Suddenly, a massive explosion shook the air and a deafening thunder of something being fired sent a cloud of black smoke into the air. A cannonball landed in the water, creating a tidal wave that threatened to swamp the ferry and, in fact, sent water spilling over the side of the wooden craft. But they were so close to shore now that all they could do was keep their eye on the dock where they could tie up and get off. Another explosion ripped the morning air and another huge wave sent the ferry bobbing up and down, but they were still intact. Only minutes later, Eric got up and leaped onto dry land, rope in hand tying it to the metal cleats on the dock and within seconds they were safely on land.

Big Gray was right where he'd been left, staring wide-eyed at the sudden commotion after a day of peace and quiet. He shied away as Dottir hurried toward him, but soon recognized her soft voice. The boys carried Orn over to the horse and helped lift him up. Dottir got up behind him and Anders handed her the reins. Eric whistled and both of the Blackwater Castle steeds appeared, as if by magic. "How'd you do that?" she asked Eric.

Anders replied, "He's got the magic touch with animals."

Dottir stared wistfully at the two magnificent animals. They'd brought her to this strange land of Valgard and now they were staying here. She knew that the boys would treat them well and they'd thrive for the rest of their days.

"We'll miss you, Dottir," said Eric as Anders lifted their father out of the craft and set it adrift in the lake. "Don't go through the forest again."

"I won't, I promise." She pulled the reins so Big Gray faced east. "Wait, I forgot. There's something in the saddlebag I need. Can you get it?"

Eric obliged, reaching in for the blanket and pulling out a small sack of food from the other side. "You always need a blanket, here, let me refold it for you."

"No, don't!" But her warning came too late as bones went flying everywhere. She couldn't slide off Big Gray because she was holding Orn upright. "Please get the bones and put them back in the blanket."

"Are they from squirrels and foxes?

Tears spilled from her eyes. "No, that's all that's left of my brother Bodie. He was sucked into a Flesh-Eating Cocoon."

Both boys bowed their heads. "We lost a brother that way, too. And a cousin and an uncle. Horrible creatures. We're so sorry."

"Not as much as I am."

They placed the blanket with Bodie's bones in the saddlebag. Big Gray had taken two steps when Eric cried out, "Wait, you forgot this."

"What?"

"The book, I think you should have it. If anybody found us with it, they'd kill us all without blinking an eye." He walked around the horse and slid it into the other pouch along with the flagon holding Orn's soul.

"Thanks. What are you going to do with your dad?"

"We know a wizard in the Forest of the Damned. He lives in an old tunnel near the boardwalk."

"We passed through it."

"He knows every spell in Etrunia. I'm sure he can help us. How about you?"

"The only thing I know is that we're going around the forest, not through it. I hope to meet someone who can bring a message to my mom and to Orn's family saying we're all right."

"We hear there's a place called Fort Ravenspur, it's the home of the Resistance, the brave men and women who are going to reclaim Etrunia and get rid of the evil rulers. Maybe there's someone there, and a good wizard, too. Perhaps you can use some of the spells in the book to reunite Orn's body and spirit."

"Thanks so much. Hopefully, we'll see each other again." She leaned over and ruffled their heads.

"Fort Ravenspur is near the village of Dobbinville," said Anders. "It's north of Southistle and not far from the Desert of Lost Souls. Now take care and good luck."

Dottir set off heading east toward Dobbinville and Fort Ravenspur hoping to find a miracle. Orn rocked with the rhythm of the horse, back and forth against her arms which soon grew weary, then numb, and Dottir knew that it would be a long day and a longer night.

She also knew she could not dismount until she reached her destination, no matter how far it was, because she'd never get Orn back in the saddle. The prospect was daunting, but she was no coward or weakling. She took a deep breath and said a prayer that she would find the strength to complete her mission and that a miracle would save them both from destruction.

PART FIVE:
FORT
RAVENSPUR

~ 47 ~

THE RETURN OF THIO THE FAIR

Back in the White City, Makka had been trapped inside Lovenfell as Brian and Rose shouted frantically from the outside, calling her name and banging with their fists. But the building seemed to want her unaccompanied and soon she learned why. The massive palace had bright, high ceilings, a floor inlaid with magnificent black-and-white marble tiles in a harlequin pattern. Banners hanging throughout the spacious rooms had colorful crests, falcons, lions, flowers and crisscrossing stripes reminding her of the shields in Thio the Fair's armory.

As Makka ascended the stairway, the legendary history unfolded through a series of murals showing bloody battles. Mirrors with faces of brave soldiers and citizens who fought valiantly to preserve the reign of the Great Pharmakeus seemed to speak as Makka climbed up the grand staircase drawn by a magnetic force. Some of the images resembled people she knew back in Granite Falls—even her mom, dad, sister and brother, Anne and Eddie.

Without realizing it, she found herself in a tower, like the one at Nideon's, a perfectly round space in royal blue and crimson, ruby and ochre, rich garnet and gleaming gold—awash in the sunlight that streamed in through the stained glass. The round, domed ceiling glowed with gilded detail work and below her feet was a thick carpet in deep garnet. Completely encircling the room were even more mirrors in all shapes and sizes. Makka raced back down the steps. As she approached the front door, she saw Brian and Rose walk in.

"Brian, Rose, get in here!" she shouted. "You have to see this. It's amazing."

Her friends swooped in. Rose wrapped her arms around Makka and Brian joined in a group hug. They were a unit again, a force to be reckoned with.

"We've been so worried about you," said Rose.

"We thought we'd lost you," added Brian, patting Makka on the back sending chills up her spine. She liked that Brian had missed her.

"Hey, that means a lot. But I was only gone a little while."

Brian and Rose exchanged worried glances.

"What?" asked Makka who seemed confused by their concern. "It was a few hours, no big deal."

Rose stared wide-eyed as if one of them was going cray-cray. "You were in there for two days. What happened? Are you okay? We were worried sick."

"That's absurd. It couldn't have been. All I know is that the door slammed shut and I couldn't open it. And then the most miraculous things began happening. I can't even explain. Come," she said breathlessly, grabbing Rose's hand, "this is beyond words. You'll see for yourself."

"We've heard all kinds of rumors about this place," said Brian.

"Well I can tell you first-hand that it's amazing. You'll see for yourselves."

She pulled them in and led them up and down the staircases and hallways, pointing out the murals and mirrors, relating the narrative as she understood it. She explained parts of the paintings.

"That's you…and me. There's Brian and our mom and dad."

"The faces spoke to me," explained Makka. "I'm not sure what they meant but everything will be cleared up—eventually. Come, let's go to the best room of all."

As they burst into the round room with the glowing dome ceiling and the deep, rich colors and mirrors, Makka felt as if she was finally home. It was inviting and comfortable, different than it had been when she had first entered—which was according to Rose—two days ago!

They stopped when they saw a golden throne and a person they knew sitting upon it. Thio the Fair had appeared, as if by magic, in the time it had taken Makka to race down the steps and back up with Rose and Brian.

"What are you doing here?" they gasped. "How…how did you get in?"

She smiled beatifically, her green tipped white hair moving like liquid as she turned her head. Instead of her pale green beaded gown she wore a dark green breastplate and riding breeches with knee-high boots. Her pale face looked even whiter in the harsh light, reflected against the metal armor. As usual, Captain Lourdes stood protectively at her side.

"Why are you wearing that?" asked Rose, confused beyond words. "Did someone send you to rescue us?"

She laughed like a thousand tinkling bells. "I don't know what you're talking about. I simply used my powers."

"Powers?" asked Makka.

Thio the Fair nodded. "This is why you are here Makka. To learn to use the powers bestowed upon you by the Ancients."

Makka shook her head as her pony tail flew back and forth. "All of this," she gestured around her. "I don't believe any of this—the talking mirrors, the murals, all this mumbo-jumbo about magical powers. Is this all a joke?"

"No, it's real. But I'll repeat some of it for your friends. From this point on, things will move with the speed of light. You'd better know what's happening or you'll be left in the dark—or worse, you'll perish—like so many before you."

Thio held Makka's gaze like a magnet. "In only a few minutes you will see the power you hold within you. So I warn you now about two things: Use these powers only for the good of Etrunia, and never let anybody trick you to using them the wrong way or we are all doomed."

Brian, Rose and Makka sat at Thio's feet as she once again related the story about how the Ancients had created *a* country they named Etrunia—a peaceful territory that prospered until fierce warriors claimed the land and war broke out. After centuries, the Ancients slowly disappeared and a succession of

Lords and wannabe Kings tried to take over the country. Finally, at the age of seventeen, the Great Pharmakeus became the ruler. He and his sister, Lady Eyrie, who was fourteen when their reign began, ruled Etrunia fairly and with compassion. There was peace and prosperity in the land.

Although her brother married, Lady Eyrie remained single. In time she became as cold as stone and bitter without compassion or empathy. The brother and sister, once so close, moved far apart. Pharmakeus built a huge fortress in Northgate to protect Etrunia from invaders and Lady Eyrie built a castle in Southistle to protect the south.

Somewhere in between lay Missilium in the Desert of Lost Souls. It was rumored to be under mountains of sand, protected from sight with a curved dome. The few remaining inhabitants went about their business in a haze, unaware and unseeing of any turmoil above the ground. They were simply spirits living in a zombie state beneath tons of sand.

They exchanged glances as Thio brought them back to the present. "I'm sure you are wondering what you are doing here." They nodded. She smiled benignly and nodded knowingly.

"We need to send you on a rescue mission and I won't lie—it will be dangerous."

"More dangerous than grabbing the Cvector?" asked Makka.

Thio nodded.

"Who are we rescuing?" asked Brian.

"You haven't met him yet," said Thio. "But I think you'll like him. He's about your age, a brave young man sent on an errand by Lady Eyrie and hijacked by Lord Hviti who sucked his soul from his body. Now he's a lifeless shell. His name is Orn Wittenberg and now his friend, Dottir Dumbledale, has rescued his body, but you must reunite it with his soul."

Rose ran her fingers through her hair. "You expect us to do what?"

Thio nodded and smiled. "Yes, it's a hard concept to understand. Souls leave the body at death. The body is no longer needed and the soul looks for another physical body to inhabit. But Orn is still alive and his soul is nearby wanting to be back where it belongs."

The three teenagers stared at Thio. Was she kidding? Was this a prank? She could not possibly be serious.

And yet she was.

"Your mission is to find Orn's physical body and the flask containing his soul and bring them both to Fort Ravenspur. That's where the Resistance movement is centered."

"What's the Resistance?" asked Makka. "We've heard that term before."

"Think about your American Revolution and how the British were defeated. That's what's going on here in Etrunia. The Resistance is going to wrest power from Lady Eyrie and restore peace and order."

Makka felt faint and swayed for a moment. She fingered the Cvector under her shirt. What did they expect of them? None of them were fighters or versed in the practice magic. She's never heard of such utter nonsense. And yet, on another level it made perfect sense.

"We can't," said Roses on the brink of tears.

Thio smiled benignly. "I'm not asking you to do it alone. There will be three of you and Dottir, who's with Orn now. She'll help you secure a red covered book called the *Book of Spells*. I would never ask you to do something we didn't think you were capable of. But take a deep breath. All of that can wait for a while."

Thio stood as Captain Lourdes snapped to attention.

"First things first. We need to eat so you have strength to carry out the mission. And we must plan the attack. Once we get started there will be no turning back."

~ 48 ~

UNDER ATTACK

Dottir rode at a snail's pace, slowly and grimly, with Orn's limp body bobbing and weaving behind her on Big Gray's back. He was like a rag doll, so wobbly it seemed all his muscle tone had evaporated overnight. Eric and Anders had tied a rope around Orn and Dottir to hold them together. She tucked his arms around her waist and patted his thigh. If he slid off the horse she'd never be able to get him back on all by herself and that was very worrisome.

The sky deepened into evening; dark clouds gathered. Fireflies blinked in the gloom and crickets began their melodious concert as they made their way slowly through the fields of large ferns, crowberry, pale yellow grass, and the occasional copse of trees. She kept the forest to her right and glanced over now and then for the Flesh-eating Cocoons. Dottir knew she had to be strong despite her sorrow and hunger pains. Her mouth was as dry as cotton but she dared not stop. Hopefully, they'd be at Fort Ravenspur by midnight—if she could even find it. The thought of being out here alone with no protection terrified her.

Suddenly, Dottir heard a rustling of wings high above her. At first she paid no attention. Birds flew to their roosting places around this time of evening to settle until dawn. Owls were the only nocturnal birds she knew of that ventured out after dark: barn owls, spotted owls, the elf owl and the great gray owls. She wondered if they were starlings, blackbirds or grackles. All of them were known to fly in large flocks. She prayed they weren't the carrion crows—ugly and ferocious predators that descended on their prey like vultures. As she glanced up, she saw two of them suddenly break from the group and head back toward Valgard. Could they be messengers from the Evil One?

She hadn't thought of Lord Hviti in hours, she wanted to put that horrid event behind her and get Orn back to normal. Only then could she return to her job with Cook. But she was far, far away from any comforts.

Suddenly, the flock dropped lower and dove straight toward her. She felt talons grab at her hair, getting tangled in the uncombed locks. A beak was pecking at her head. She let go of the reins and swatted at the birds. Another landed on Orn and she knocked it off with her hand. Then three of them landed behind her, startling Big Gray so that he bolted forward.

Panic swept over her. Never in her entire life had she felt as vulnerable as she clung to the saddle horn. They cawed and cackled above her—swirling like a monstrous black whirlwind plunging down to peck her cheeks, hands and Orn's lifeless body behind her—each time drawing blood or unraveling a bit of their clothing.

The screeching made her ears throb and the flapping wings blotted out the dusky sky. Where were the farmers tending their fields? There was nobody to save them as the noise became an endless ear-splitting screech of caws, rattles, and clicks multiplied a thousand fold as they continued their unmerciful attack. Blood dripped into her eyes as Orn slipped off Big Gray and landed on the soft ground with a horrible thud pulling her down too.

She threw her body on top of his. She needed a blanket to cover them but Bodie's bones were wrapped in it. As if he knew the situation, Big Gray walked over and shielded their bodies by straddling them. He whinnied and snorted as the birds continued their relentless assault, swishing his tail and tossing his mane.

Dottir felt as though she should give up, just let the birds peck them to death and be done with it. But the thought of her parents grieving over two lost children gave her the strength to hang on. She flattened herself over Orn's back wondering why God wanted them to die in such a hideous way. Then again, was it any more gruesome or shocking then being sucked into a flesh-eating Cocoon?

After what seemed like an eternity, her mind simply could not take any more abuse and shut down. The carrion crows continued their raucous aerial maneuvers as everything went dark.

~ 49 ~

THE REFUGE OF RATIONS

Thio led Makka, Rose, and Brian down the stairs to the Refuge of Rations. They were all famished. Rose told Makka she'd been in Lovenfell for two days, but she hadn't slept or eaten. Weird didn't even begin to describe how she felt, as though she was in somebody else's body with someone else's brain. Nothing computed. Nothing made sense. The days had passed as though she was in a dream state—or perhaps a nightmare—from which she could not awaken.

Now she recalled that early in their journey through Etrunia, Captain Lourdes had remarked: "Time has no meaning here."

Is this what he meant? It certainly felt that way. But hunger was a very real sensation and she would have traded her shoes for a chocolate bar and a bowl of angel hair spaghetti smothered in sauce or a cheesy pizza. Her mouth watered.

Thio's hard-soled boots tapped rhythmically on the marble floor as she strode across the room, her hair swaying, the green tips of her white hair mesmerizing the three American teenagers as they followed her along the hallway, past the murals of bloody battles, all of their heads swiveling right to left as they tried to consume the history of Etrunia and understand how they fit into the picture. Hallways were decorated with banners and mirrors. Eyes followed them and whispered stories of ages past.

Thio seemed unaffected as she hurried along in search of food to feed her disciples with Captain Lourdes following closely behind. Makka wondered if she was going to produce baskets of fish and gallons of red wine like the story of Jesus. She didn't care much for fish and her mother would have a cow if she drank real wine. Then again, her mother wasn't anywhere near here and if Thio offered wine, she'd definitely drink it. After all, she deserved some reward for all of this, didn't she?

"I don't know how she doesn't get lost in here," said Rose. "Nothing makes sense. How does she know where the hallways lead?"

"It all makes perfect sense to me," Makka replied. "The palace is built in the shape of a Latin cross."

Rose stopped short. "How do you know that?"

Skidding to a stop and nearly colliding with Brian, Makka shook her head. "I don't know, but it seems so familiar, like I've been here many times before. I seem to have somebody else living inside me."

And then she heard a whisper, *Davina of Saragon.*

She asked aloud. "Who's that?"

"Who's what?" asked Brian.

Rose, eyes wide with fear, said, "What's going on guys? I'm freaking out here."

They heard Thio calling from a distance, her voice sounded like delicate cymbals clinking and reverberating. "We have to hurry. There's a lot for us to do before the day is over."

"I wonder what she means by that?" asked Brian.

"I suppose we're about to find out," Rose answered.

But Makka had nothing to say, the name Davina of Saragon kept echoing in her brain.

They caught up with Thio just as she descended a flight of stone steps and entered a huge open chamber filled with mouth-watering aromas. Their stomachs growled unmercifully. "I guess I'm hungrier than I realized," said Brian.

"You're always hungry," retorted Rose.

"Over here," Thio the Fair called as she turned the corner and passed through a low-ceilinged stone archway from which several rooms branched off. Thio motioned to the chambers. "Go in and freshen up. You've been on a long journey since we last met and I'm sure you need a change of clothing and some warm soap and water."

Sure enough, Makka found a wash basin and a table with a pitcher filled with warm water. Clean tan colored pants and a sweater had been laid out on a chair. She was just dipping her hands into the water, ready to splash some on her face, which was smudged with soot and grime; her hair was a holy wreck.

Then, in the blink of an eye, she was surrounded by a swirling dark cloud. She tried to scream but no sound came out. Her face was wet and then dry, her hair tugged in a thousand directions and she felt a chill around her body and then a warmth she hadn't felt since the last time her mother tucked her into bed. She hadn't had that feeling in what seemed like a million years. The entire episode was over in a minute and she stood perfectly still gazing at herself in the mirror. Was this really her?

The stunning sweater was a shade of goldenrod that made her freshly washed skin look radiant. It fit her like a glove. Looking down, she realized her pants had been changed without her feeling a thing and even her shoes were new—handcrafted boots of the finest leather with golden laces. But it was her hair that took her breath away. The messy pony tail with burrs and twigs had been cleverly braided with gold and silver ribbons that glowed in the lantern light. She turned around to see it over her shoulder and ran her hand lovingly over the ribbons.

"Who's there?" she called out.

Nobody answered. She was all alone.

Before leaving the room, Makka made sure the precious Cvector was still around her neck. It was. Then she patted her pants pocket and felt the familiar outline of her precious cell phone. She couldn't resist pulling it out to check the screen. She tried to power it on, but it was dead and there was no charging cord. Heck, there wasn't even an electrical outlet in all of Etrunia, much less a cell tower.

But she took comfort in having it, useless as it was. It reminded her of home—of her mother, Elizabeth, her father, Michael, and her sister and brother. She tucked the pink case into her back pocket for safekeeping and stepped outside.

She saw Rose first, her brunette hair neatly combed and held in place by tortoise shell barrettes. She wore an embroidered blouse with a lamb's wool vest over it and dark broadcloth pants. Brian was clean-shaven wearing a denim shirt that matched his eyes and a leather vest with silver stitching and buckskin pants. His hair had been slicked back and he looked older and wiser.

They all broke out laughing. "What the heck just happened?" asked Makka.

"Damn if I know," Brian replied.

Rose ran her hand over her hair. "All I know is that it was the fastest I ever got washed and dressed. And these clothes are awesome. I feel fantastic, don't you?"

"Yes," Makka replied. "But it was like being sucked up into a tornado. Something weird is definitely going on."

Brian patted her shoulder. "Are you just figuring that out?"

Laughing and in high spirits from their extraordinary changeup, they followed Thio to a cavernous dining room where long wooden tables and benches were placed along the far walls of the great hall. In the center was an enormous polished mahogany table with red velvet upholstered chairs and candelabras. Places were set for five people although another two dozen could easily have fit.

Thio sat at one end with Captain Lourdes to her right. Makka sat the far end, her silver-and-gold flecked hair sparkling regally under the crystal chandelier with its flickering candlelight. Brian and Rose were in the very middle, opposite one another. They had crisp white napkins and plates trimmed with gold leaf. The cutlery was made of gold and cut glass vases held gorgeous bouquets of flowers in autumn colors. Aromas filled the air and great loaves of barley, rye, and wheat bread were spaced out between the tureens of bisque soup, stews, sweet buttered corn, and herb-crusted potatoes. Rose wanted to eat an entire loaf of bread by herself.

An enormous roasted pig sat square in the center of the table with a red apple in its mouth. It was flanked by two sturgeons, fish eyes staring blankly and scales glittering even in death. Makka looked away and concentrated on the colorful roasted root vegetables and delicious looking meat pies. Bowls of mustard were placed at each setting along with goblets of something red.

Thio held up her goblet. The table was too long and they were too far apart to clink to their good health so they held the pewter chalices aloft.

"A toast to Makka," said Thio. "Welcome back. Let's celebrate your triumphant return." She took a sip and everyone else followed—except Makka who didn't believe her ears.

Did she just say triumphant return? Return from where? What the heck was happening?

"Yes," they replied in unison taking sips of the homemade brew.

Thio smiled benignly. "This is sugar wine which we use for special occasions. It's made of beauty berries mixed with honey and spices. But it's not fermented so it's not *real* wine. And anyway you're all too young to drink alcohol." She took a dainty sip and held the pewter stemware aloft looking at Makka. "This has always been your favorite."

Makka was dumfounded. What did she mean by *always your favorite* and *welcome back*? She'd never been here before, except for the two preceding days that she could barely remember.

Just then she felt a presence nearby and distinctly heard the words *Davina of Saragon*. Her hand shook so violently that sugar wine spilled over the top of the glass and onto the white napkin in her lap forming a blotch that resembled her dog Sasha. *No, that was impossible* This was absolutely crazy, beyond her wildest imagination.

But it got even more bizarre as the platters in the center of the table began to move, lifted into the air, circling the table as unseen beings placed food on each of the guest's plates and then returned the pots to the table without making a single sound.

Rose and Brian stared in utter disbelief as Thio was served first and Makka second. She shook her head to the fish and nodded as a slice of meat pie was placed on her plate along with the root vegetables. Her goblet was refilled by a pitcher that appeared to be suspended in the air.

"Please don't be alarmed," said Thio soothingly. "The Wraiths are acting as our helpers today. I think each of you has already met them when you changed a little while ago. They are here to assist, not to harm anybody, so please let them know what you want to eat."

Rose opted for a slice of fish, a piece of pork and half a loaf of bread. She didn't want the root vegetables but nodded enthusiastically when the bowl of potatoes came floating around.

Brian acted as though this kind of service happened every day of the week, but his face was ashen and his hand trembled as the fork brought a slice of ham to his mouth.

Captain Lourdes ate heartily. Thio only nibbled on a crust of bread while consuming endless glasses of sugar wine. No wonder she's so thin, Rose thought to herself. She doesn't eat any carbs. But the food was delicious and like nothing they had ever tasted and soon Rose was sound asleep in her chair.

Without waiting for dessert and without waking Rose, Thio, Brian and Makka left Captain Lourdes to stand guard over Rose who was snoring softly.

~ 50 ~

LEGEND OF THE WRAITHS

Thio the Fair, Makka, and Brian followed their footsteps back down the hallways, through the great room with the colorful banners, and up the spiral staircase to the circular room where Thio settled on the throne and motioned to Brian and Makka, to get seated on two low stools in front of her. Still shaken by the shadows—called Wraiths—Makka had so many questions she didn't know where to start. Before she could open her mouth, Thio the Fair began to talk.

"You both saw and felt them, didn't you?" asked Thio. Makka nodded.

Brian said, "The pots and bowls moving around were pretty awesome. So was being stripped down and dressed by ghosts."

Thio nodded. "You're right. Those are the Wraiths."

"Wraiths?" asked Makka.

"It's complicated, but I'll try to keep it simple. These Wraiths were once living here, in Lovenfell, but they didn't die—at least not in the traditional way. They are simply a shadow of their former selves, like a ghost or spirit of the undead."

"I don't get it," said Makka, shaking the cobwebs that seemed to be wrapped around her brain.

Brian spoke up. "Last year we studied Scottish poets and they used the word to mean an apparition or manifestation of someone who was once alive. And sailors often saw billowy figures in the fog that they believed were ghosts of sailors who died in storms."

"Close enough," said Thio. "The point is that these shadowy figures have stayed here since you left. They had no reason to live but no reason to die either, and thus they became Wraiths."

Makka thought she'd faint. "What do you mean since I left? I only got here a few days ago and haven't gone anywhere and why would they have no reason to live? It makes no sense whatsoever. I'd like to go home now."

She stood up and brushed off the seat of her pants and then reached over to pull Brian up. But he sat ramrod straight, eyes wide open as though in a trance.

"Brian, Brian!" She shook his shoulder. "Wake up. Where's Rose? What's happening?"

Thio smiled and remained still while Brian sat immobile, unable to move, and Makka became more distressed. Panic welled up inside her and she felt her heart pound so fast and loud she thought for sure she'd have a heart attack—a heart attack at fourteen. This wasn't really happening. She was freaking out in this palatial twilight zone as Thio turned her head toward the doorway and Makka realized that a swarm of Wraiths had entered the room. They slowly took shape, turning from vapor into semi-transparent objects with faces and clothing—they looked like butlers with dark trousers and white shirts and maids with caps and aprons.

"These were some of your loyal subjects," said Thio. "Makka, meet the Wraiths."

Makka heard a jumble of whispers all around her as the number of Wraiths continued to swell until the room was crammed. Brian still sat ramrod, unable to see or hear, although he was quite alive. She could see the vein throbbing in his forehead, which was covered with perspiration.

And then she heard it, rising like a wave at a ball game, a chorus of voices starting like a vibrating hum, the volume swelling with each passing second: *"Davina of Saragon, Davina of Saragon, welcome, welcome, welcome, Davina of Saragon, Davina of Saragon, welcome, welcome, welcome home, welcome home, welcome home."*

The voices reached a crescendo, filling the air to the stained glass panels near the ceiling and through every crevice and crack of the round and richly decorated tower chamber.

Makka's breath was sucked from her lungs. Her body went limp and everything went black.

~ 51 ~

RIDDLES OF THE PAST

When she came to, Thio was still on the throne. Brian and Rose looked well rested. They were seated beside her on the same kind of tapestry covered stools. Captain Lourdes stood to Thio's right and between them was a pedestal with a huge crystal quartz ball about the size of a bowling ball. It had been right there when she first surveyed the room when she was all alone.

Then, somehow, it vanished when she showed her friends around, and now it was back again. What kind of weird magic was happening here? Certainly it could not be explained and she simply had to accept it, as she had for everything else that had transpired over the past few days—or weeks.

Thio leaned forward. "Makka, do you remember when you spent time with me at the Morass and I told you that you are here for a purpose—that your flight through the portal chasing Jesper, who had stolen something you valued, was no accident?"

Makka wracked her brain to recall that conversation, but so much had happened since then—the armory, the heat shield around Nideon's Tower, stealing the Cvector, the three little men—what were their names? Melker, Agmar and Thorvi—and their missing limbs and terrible tales of the wicked Lady Eyrie and bitter, brooding Lord Hviti and the band of men called the Resistance. She recalled traveling to the White City and being chased by men in dark hoods on black horses. Then she, alone, was let into Lovenfell to behold the talking mirrors and bloody murals and conversations with people who were long gone. And now she was supposed to recall a conversation that she had a million years ago with Thio?

For a few heartbeats nobody spoke.

Thio continued: "I said all will be revealed over time and in many different ways. Let me start now by telling you about this crystal and Lady Eyrie and why you have been brought to Etrunia and—most important—where you go from here."

Over the next few hours, Thio the Fair led the three Americans through the history of Etrunia, from the loving sister and brother who grew into adversaries and how Lady Eyrie had vanquished Pharmakeus—but not before he had established the ancient city of Missilium that lay hidden under the hot sands of the Desert of Lost Souls. She reminded them that when they left the Morass they'd been on a mission to take the precious Cvector from Nideon, the highly-coveted amulet that could find the ancient city of Missilium. She congratulated them on a job well done. They had accomplished their mission. But that was only the beginning.

"You were successful," Thio reminded them, as Makka fingered the amulet under her clothing. "You have it now. But this is not the time to use it. I need to explain who Davina of Saragon is and why she is so important to this story. And then I will show you how to use this ball and send you on a quest—one that's a matter of life and death.

Aren't they all? Makka wondered. But she remained silent.

"The truth is very simple," said Thio. "YOU, Makka, are Davina of Saragon."

"You are?" Rose piped up. "Why didn't you tell us? You said you were Makka Sinclair."

"I am."

"You are," said Thio, "and yet you're not."

"This is harder to understand than calculus," added Brian, scratching his head.

"All of you actually lived here before. You knew each other then and have been reunited to save Etrunia from the evil forces that have taken over. They will destroy all of us one day—if Lady Eyrie, the Grand Wizard Archite and Lord Hviti, who harbors a bitter rage against everyone and everything—are not destroyed. If a new ruler is not put into place soon, we will all perish in the most hideous ways imaginable."

Silence filled the room. They dared not breathe. Rose's face was the color of a ripe red apple and Brian's breathing had become a rattle in his throat.

"I think there's been some mistake," Makka finally croaked out.

"No, no mistake." Thio shook her head, hair swirling like a beautiful white beta fish in a clear pool of water. Captain Lourdes smiled and nodded sympathetically as she continued.

"You were special then and you are special now. You were the daughter of the trusted advisor to the Great Pharmakeus. Rose and Brian became your best friends. They were the children of Pharmakeus and Aurora. When Pharmakeus was destroyed by his sister, he reappeared many decades later in Granite Falls as Royal Abadon and had two children—Brian and Rose. Your new parents lived in Florida. So it was no accident that they moved north so you could meet the twins. It was your destiny."

Rose, Brian and Makka stared at one another and shrugged their shoulders. They couldn't have seen this coming even if they'd had their own personal crystal balls.

"The reasons are fairly clear," said Thio. "The three of you were together then and you have been reunited with a new purpose. The switcheroo is that although Brian and Rose were born into royalty, *you* Makka were the Chosen One.

"The future will bring the answers you crave. Suffice it to say that we know all about your American parents, Michael and Elizabeth Sinclair, as well as your siblings Anne and Eddie. You were named Davina of Saragon when you lived here because everybody admired your wisdom, fairness and great powers."

"No way," Makka protested. "You're making this up to frighten me."

"I speak the truth. You have the power that we desperately need."

"You've been watching too many movies. I have no powers."

"What's a movie?"

Brian spoke up. "Listen Makka, if we ever want to get back to Granite Falls you'll have to go along with this. I'm sure that Thio the Fair knows more about this than we do and we have to trust her."

"I agree," said Rose. "You will be our leader."

"Come," said Thio. "Stand up and come here."

Makka did as she was instructed. "Touch the crystal."

Her trembling hands lifted slowly and felt the cool, dry and remarkably smooth orb, which immediately began to glow and pulsate—turning sea green, aqua, lavender, rose, ginger, lemon yellow, and back to clear.

"Look deeply," Thio instructed. "You'll see something as soon as the fog clears."

A vacuum of silence filled the room as the ball swirled and something came into focus. It was dawn, with streaks of violet and pink. She saw a large gray horse, saddled and grazing in a field. What was so remarkable about that? Then she noticed a body—no, make that two bodies—one lying upon the other—a girl and a young man. They were on the ground, their clothes in tatters, dried blood caked in her hair and on the fair skin of her face and hands. What had happened?

"Are they dead? Do you want me to bring them back to life?" Makka asked, her throat dry. "I can't do that you know. I don't have any powers at all."

"Think positive. I'll show you."

Thio instructed Makka to slide her hands around the crystal. "Now you are holding the people and the horse. Nearby is Fort

273

Ravenspur. I want you to move your hands slowly, lifting them high up in the air until you find the fortified wooden wall and then I want you to slowly set them all down inside. They are alive, but barely. You will save their lives when you accomplish this task."

Everybody held their breath as Makka followed Thio's instruction. The horse was heavier than the two bodies, both of which were limp and threatened to slip from her grasp. The horse's eyes looked startled, wide with fear and alarm, but he didn't struggle and she was grateful. A few seconds later, the wooden fence came into view and she saw the roofs of huts and a clearing.

Gently she lowered the horse and the bodies to the ground. Almost immediately there was a rush of soldiers clad in brown, most of their clothing frayed and dirty. They stared at the bodies that flowed through the air then ever so gently landed on the ground and called for help. Others came running with clean cloths, a bowl of water and bandages. The crystal ball clouded over and then went dark.

Captain Lourdes replaced the cloth cover.

Thio stood up and clapped her hands slowly and steadily. Indeed, Makka had the powers! "Davina of Saragon is back. Long live Davina."

~ 52 ~

FORT RAVENSPUR

Dottier felt strong arms lifting her up; she heard voices calling for water and bandages. She tried to open her eyes, but they were swollen shut. "Orn," she whispered hoarsely, "where are you? Are you alive?"

"He's a few feet away," someone answered—a man with a deep and friendly voice. "He's out cold, covered with scratches. What happened? Who are you?"

Tears trickled from her closed eyes creating puddles in the dirt upon which she had been placed. "I have to save him," she cried in anguish. "Don't let him die."

"Calm down, it's going to be fine."

"Am I still in Valgard?"

"Not really," said a soothing voice. "I mean, we're on the edge of the land owned by Lord Hviti, but you're safe inside Fort Ravenspur. You're surrounded by soldiers of the Resistance army. We're going to make sure you're patched up good as new."

"But Orn…" Her voice trailed off as sobs shook her body.

"We've cleaned up his wounds and he doesn't seem to have any broken bones. But he appears to be in a trance."

"And Big Gray?"

"If you mean the horse, he's fine," said the soldier tending to her. She felt warm water on her face as salve and bandages were applied. "We've given him oats and a bucket of clean water. He looks like he was attacked by a flock of buzzards."

She lay silently on the ground, letting the healers do their job, feeling better knowing that Orn was alive and that Big Gray had suffered no permanent damage.

"Can you sit up?" asked the soldier, gently placing a hand behind her head and pushing her into a sitting position.

Dottir opened her eyes a crack. She could feel the lids were swollen and the light caused a major headache as she looked around at the dozens of huts in front of her. Big Gray was not far away and Orn lay sprawled nearby like a broken scarecrow that had escaped from a horrible battle. She couldn't figure anything out, nothing made sense.

The last thing she remembered, she and Orn had slid off the horse while being attacked mercilessly by the carrion crows and Big Gray had stepped over them to shield their bodies. She could not possibly have gotten Orn's limp and nearly lifeless body back on the horse and navigated through the night over unfamiliar terrain to a fort that she didn't even know for sure existed. Something was definitely weird and extraordinary.

"How did I get here? Did your sentries find us and carry us back?"

He shook his head. "By the way, I'm Captain Alabaster."

She peered at him closely and was surprised that he was indeed chalk white—from his hair to his pale complexion and even his eyes, which appeared the palest of aqua with just a hint of blue. He was a slight man, thin with calloused square hands and pointy ears that stuck out like pale appendages. A shock of ivory hair hung over his furrowed brow. The captain was dressed in forest green, which provided a stark contrast to his pallid complexion. But his expression was kind and his voice was soft and sympathetic.

"I've asked the sentries and they didn't open the gate last night to anybody. We're under strict orders to search anyone who comes in."

"Then how did we get here?"

He shook his head in dismay. "The only answer I can give is magic."

She stared in disbelief.

"Wait, I'll ask General Darogan. Maybe he has some answers."

Without moving or making a noise, a tall, imposing man suddenly appeared—like a gust of wind had blown him to their side.

"General Mach Darogan at your service," he said, bowing to Dottir. Nothing was logical here. Why was a general bowing to a kitchen maid? She feared looking into the eyes of this powerfully built man who was darker than ebony and as tall as a small oak tree. His teeth gleamed white against his skin and his nose sniffed the air for scents. Huge hands were balled into fists.

Unlike Captain Alabaster who dressed in forest green, General Darogan wore cream colored fatigues. But his eyes were the most mysterious part of this strange and commanding man. Glancing into them, Dottir felt as though she was falling into a bottomless pit. She looked down at the ground to keep herself from dissolving.

In a deep throaty voice, General Darogan explained that nobody had come in or gone out through the fortified gate since the preceding day. He was extremely concerned they might be spies sent from Lord Hviti, but dismissed that theory when he saw how damaged they were. Sternly, he demanded to hear Dottir's story.

She stood up on wobbly legs and began her story about meeting and Anders and Eric their plot to invade the Dark Fortress to rescue their father and Orn, who had brought a message and was destined to die for it.

She explained that they had been only partially successful—that the bodies had been saved—but not their souls.

"So he is essentially one of Hviti's ghouls?" asked General Darogan, his voice modulated to contain this potentially overwhelming piece of news.

"No, no," Dottir cried out. "He's not a ghoul. In fact, I have his soul."

Alabaster asked, "You have his soul? Where?"

"In the saddlebag." Dottir pointed to Big Gray. "And there's also a book that we borrowed."

"Were you planning to return it?" asked General Darogan.

"No," she shook her head until it ached. "We didn't know what it was but it seemed important so we just grabbed it along with the flask containing Orn. But he has thousands more. It was awful."

"You know what Lord Hviti does?" asked Captain Alabaster, his white skin gleaming.

"Yes." She nodded her head. "I've seen it with my very own eyes!"

The two soldiers stepped aside to confer while Dottir wiped her face with the hem of her apron and brushed the dirt from her sleeves and bodice. She looked a fright. Good thing she didn't have a mirror. But most important was getting Orn's soul back into his body so they could go home.

"Come with us," said General Darogan. "We will move Orn into one of the huts and then check the saddlebags to see what you have in there."

She followed them dutifully having no idea how they could make him whole again so they could leave. Would they even be allowed to return home? There were so many questions and not one single answer. Her world looked as bleak as the Fort with the tan dirt and tan huts and brown fence and not a tree in sight or splash of color. Her heart sank to her dusty shoes as she followed them over to Big Gray.

She said a silent prayer that she would survive the day and night and that Orn would get his soul back and they'd be allowed to leave. It wasn't asking a lot, was it?

~ 53 ~

THE DANGER ZONE

In Lovenfell, the cloth was again pulled off the crystal and Makka, Rose, and Brian continued to stare into the crystal ball as the drama between Dottir, Captain Alabaster, and General Darogan unfolded.

They watched in awe as the three of them walked over to Big Gray and rummaged through the saddlebags. They saw Dottir place a hand on Captain Alabaster's as he started to pull out the blanket that contained her brother's bones. She shook her head and pleaded silently. They couldn't hear her words but the expression of horror and sorrow on her face was unmistakable.

Then she rushed over to General Darogan as he pulled out the flask holding Orn's soul. She held out her hands and he gently placed it into her palms and then dug out the massive red book.

Makka called to Thio who had sat down on the throne and closed her eyes.

"Please, come see this. What's in there?" She pointed to the volume being laid on a dusty trestle table in a courtyard outside the hut where Orn lay. The flask with his agonized face still pressed against the glass was clearly visible. Thio rose elegantly and strode over to the crystal ball, gazing down into it, running her hands silently over the top and sides as it began to swirl with a profusion of colors. Then she exclaimed: "Yes, yes! That's it. The book I've been searching for—it disappeared from the Morass when our forest castle was destroyed by Lady Eyrie's evil forces."

"What's in it?" asked Rose.

"The *Book of Spells*. Everything you need to know about magic is in there. The person who controls it governs the universe."

"The whole universe?" asked Brian.

"I'm not sure exactly, but Etrunia for certain," replied Thio the Fair, tossing her white-green hair. "You must retrieve it."

"We?" asked Makka. "Aren't you coming?"

"I must return to the Morass. My people need me."

"But..." Rose protested. She was clearly disappointed and definitely fearful.

"We'll be okay, Sis," said Brian, putting his arm around her shoulder. "Makka will be in charge."

"Me? Why me?" She put her hands on her hips and stared without blinking. "Don't for a minute think that the myth about Davina of Saragon means that I have any kind of supernatural powers. I'm just a teenager from Florida who stumbled into Etrunia by way of Granite Falls."

"Everything happens the way it's supposed to," said Thio, nodding to Captain Lourdes. "I'll leave you now. You know how to use the crystal; you know that this is your home and your safe haven. Now go help Dottir and use the *Ancient Book of Spells* to introduce his soul back into his body. You can return it to me when you're finished. But don't, under any circumstances, let it fall into the hands of Lady Eyrie or..."

"Or what?" asked Makka.

"We will all be doomed."

With that astonishing proclamation, Thio swept out of the throne room as Captain Lourdes held the door open for her. She stopped suddenly in the doorway and said, "Go out to the courtyard. They will deliver you safely to Fort Ravenspur." Use the map in the saddlebag to guide you.

"Who's they?" asked Rose, but Thio was gone.

When they were alone Makka asked, "Now what?"

"I guess we go outside," said Brian. "There must be horses out there."

Makka glanced around at the magnificent room that was beginning to feel like home. She had a sinking sensation that it would be a long time before she'd be back in this splendor again.

They went through the hallway, heads swiveling at the scenes depicted in the murals and slowly down the stairs as though trying to stall their arrival in the courtyard and the perilous future that awaited them—not wanting to leave their glorious surroundings.

As they passed the murals again Brian cried out, "Look, here is a new one. It's Makka sitting on the throne with the crystal ball in front of her and it seems as though those are the Wraiths surrounding her. Who painted this...and when?"

"In time all will be revealed," said Rose.

"You sound like some wise old soul," quipped Brian.

"Maybe I am. You can never tell. After all, look at Makka, I mean Davina of Saragon."

They raced down the final corridor, Brian and Rose trying to beat each other the way siblings do, and burst out of the White Palace through the back gate where they spotted three horses, saddled and ready. Like a carousel, they walked around the snorting animals that pawed the ground restlessly. Brian cried out, "Look at the harnesses, they have names. I'm taking this roan called Warwick."

Rose quickly claimed the beige horse called Pyros. Makka took the powerful chestnut stallion named Arion.

Within seconds they were up in their saddles, leaving the White City, trotting over the cobblestone streets and into the fields of tall dry grass following the map as they rode along. The sun rose high in the blue sky and the temperature climbed steadily until they were hot and sweaty. Makka, in the beautiful goldenrod sweater, had the sensation that she was melting—like she had when they reached the heat shield outside Nideon's Tower.

"We need to get to higher ground," said Brian, turning his horse toward a hillside to the left. The grass was shorter and the temperature dropped as they rode between small clumps of alder trees. A small breeze whipped up and they were able to enjoy the scenery as they continued toward Fort Ravenspur and the nearby village of Dobbinville. Above them, they heard birds chattering in the swaying branches and dragonflies fluttered around their heads.

"I hear something," said Rose, turning in her saddle to look back at Brian. Makka had her eyes glued to the horizon, hoping to see the high fortified wooden wall of Fort Ravenspur. She didn't hear Rose as the rumble grew louder.

Then, out of the blue, Brian caught up with her and yelled, "Go! Go as fast as you can."

"What's going on?"

"Don't look back, just go!"

As the words spilled out, Rose, astride Pyros, zipped past Makka and galloped away in a cloud of dust. Makka kicked Arion who responded to the slightest touch, bolting forward so that she was thrown backward, nearly toppling off. They galloped as fast as they could while Makka, unable to resist looking back, was horrified to see a herd of wild boars with long, sharp tusks coming straight toward them. She couldn't count how many, but she estimated at least two hundred—maybe more!

Where had they come from? What did they want?

"Faster!" shouted Brian over the deafening sound of hooves beating the earth. The ground seemed to shake and quiver as the noise of the snorting beasts, some weighing five-hundred pounds, closing the gap between them.

Makka didn't know much about them except that they were feral pigs, but far more deadly with thick, razor-sharp tusks. These were not like domesticated pigs that some people keep as pets, but aggressive, unpredictable and extraordinarily dangerous. They eat anything they kill and these beasts looked hungry.

Brian wondered where they came from, but uppermost in his mind was how they could get away without being trampled to death?

As the life-threatening seconds ticked by, the wild boars gained inches, then feet, closing the gap between the riders and their sharp-edged tusks. The horses' flanks were covered with sweat and their eyes were wild with fright. Up ahead was a thick grove of alder trees with thin trunks and low-hanging branches. If they weren't careful, they could have their heads lopped off or cause grievous injury.

"Hurry," yelled Brian to Rose and Makka. "Let the horses take the lead; they'll know when to slow down."

He smelled the stench from the herd of wild animals and their hot breath on his back as the herd surged forward.

"We're going to be trampled," yelled Rose over the thundering of hooves. "I don't want to die."

"We won't die!" screamed Makka. "We have to get the *Ancient Book of Spells* for Thio." She wished she knew how to work the magical powers she supposedly had as a thousand cloven hooves hit the ground. They could barely hear each other. Grass and dirt were flying as Warwick, Pyros and Arion kicked into overdrive.

Suddenly, Brian took over the lead. "Follow me." He steered sharply around one tree and then another. Behind them, the wild boars split up, some going to the left, others to the right—always on their heels. Then, to Rose and Makka's astonishment, Brian grabbed a branch and swung himself up into a tree as his horse continued on without him. Rose, finding strength she never knew existed, followed a few seconds later, letting out a loud "oomph" as the branch hit her stomach. But she was safe as Pyros galloped away, eyes wild with dread.

Ever so slightly, Makka stood in the stirrups and let go of the reins as another tree approached. She grabbed hold as her body jerked back and her legs dangled in the air, just above the hairy backs of the feral beasts.

She held on for dear life as Arion thundered away and then wedged herself into the crook of the branch, hanging onto the tree trunk. Her body ached, her heart raced, her sweater was ruined and her neatly braided hair was a tangled mess.

But she was still in one piece as the herd continued to chase the horses and their adrenaline subsided.

They were safe—for now—but without transportation to Fort Ravenspur. They had no idea how to get there. Each of them wondered if Lady Eyrie had something to do with this unexpected attack.

Was she really that powerful?

~ 54 ~

CAPTURED

Cautiously, they climbed down from their perches and surveyed the damage. The ground had been trampled and some small trees knocked down.

"Is everybody okay?" asked Makka. The twins nodded. The small grove of trees allowed the sunlight to shine through the branches and the air was crisp as the dust settled. "We have no choice but to try to find the horses and pray that the boars have left them alone."

As the sun rose, they set out on foot. Makka tried to communicate with Thio the Fair by telepathy; it was definitely worth a try. She'd never done it before but she prayed someone would become aware of their plight and come to their aid. Just as she sent a plea for help, Rose cried out, "Up ahead, look, something is in the grass."

"Careful," warned Brian. "If it's a wounded boar we could get gored."

Slowly they approached until Rose cried out, "It's Pyros!" The horse was clearly dead, eyes glazed with a film, no longer breathing or in pain. Rose burst into sobs and threw herself on the animal even though they had only been partners for a few hours.

Brian and Makka knelt near her, putting their arms around her to console her anguish. Makka felt Brian's arm on hers and her heart beat faster. This was not the time to think about anything except getting to the Fort.

Still, her brain and heart were connected in some mysterious way and the electricity that passed between them was tangible. He glanced at her and smiled sadly. He felt it too, but their collective pain and fear overrode any romantic notions they might have had.

Brian patted his sister on the back. "She feels no more pain. She's off to a better world and she didn't suffer. It was over in an instant."

Makka, at a loss for words, simply kissed Rose's flushed and dusty cheek. "We need to move along. Come, let's get up and find the other horses. You can ride with me."

Rose stroked the horse's soft, velvety muzzle and then stood up on trembling legs. That was a close call, far too close for comfort. None of them were ready to die. They had to get to Fort Ravenspur as quickly as possible. But Lady Eyrie had other plans for the American teenagers.

As they trudged along a stream that wound from east to west, they stopped to drink deeply. They were filthy, covered with dust from the stampede and hungry—despite the huge meal they'd eaten a few hours ago. As they bent over to splash water on their faces, they heard the flapping of wings—a thunderous whooshing sound high above and a sound Makka had heard only once before.

It wasn't the sweet trilling of mourning doves or the brash cawing of a flock of crows. It sounded as though an orchestra of big bass bassoons was descending onto their heads. Makka covered her ears as Brian gazed up. "The Grizzards!" he exclaimed. "They've come for us."

The girls looked skyward and saw three gigantic brownish black birds with huge curved beaks soaring in circles, coming ever closer, talons out and beady eyes fixated on them. Makka, who had no experience with these avian giants, felt herself shrinking behind Brian's back.

"It's okay," he said, patting her hand, sending a shock up her arm. "They're friendly. They've must have come to take us to our destination."

Makka simply nodded unable to speak as the Grizzards circled ever lower, the wind swirling dust around their heads as the birds finally skidded to a stop at the edge of the stream, dipping their huge heads into the water and then tilting them back to let the cool, clear water drop down through their long, thick necks.

Then each bird—almost as large as a small aircraft—waddled over. Brian helped Rose and Makka climb on. Rose had flown on them before, but Makka didn't know how to hold on. Brian showed her a leather strap that was cleverly wound under the wings and around the neck. "Just try to relax," he cautioned. "Taking off is scarier than hell, but once you're up it's a smooth ride."

"Once you get used to it, it's the only way you'll want to fly," Rose added with a smile. "I love it."

Brian climbed aboard and they were off, first running to gain speed as Makka's silver and gold ribbons streamed behind her. She scrunched her eyes shut, unable to bear the sensation at liftoff, her tummy jumping into her throat and feeling as though she would tumble off and into space at any second. But then they were up, flying high above the trees, above the forest animals and the stream, which sparkled in the sunlight like diamonds winding in a path below them.

As they continued, they could see the Forest of the Damned and Fort Ravenspur. But between their flight path and their destination lay the trap set by the wicked Lady Eyrie, who was bitter and furious that the Cvector had been stolen right out from under her nose.

She had sent Councilor Simeon and his finest soldiers to find the invaders. They would have to pay for their insolence; they would be sacrificed for the good of Etrunia so the evil forces could govern the masses for eternity—or even longer—until the end of time.

She cackled as she watched the drama unfold in the smoky crystal ball from the comfort of Blackwater Castle. The beginning of the end was upon them.

~ 55 ~

MORTAL DANGER

As Brian looked down, he realized that between their flight path and the Fort was a meadow and covering the grassland were dozens and dozens of tents set up in perfectly straight lines forming a large square. At each corner there was a narrower, taller tent with a guard stationed, keeping watchful eyes over the surroundings and the airspace above them. Between and around the structures were scores of soldiers, each armed with a sword and a cross bow. The soldier gazed up as they heard the loud flapping of the Grizzards' wings.

"Come down," they shouted. "Land those birds now in the name of Lady Eyrie!"

The army of the Wicked One looked up and aimed their arrows upward. Councilor Simeon appeared in the midst of the shouting and nodded with approval. This is what they'd hoped for—their prey walking, or in this case, flying—right into their well-laid trap. Lady Eyrie would be overjoyed, although she would never show it.

Now she would have the Cvector that she so ardently desired, the magical amulet that would make her the happiest and most powerful person in Etrunia and far beyond its borders.

Brian shouted over the wind that whistled past his ears, "Fly north, quickly, and follow me." He yanked on the leather thong directing the powerful bird to the right. Makka did the same, but just as Rose began to turn, an arrow—sent by one of the soldiers below—flew through the air and struck home. With a sickening thud, it pierced the bird and was followed by a gut-wrenching screech. The Grizzard, with a wingspan of nearly twenty feet across, began a death spiral nosedive. It cawed helplessly, its cold black eyes already giving up any hope of survival with an arrow through its neck.

"No! No! No!" Makka screamed as Rose tumbled off the dying bird, its eyes glazed over with death as it fell toward earth. As Rose slid off the bird's back, Makka saw an arrow going through Rose's right shoulder. As though in slow motion, Rose tumbled into the air, now separated from the dying bird, as she searched frantically for help, and the soldiers continued their assault.

Brian's face was etched with horror and determination. This was his twin sister; they had been together forever and joined at the hip through this bizarre adventure. Another glance at the spiraling Grizzard made Makka sick and Rose's blood-stained clothing was horrifying. They could not let her die. No way! What would they tell Mr. and Mrs. Abadon? How would they ever contain their grief?

She could not let her friend die. Would not!

The soldiers cheered jubilantly as Rose let out an ear-piercing scream that chilled Makka to the core. But Brian and Makka were horror-struck, wild with grief, sickened and revolted that these soldiers would stoop low enough to shoot down an unarmed civilian—a teenager no less!

As another barrage of arrows flew toward them, Makka felt a strange and powerful urge to release the leather strap of the Grizzard. It felt as though something or someone had taken over her body. She was charged with a million jolts of electricity as she let go of the leather strap and stretched out her palms to deflect the thin razor-sharp spears aimed right at them. As though deflected by an invisible shield, they bounced away. Nobody was more surprised than Makka as Brian stared in astonishment.

Then he turned his head toward Rose and shouted, "Rose! Rose!" as she continued to tumble to the ground drenched in blood. With the arrows deflected, Makka pinched her fingers together—as though gathering an invisible thread—and pulled upward. Rose, whose limp body was plummeting through the static-charged air, slowed the descent and began to rise up again. Makka urged the Grizzard higher so she could pull her friend up and out of danger by the invisible thread.

Both Makka and Brian were stunned at the magical phenomenon playing out right before their eyes. Rose, who was nearly unconscious, smiled as she felt the tug of gravity release its death grip and her body begin to rise up in the air and away from the arrows that now fell back to the ground without hitting their marks.

Makka, holding one hand palm up to keep the arrows at bay, continued to pull Rose upward. She called out, "Brian catch her."

Deftly, as though steering a sleek sports car, Brian maneuvered the mighty bird under Rose and held up his hands to grasp her limp body. But just as Brian was about to grab Rose something

293

else drew Rose away and downwards. Brian looked at Makka, who in turn gave him a surprised and horrified look. Makka turned her full focus to Rose, pinching her fingers together trying to pull Rose back up, but, it didn't work. Something else was tugging at Rose and Makka didn't know how to combat it.

She suddenly felt eyes staring at her—hard, evil eyes. The eyes smiled wickedly and Makka lost her mental focus and Rose tumbled to the ground, turning twisting, falling toward the unforgiving ground. Makka lowered her arm and looked helplessly at Brian.

"What now?" she called out.

With despair in his voice, he shouted, "Head to Fort Ravenspur. There's nothing we can do here!"

They commanded the Grizzards: "Fly to Fort Ravenspur NOW."

Thio the Fair had sent them on this mission to retrieve the *Book of Spells* so they could resurrect the ghouls and put Orn's soul back into his body. But now Rose was severely injured, perhaps fatally! And they were in deadly danger, completely exposed and in dire need of a safe haven themselves.

The wind howled around them and the horrid caws of the Grizzards that mourned the loss of their brother. She held onto the rein with one hand while deflecting the arrows that still came precariously close. Another casualty was not an option.

"Please let Rose be okay," Makka whispered to herself. "Hang on my friend; help will be sent to you."

In Blackwater Castle, Lady Eyrie watched the events unfold through her crystal ball. She laughed as the dead bird spiraled to the ground and Rose fell through the air pierced by the arrow. Lightning shot from her fingertips as she easily thwarted Makka's powers—enough to stop Rose from being saved. An evil grin crossed her face as she thought about the upstart who dared challenge her powers as the ruler of Etrunia.

This young girl, the intruder with her worthless friends, had powers—that much was clear. The powers were weaker, of course, but they were powers nevertheless. She covered the crystal ball with a soft cloth and turned away. These invaders could become a serious threat. But it was easy enough to stop them dead in their tracks.

She was only biding her time until their plan unfolded entirely and she could see what benefit she might derive from it. Otherwise, they would become yet another blip in the long, twisted history of Etrunia.

Makka tightened her grip on the Grizzard's leather strap, wishing with all her heart she could change the plot, stop the movie, and halt the action. But that was impossible and she quickly turned her thoughts around. Once they landed within the fortress walls they would alert the soldiers and find the leaders who could execute a plan to rescue Rose. The urgency of the situation could not be ignored. Everything had changed. They needed a new plan immediately. Sooner!

A final glance down revealed the dead Grizzard lying on the ground. Soldiers poked its lifeless body with their boots which made Makka sick to her stomach. Another soldier carried Rose in his arms. She was limp and pale, ghostly white and drenched in blood. Makka sent up a silent prayer that she would be all right.

Revolted by the scene, she quickly turned away. There was nothing she could do at the moment. Nothing could be done until they landed in Fort Ravenspur and put together a rescue party.

"It can't end like this," Brian said to Makka. "We cannot allow it."

Makka nodded solemnly. She had no words that could make him feel better.

There was nothing more to say. Now they had to act!

~ 56 ~

HOME

As they made their way to the Fort, Makka knew there was only one mission after Rose had been returned to safety. They had to vanquish the malevolent and powerful Lady Eyrie. She had to be destroyed, along with Lord Hviti and his fortress of dead souls.

She had no choice but to accept the mantle of Davina of Saragon and steel herself for the inevitable challenges and battles that inevitably lay ahead. She'd throw herself into any test they could invent, no matter how grueling, challenging, or treacherous. She would not quit and she would not die quietly or without struggling with every ounce of strength in her body.

This was not the end but simply a beginning. A new day would dawn. Freedom and victory lay ahead. Nothing would get in their way. Nothing.

All she needed was a plan.

Suddenly, Makka's phone buzzed and then buzzed again louder. What was going on? A third incoming message roused Makka from a deep and profound sleep. She was in a room, under the coverlet, lying on a beautiful four-poster bed. The gauzy canopy was waffling in the breeze that spilled in from the open window.

She pulled herself awake and looked around feeling totally disoriented.

Was she back at Lovenfell in the White City?

Had she fallen asleep on one of the beds there?

This wasn't her room, certainly it couldn't be. She's never seen this gorgeous bed before or the heavy oak chest of drawers over there and the two matching side tables or the stunning rug in blue-gray swirls that covered the wooden floor. She heard something whine and there, at the foot of the bed was a black-and-white beast. Was she dreaming? She sat up.

"Sasha?" she asked. "Where am I?"

"Good morning, sunshine," said her mother, looking tired and pale. "It's early little one, go back to sleep."

"Whose bed is this?"

"Yours. Who else's would it be?"

"But I went to sleep on an air mattress last night."

"That was a few nights ago. The furniture came yesterday, exactly what you wanted, remember? Don't you like it?"

Makka wasn't sure about anything. Wasn't she just in Etrunia helping Rose? OMG, Rose! She's bleeding out. "I have to go somewhere," she said, flinging the covers back.

"Where are you going this early? Nobody is up yet. Take Sasha out and I'll be down soon."

Makka was stunned. What was going on? Her mom was acting like this wasn't any big deal but it was a VERY BIG DEAL.

Rose needed help. Where was Brian? She had to get to the Abandon's house to find her friends. There wasn't a second to spare.

She wondered if this had been a dream. What if Rose and Brian thought she was crazy—or worse, a liar? What if they never talked to her again? They were her only friends in Granite Falls. They were the only ones who could confirm that Thio the Fair really existed with her blonde-green hair. They were the only ones who'd seen Lovenfell and could confirm that it had been real and not a figment of her imagination. Only Brian and Rose would know if Grizzards did exist?

Or was all a crazy dream? Any semblance to reality was impossible. Etrunia was just a dream and certainly she had no magic powers. Gnomes didn't run through portals. Crystal balls couldn't tell the future. There was no place as Etrunia.

Brian and Rose were probably safe at home, just as she was.

The whole adventure was just a bizarre dream. An aberration.

And yet—it was so real.

Makka threw off the covers and slipped out of bed and into a pair of black leggings, white tee shirt, and dark hoodie. She opened the door to let Sasha out as a strange looking object on the dresser caught her eye. Slowly, she walked towards it, picked it up and gasped in astonishment.

Makka clutched it to her heart as she ran after the galloping dog, flinging the front door and racing out into the early morning mist.

Slowly, she glanced down at the ornate metal object that glowed in her hands. She knew exactly what it was:

The Cvector!

THE ETRUNIA SAGA

Book Two:
The War of the Crystals

~ 1 ~

Into the Mist

Makka awoke just before dawn and threw back the coverlet on her four-posted bed in their new house in Granite Falls, Minnesota, to let her Great Dane, Sasha, outside to do her business. As she hurriedly pulled on a pair of black leggings, white tee shirt, and dark hoodie, she spotted a shiny object on the dresser and grabbed it, shoving it down into her pocket.

In the kitchen, she yanked her pink cell phone off the charger, checked for messages and saw none. She noticed a navy blue backpack with a school insignia. Could this be the first day of school? Impossible! It was still summer, wasn't it?

A jumble of memories began to surface as she stuffed the silver object into the pocket and thought about the dream that filled her thoughts—something about giant birds and arrows. She broke out in a sweat. Rose! Rose and her twin brother, Brian, had been with her in the dream—a wild adventure in a place called Etrunia.

"You're being silly," she said aloud. And yet she couldn't shake the nagging feeling of impending doom.

She called Sasha to come inside but the dog wasn't interested in obeying. At fourteen, Makka had no patience for his disobedience.

"Get in here now!" she hissed into the dark yard as mist rose from the wet grass. Obediently, the dog trotted to her side, drooling. "Sorry, but I have to go," she said, scratching its massive head. "I'll be back soon and then we'll play. Promise!"

She filled the dog's bowl with water and set out clean kibbles. "You stay here girl and I'll be back in a jiffy." She grabbed a bottle of orange juice from the refrigerator, jumped on her bike, and headed in the direction of the Abadon house.

It seemed as though it had been ages since she'd been here last—and yet it was only yesterday. She *thought* it was yesterday.

The vapor from the street lamps glowed eerily in the misty morning as the sun's rays cast broad shadows on the horizon.

The Abadon home was an imposing structure of fieldstone and granite, from Granite Falls she assumed, and completely dark. She pulled up to the gate and leaned the bike against the post, peering into the empty courtyard. The ground was dewy and the assortment of gnomes seemed sad and forlorn. The grass was overgrown, riddled with weeds.

She pushed on the wrought iron gate and was surprised that it opened with a loud squeak. It had been oiled the last time. In fact, it didn't even seem to be the same house. But there was a big "A" on the bars. She slipped through and jogged past the courtyard to the front door, knocking softly. She called out, "Brian, Rose...I'm downstairs."

She banged louder and pulled out her phone, calling each of them but received no answer—even as she heard the ring tones chiming faintly inside the house. Where was everybody?

Then, suddenly, she remembered how in her dream she had followed a gnome down a winding staircase into their basement and through a portal. She had to find that portal again.

She threw pebbles at the window where Rose's room was located and shouted her name, not caring if she woke up the whole neighborhood. Despite the chilly morning fog, Makka was sweating. And then she nearly jumped out of her skin as her cell phone rang, slicing through the quiet dawn and her frantic thoughts. Her mom's photo appeared and she quickly swiped the green button.

"Where are you?" Elizabeth hissed.

"I'll be back soon. I had to run an errand."

"An errand this early in the morning? Makka, what's going on? You're making me nervous and I hate feeling this way. Didn't you see the backpack? Don't you know what day it is?"

Makka stared silently at front door. Just yesterday she had been inside, wondering about the gigantic fireplace and the suits of armor.

"What day is this?" she asked her mother.

"Are you all right? Do you have a fever? Are you coming down with something?"

Makka wondered if she had amnesia or Covid. She took a sip of juice. It was sweet and delicious.

"I'm fine. I just need to check something out. I'll be home soon."

Elizabeth shouted into the phone, "This is the most important day of the rest of your life. I need you home right now."

"I'm okay," she reassured her mom. "I'm at the Abadon house making sure Rose and Brian are up so we can ride to school together. Don't be such a worry wart."

"The Abadon house?" she asked incredulously. "But you never met them. They all disappeared a long time ago. How did you even hear of them?"

Her hand began to tremble. "I was here yesterday. Everything was fine."

"Makka," her mother said slowly. "Listen sweetie. There was a terrible accident. I'm sorry to say that both Rose and Brian died tragically. After that, Mr. and Mrs. Abadon couldn't bear to be here any longer and they simply vanished. Nobody knows where they went."

But Makka knew. She knew exactly where they went—where they ALL went.

As she looked around, it *did* seem as though nobody had lived there for a long time. The weeds were overgrown and the gnomes were gone. And then something caught the corner of her eye and everything became crystal clear.

"I've gotta go," she said, disconnecting the call. Slipping the phone into the pocket of the hoodie, she followed the small figure with the pointy hat until it disappeared into the mist.

Made in the USA
Columbia, SC
01 August 2023

21054028R00174